King Harald's Snow Job

A Canine Cozy

by Richard Audry

The Third King Harald Mystery

Visit drmartinbooks.com & facebook.com/richardaudryauthor
Contact the author at drmartin120@gmail.com

Chapter One

King Harald was sprawled on the living room rug, watching the boss do another one of those inexplicable things he did. Yammering away with that shiny, little rectangular object held up against his ear. He clearly wasn't talking to Harald. But as far as Harald could see, there was no one else around.

"Sorry for calling so early, Phil," the boss was saying. "Listen, I know I promised I'd be down in time for happy hour. But this thing has come up with my aunt."

The boss stopped talking, and Harald heard some teeny-tiny noises coming out of the little shiny object, as if a mouse were in there.

"Yup. The one who tricked me into running for mayor. I don't think she has anything quite so devious in mind this time. It's just that she got herself a new job and she needs some extra muscle today. Anyway, I might be a little late for happy hour. You guys hold down the fort and save me a few beers."

There was another silence from the boss and more teeny-tiny sounds from the object.

"Oh yeah, *well* up in her sixties. But she's got energy to burn. She snagged a gig as assistant events manager at this resort up in Hobartville. And they're having a big bash—the Girls' Weekend Out and Holiday Faire. But here's the kicker. A week before the event, Aunt Bev's boss goes mountain biking and ends up with a bad compound leg fracture. So Aunt Bev's gotta handle the whole event, and she needs a little help setting up."

The boss went silent for a bit, then laughed again. "I know, I know. Me and a hotel full of women. Every macho man's dream come true. But fool that I am, I'd rather be down in the Cities, chillin' with my chums."

The boss talked a while longer, then slipped the shiny object into his pocket. He headed out of the room, so Harald lurched to his feet and trotted after him. They ended up where the boss slept at night.

He began to stuff things into his blue bag and Harald knew immediately what that meant. The boss was going away. He would take Harald to another house. And then Harald wouldn't see him for days.

Normally, being left at another house wasn't a big deal for Harald. There was always someone around to play with and plenty of food to eat.

But this morning, for some reason, the idea of leaving home felt different. Felt wrong.

There was something in the air that Harald sensed. Something dark and heavy and dangerous. Some kind of trouble out there.

But the boss seemed oblivious to it. Harald needed to get his attention. So he used his time-tested method for letting the boss know he was making a mistake. He whimpered.

The boss looked down at him. "Hey, what's wrong there, dude?"

Harald gave him his best poor-little-puppy-dog look and whimpered again.

The boss came over and rubbed Harald's head. It always felt good when he did that.

"No reason to act so sad, big guy. You're gonna meet lots of people at the resort. You know how much folks like to pet you. And this afternoon when I head down to the Cities, I'll drop you off with Uncle Frank and Crackers."

Harald perked up, hearing that name. He and Crackers always had fun together—running and barking and wrestling.

"I'm going to spend the weekend with some friends," the boss said as he zipped up the blue bag. "We're gonna catch a basketball game tomorrow afternoon and the Blitzers concert in the evening." He looked back down at Harald. "And I wasn't going to tell you, but Phil and his wife lined me up with a date for the concert. A nice-looking lady I knew back when."

Harald cocked his head and gave a little woof.

"Yeah, I agree. We could use a new girlfriend, couldn't we?"

Harald could tell the boss was happy about something. And normally, a happy boss meant a happy dog.

But Harald couldn't stop feeling that leaving the house today—even just going out the door—was a bad idea.

A *very* bad idea.

Chapter Two

"Sorry I'm late, Aunt Bev."

Andy had promised to be there by eight. But when he arrived at his aunt's cubicle at the Beaver Tail Resort and Conference Center, the clock on her desk said eight-thirty.

"I don't know what the heck was wrong with Harald," he said, setting down the grocery bag that contained dog chow and a couple of plastic bowls. "He just wouldn't budge."

Harald, slumping gloomily, didn't even bother to look up. He was clearly not a happy hound.

From her fancy office chair, Aunt Bev regarded both of them with a preoccupied expression—not something Andy was used to seeing on Beverly Engebretson's face. She looked quite the professional in her navy blazer with a Beaver Tail Resort patch on the pocket. Not a single gray root showed in her immaculate henna dye job. Her desk, on the other hand, was a mess, with piles of papers strewn all over it. On a file cabinet next to it was a stack of business books. Andy squinted at a couple of the titles—*Piloting Your Career to Supersonic Success* and *Seventy Is the New Fifty: Career Plans for Older Workers*. It seemed Aunt Bev was dead serious about making a go of it in the corporate world.

"Dogs can be peculiar sometimes," she said distractedly.

"I mean, he literally wouldn't budge," Andy continued. "I kept telling him we were going for a ride in the Silverado. He loves riding in the truck. Can't hold him back usually. But this time, I had to put the leash on him and haul him out. Thank heavens I didn't have to lift him into the seat. Could've given myself a hernia or something." He glared down at the big, ginger pooch. "Thanks for nothing, Mr. Lead-in-the-Butt."

"Yeah, that's kind of strange," Aunt Bev sighed.

She didn't sound like her normal self—cool and confident, ready for any challenge. Andy wondered if she was just stressed out over the big event. After all, she had been expecting to be the assistant for the weekend, not the top honcho.

"Is there anything wrong, Aunt Bev?"

She put on a brave face. "No. It's just been a bit hectic here this morning. The phone keeps ringing, and I can't get anything done. I'm trying real hard to exercise visual management, but I just don't see it." With that, she knocked a pile of papers onto the floor with her elbow, barely missing her big to-go cup of coffee.

"Oh fudge!" she spat.

Bending over, Andy helped her pick them up. He hadn't exactly been thrilled to get her SOS a couple of days before, what with his big weekend plans. But now that he saw how frazzled she seemed, he was glad he had agreed to pitch in. In addition to providing some muscle, maybe he could give her a bit of moral support. And in any case, he'd be on the road by two.

"So, what's on tap for the weekend?" he asked, straightening up.

"Plenty," Aunt Bev said, rubbing her forehead. "The first weekend in December is always slow for the resort. So, a couple years ago, Rosemary—she's my boss—came up with the idea for the Holiday Faire." She grabbed a flyer from one of the stacks on her desk and handed it to Andy.

He glanced at the promotional copy. "That's gotta be a sure-fire bet this time of year."

"Oh, it's very popular. We've got forty-plus vendors setting up in the conference center today. The doors open at two. That's why I needed you here this morning—to go around and make sure everyone is good to go."

Andy nodded. "Easy peasy. I might even do some Christmas shopping while I'm at it—looks like some great gift ideas. Bet you'll draw a good crowd for this."

"We always do. But the problem is most of the folks come and shop and leave. They don't spend the night. They don't eat here. So Rosemary had another idea. The Girls' Weekend Out. To piggyback onto the Holiday

Faire. It's a two-night package, with breakfast included. We planned a bunch of fun GWO events, too."

"Smart idea," Andy said, plopping down in the cubicle's guest chair. He remembered when Tracy, his ex-wife, would go off on weekend jaunts with some of her gal pals. "Estrogen bonding," she called it. She always came home relaxed and happy, ready to face another stressful workweek.

"Yeah, it *was* a smart idea. Until Rosemary fell off that darn bike." Aunt Bev glared at her desk, as if it bore some responsibility for the unfortunate accident. "And if I had been in charge from the start, I wouldn't have booked in Logan Kennedy's big event, *too*."

"Logan *who*?"

"Logan Kennedy. She's a Herkimer County girl who's written those best-selling novels. I haven't read any myself." Aunt Bev paused. "They're supposed to be kind of, well, *raunchy*."

Andy made a mental note to check them out. "So you have to handle logistics for that, too?"

"No, thank goodness. Her people are taking care of it. But we still have to coordinate with them. Her book launch is at five tomorrow, and I don't know if our New Bergen buses will be back in time. I'm sure some of the gals going down there will want to attend the book launch, too."

Aunt Bev and Andy's sister, Kirsten, had cooked up the excursion to New Bergen. The GWO ladies would lunch at Kirsten's restaurant, Ansel's Café. Then the gals would have a couple of hours to shop Skjegstad Street.

"Beverly, did you get those contracts delivered to the accounting office?"

Andy turned to see a trim, thirty-something man walk into the cubicle, in a navy blazer identical to the one Aunt Bev was wearing. When he saw Andy, the expression on his face went from grimly businesslike to superficially warm. "Oh, excuse me. I didn't realize you had a guest."

"Tim," said Aunt Bev, "I'd like you to meet my nephew, Anders Skyberg. And Anders, this is Tim Fisher, our resort manager."

The two men shook hands and made the requisite noises about how pleased they were to meet each other.

"Anders is going to help out today. As you know, we're a little short-handed."

Suddenly, Tim's narrow face returned to grimly businesslike. "He's a temp? Who said you could hire a temp?"

"Rosemary gave me the go-ahead," Aunt Bev said evenly. "She put a line item in the budget for extra manpower, in case we needed it."

"Rosemary, Rosemary, Rosemary." Tim shook his head with each pronunciation of the name. "A week before the Girls' Weekend Out, Rosemary—who is almost old enough to qualify for a senior discount—has to go mountain biking. In Arizona. With a boyfriend half her age. And she breaks her leg. In two places. So now we're stuck with you, Beverly. To handle our two biggest events of the month."

Andy's jaw dropped. What kind of boss calls out an employee like that in front of her own nephew? Who did this joker think he was?

Aunt Bev stiffened visibly. "I'm up to the task, Tim. Don't you worry. I've got this."

"Well, make sure your nephew fills out the correct paperwork, and get it to Jane in accounting." Then Tim's eyes fixed on Harald and he scowled. "What is that mangy animal doing here?"

From the look on the dog's face, Andy could tell Harald understood that "mangy" was not very complimentary. On a scale of one to ten, Andy had to give Tim Fisher a zero for making a good first impression. What a creep.

"Oh, that's King Harald," Aunt Bev explained. She looked at the dog and, for the first time since Andy arrived, her face seemed to relax. "He's been on the news, you know, for his crime-sniffing exploits. Both he and Anders."

Tim's eyes went wide. "You're not expecting any criminal activity here this weekend, are you?"

"No, of course not," Aunt Bev quickly assured him. "Harald just needs a place to hang out for a few hours while Anders is working. One of the vendors agreed to dog-sit him."

"Well, keep him out of the way," Tim huffed. "I don't want anyone tripping over him." He gave Harald a wary look. "I assume he's housebroken."

Harald looked even more offended. Andy didn't think that highly uncalled-for remark even deserved a response, but he gave a short one: "Not a problem." He almost added: *"And he's better behaved than you are."*

"By the way," Aunt Bev said, "Anders here is the mayor of New Bergen."

Tim seemed dubious—as if his leg were being pulled—then realized she wasn't joking. His face subtly transformed from peevish to reasonably cordial. "Sorry, Mr. Mayor, I didn't know. Good to have you with us. If you ever need facilities for meetings or events, please keep us in mind. Now if you'll pardon me, I've got a million things to do." The peevish expression flipped back onto his face, and he strode off.

"A bit full of himself, isn't he?" Andy observed.

Aunt Bev shrugged. "He's young and ambitious. A rising star in the corporation. Aiming for one of the company's big resorts in Florida or Arizona." She shook her head. "But I am *not* letting him get to me. I need to stay focused."

The tone in her voice, though, convinced Andy that she was feeling less confident than she was letting on. "Are you sure everything's okay, Aunt Bev?"

She squared her shoulders and gave him a big smile. "Listen, kiddo, I just have to make it through the weekend. And really now, how much could go wrong in two days?"

Chapter Three

Andy and Harald emerged into the resort lobby through a door next to the main check-in desk.

Aunt Bev had given him his marching orders. He was to go around and greet the Holiday Faire vendors as they were arriving and setting up. And to touch base with them throughout the morning, to see if they needed anything. She told Andy to keep an eye peeled for Butch Behr, the facilities manager, and introduce himself. If there were any mechanical or technical issues, Butch could handle them.

Andy knew the resort pretty well. He had eaten a number of times in the Voyageur restaurant and imbibed not a few Biberschwanzes bellied up to the Homesteader's bar—both located off the lobby near the main desk. The Lumberjack Café, on the opposite side, made the best Eggs Benedict in the county and a killer huevos rancheros.

The lobby was done up in a piney, rustic northwoods style, with stuffed leather chairs scattered around and a massive stone fireplace. Holiday lights glinted and blinked all over. Through the broad front windows, Andy could see his blue Silverado off a good distance in one of the parking lots. His packed suitcase was in it. When he was done at two, it was a quick spin down the interstate to New Bergen, where he would drop off Harald with Uncle Frank. Then it would be time to whoop it up with old friends down in the Cities.

The resort wasn't busy at the moment. A few people were lined up at the front desk to check out. A small group was taking selfies in front of the big Christmas tree by the door. Another clump had posted themselves in front of the huge Samsung flat screen. It was tuned to the weather station, and Andy could see a blonde meteorologist waving her hand over a map of the tri-county area, which included Beaver Tail.

"*Ohhhh!* Who is this beautiful baby?"

Andy suddenly found himself surrounded by four women in yoga pants and T-shirts. One of them, wearing a hot pink top, had gotten down on her haunches and was going nose-to-snout with Harald.

"You are such a good boy, aren't you?" she said, petting his head and neck. "Yes, you are. Yes, you are!"

Harald seemed uncharacteristically unenthused, but he tolerated her attention with a certain forbearance. Still down in the dumps, Andy figured. He'd love to know what was bugging his canine sidekick.

The woman stood up and smiled at Andy. "Your dog is *so* sweet. What's his name?"

Andy smiled back. "His full name is King Harald, but we usually just call him Harald." He waited for one of the women to say that she had heard of the crime-busting mutt—that's what usually happened these days. But not this time. Andy was actually a little disappointed.

"Well, you are darn lucky to have him," Harald's pink-clad admirer said. "I just adore a big, friendly dog like him."

"So, are you ladies here for the Girls' Weekend Out?"

"We are," replied a grinning woman in a sky-blue T-shirt. "We drove over from Watertown. Left at six this morning. We usually go to Vegas in December, but this sounded like so much fun. There's that smorgasbord tonight. And a karaoke party tomorrow. We all love to make fools of ourselves singing in public." The other women giggled.

"Well, speaking for myself," said the short gal in mint green, "I'm here to do some power shopping. We're taking the bus down to New Bergen tomorrow. The brochure said it's jam-packed with wonderful stores. Sounds like a charming little town."

Andy almost boasted about being mayor of that "charming little town." But he didn't have time right now to do his New Bergen cheerleader shtick.

"A little early for check-in, aren't you?"

"The hotel let us check our bags until the rooms are ready," said the woman in lemon yellow. "We booked half a day at the spa."

"So by midafternoon we'll all be gorgeous. Massaged and pampered and ready for a glass or two of Merlot this evening," said Mint Green.

"A glass or *two*?" Hot Pink repeated with an exaggerated look of horror.

"Try six or seven," laughed Sky Blue.

"Are you attending, too?" Mint Green asked. "I know it's *Girls'* Weekend Out, but it would be nice to have some fellows around."

"Just don't tell our husbands." Lemon Yellow gave him a flirtatious wink.

A grin froze on Andy's face. He liked women. He really did. Some of his favorite people in the world were women. But the thought of being trapped amid dozens and dozens of them practically gave him hives. There was always so much laughing and giggling going on when women gathered in regiments, and it made him nervous. *No thanks.* Andy preferred the ladies in smaller numbers, or, even better, one-on-one.

"Nope, I'm not a guest or anything. Just here to work a quick temp job. Help get things set up for the Holiday Faire in the conference center. But I'm sure you gals will have a lot of fun."

"Oh, you betcha," enthused Mint Green. "But if I see you at the karaoke party tomorrow night, you and I are gonna dance! Don't even think of saying no."

The T-shirt quartet all burst into laughter and headed off toward the spa.

Standing there, watching them go, it occurred to Andy that he hadn't danced with anyone since he had dated Cass Conlin. They had taken swing and line dance lessons together and danced a few times down in the Cities. The former deputy sheriff didn't exactly have twinkle toes, nor did Andy. But they had a good time tripping the light fantastic.

Andy missed having someone of the opposite sex to hang out with. And to canoodle with. And to just plain talk with. He hadn't had much luck in that area since his divorce. But maybe his date this weekend would change all that.

When Phil had called a month ago, he asked Andy if he remembered Paula Kroeger. Andy did. She and her husband had traveled in the same circles as Andy and Tracy, his ex. Paula, a middle school teacher, was cute and vivacious. But her husband had proved to be a tireless skirt-chaser. Paula dumped him about the time Tracy was dumping Andy for her hot Pilates instructor. Phil had wondered if Andy would be interested in Paula as his plus-one for Saturday evening. Andy thought it was a great idea.

Phil recounted that when he had suggested it to Paula, she confessed that she had always thought Andy was a "hunk." Andy laughed when he heard that, protesting that she must have confused him with someone else. But he was flattered that the lady was open to a not-so-blind date. He couldn't wait to see her again.

Other than lacking female companionship, Andy's

life was ticking along pretty well. His sister's Nordic Deli and Gallery had its groundbreaking ceremony a few weeks ago. Andy would be in charge of curating the art gallery. Just in the last month, he had sold two of his own paintings—one a commission and the other a big canvas of a birch forest. And he had recently come into a tidy sum of money, which nicely augmented his minuscule retirement nest egg.

Andy made his way to the corridor that led into the conference center. He could hear a confused sort of clamor. Voices shouting and directing. Hammers hammering. Electric tools whirring. Inside the large exhibition space, booths were in various states of completion and merchandise was being unloaded. The Holiday Faire had two main aisles and four rows of booths. Andy glanced at the sheets Aunt Bev had given him and confirmed her count of more than forty exhibitors.

Stopping a guy who looked like a custodian, Andy asked where he could find Butch Behr, the facilities manager. The guy said the last time he saw Butch was by the conference center's main entrance, at the opposite end of the hall. He told Andy to look for a beefy guy with a bushy mustache.

Before he did anything else, Andy had a stop to make. Looking at the floor plan, he led Harald down the west aisle, past booths offering chocolate delicacies, beeswax candles, new age goods, and textile art. Toward the end of the aisle, they stopped at a booth with a banner proclaiming "Hofdahl Farm Cheese."

Thor Hofdahl, Andy's best New Bergen buddy and noted cranky socialist, was helping set up a photo display of the goat cheese operation that his wife, Sonny, owned. As he usually did when he was selling cheese, Thor had on a red plaid flannel shirt under blue bib overalls. The septuagenarian said his attire was part of the branding. Folks wanted to buy cheese from someone who looked like a farmer—or at least what they *thought* a farmer should look like.

"Well, there's our canine ward," Thor said when he spotted them.

"I gotta tell you, today he's more like canine weird," said Andy, handing over the bag that contained dog chow and plastic bowls. "He's got some kind of burr under his collar. Didn't want to leave the house this morning. Practically had to carry him to the truck."

"Maybe it's the weather coming in," Thor said, crossing his arms. "Change in barometric pressure and all that. Animals are more sensitive to those things than we are."

"Is that what's bugging you, big guy?" Andy asked, leaning over and giving Harald a scratch behind the ear. "Well, don't worry. It's only going to be a couple inches." Andy had watched the weather report last night before going to bed, and it didn't sound like it would be too gnarly.

"Could be more than that," Thor noted. "I think they said something shifted in the storm track. Not sure how much snow yet."

Andy frowned at the news. He sure hoped it wouldn't be a lot more. But the Silverado, even without 4-wheel drive, was a champ in the snow. He had no doubt that getting down to the Cities, even in eight or ten inches, would be no problemo.

B-ball, big date, and Blitzers. Yes siree!

Andy Skyberg wasn't going to let a few flakes spoil his weekend.

Chapter Four

Leaving Harald with Thor, Andy headed toward the main entrance in search of Butch Behr, the facilities manager. As he was scanning the place, he spied Aunt Bev scurrying around the corner of the other aisle, carrying a role of paper towels in one hand and her cell phone in the other. Andy always thought his aunt had the legs for competitive race walking. She only had one tempo—full speed ahead.

He caught up with Butch right by the conference center's main doors, where vendors were rolling in merchandise on handcarts and platform trucks. Butch seemed to be in an intense discussion with a stout little woman who didn't look happy. Andy recognized her. She owned Beaver Tail County's top travel agency, and she always ran ads in the *Chronicle* with her picture in them—usually wearing an aloha shirt and a lei.

"We were assured that our Wi-Fi connection would be up to snuff for showing high-definition videos," the woman was saying as Andy approached. "We go to a lot of trouble to find quality footage of our destinations, and your Wi-Fi just keeps freezing up on us, Butch. And we need it fixed immediately."

Built like a Mack truck, Butch didn't seem much discomfited by the travel agent's irritated tone. "Don't worry, Anita. We've got a couple options. First, we'll try a special antenna with your laptop. If that doesn't do it, we can run an Ethernet cable. Let me get on the horn with our tech nerd, and he'll be right out to help you."

As Anita trotted off, looking mollified, the beefy manager shifted his gaze to Andy. A small smile turned up the corners of his mouth beneath that bushy mustache.

"Let me guess. You're Anders Skyberg."

Andy stuck out his hand, which Butch grasped in an over-strong grip. "Please just call me Andy. Guess my Aunt Bev warned you I was coming."

"She did." Butch nodded. His voice was kind of gravelly—a smoker, maybe, or a drinker. "That aunt of yours is a real dynamo for a lady her age."

"Yup, that she is." Andy thought Aunt Bev was a real dynamo for a lady of *any* age.

"And I'm glad she asked you to help out," Butch continued, "what with Rosemary being out of commission. She's still trying to pitch in by phone from her bed. But Tim and I have a lot more to handle, with all the security issues."

Andy raised his eyebrows. "Are you worried some of the ladies might get out of hand?"

Butch laughed. "Nah, not this crowd. But we've got a lot of valuable merchandise in the hall, and we gotta keep our eyes peeled for sticky fingers, if you know what I mean."

It hardly seemed to Andy that goat cheese and beeswax candles required much security. But then, who knew what kind of evil lurked in the hearts of middle-aged moms and grandmoms?

"Anyway, work on that list that Beverly gave you," said Butch. "Find out what people need. Check 'em off as you go. Any issues, get back to me or your aunt. I'll be circulating, too. And we'll do our best to get it all done by two o'clock, when the doors open."

"Sounds good. I know Aunt Bev will be relieved when everything's finally up and running."

Butch went silent for a few seconds. "How's your aunt doing?"

"What do you mean?"

"Bearing up okay?"

"Don't understand what you're asking."

Butch sighed. "Since Rosemary got took out of action, Tim Fisher's really been on Beverly's case. Kinda crummy, since she's so new. Not fair. The assistant manager told me Tim's not sure she fits in here. You might wanna give her a heads up. Her weekend might not be too much fun, if Tim's gunning for an excuse to can her."

So the little weasel wanted Aunt Bev out. Well, Andy was going to make darn certain that none of the

Holiday Faire vendors would have any cause to complain about her.

He started in the northeast corner of the conference center with Tollefson's Bed and Breakfast, which was touting romantic weekend packages. The B&B was located in Solberg County in a restored farmhouse on the edge of an old-growth oak forest. Andy had almost booked a weekend early last summer in its "Rub-a-Dub-Tub Suite," so named for its little patio with a hot tub. But his procrastination had proven prescient. He had broken up with Deputy Sheriff Cass Conlin shortly thereafter. If things clicked with Paula this weekend— fingers crossed—he might try again.

But things were not clicking in the B&B's booth. Joan Tollefson complained that a big rug she had been promised hadn't shown up yet. "We'll get right on it," Andy assured her. He called Aunt Bev immediately and left a message.

It was smooth sailing for a bit, as he went down the east row of exhibitors. The lady who owned the Cat House, with its abundance of feline merchandise, said they were ready to rock and roll. The Beaver Tail Potters' Cooperative and School was all set up, with shelves full of lovely, artistic pieces, as well as lots of functional cooking pots and dinnerware. Andy spotted some cobalt blue mugs rimmed with Viking-looking scrollwork. They would make perfect host and hostess gifts for Phil and his wife.

The jams and jellies booth was looking good. And so

was the Peaceful Hands Massagery booth, with its offer of a ten-minute chair massage for ten bucks.

Nobody was on duty at Written On Skin, though several tattoo machines, ink bottles, and other supplies were arrayed on a table, ready for a busy day of tattooing. A flat screen TV by the aisle ran a slideshow of the artist's work, and Andy watched it for a bit. Bare arms, backs, legs, and necks appeared, one after the other, like living canvases. There were things that Andy had seen in many a bar—gothic emblems, heavy metal symbols, and biker art.

But the proprietor, Damian Powers, had a more elegant, innovative side, too. His way with botanicals, animals, and script seemed wonderfully expressive. A helix of larks ascended a woman's bare back, right up her neck. An expressionistic wolf with intense, dark eyes stared out from a muscular forearm. A vine wended its way up a woman's thigh.

"Thinking of getting a tat?"

Andy turned and found himself facing what J. J. Lindquist, head waitress at Ansel's, would have called "a big sweet hunk of man candy." With his combed-back dark hair and sinewy build, Damian Powers would not have looked out of place in one of the hipster joints down in the Cities. He was wearing tight black jeans and a long-sleeved black shirt.

"No, no thanks." In fact, Andy had a tattoo already— one that he wanted to get rid of. "Just admiring your handiwork. Gorgeous stuff. Have you ever thought about doing real art?" The instant those words came out, he regretted them. "Sorry, I didn't mean it that way."

Damian flashed a good-natured grin. "Not the first time I've heard that. So not a problem. And to answer your question, I do some oils on the side."

"Me too. I have a studio in New Bergen. Anyway, I'm checking with all the exhibitors to see if everything's okay. Anything you need?"

"Nah, I'm in good shape. Butch Behr helped me unload the van when I got here and a couple of my employees are due to arrive any minute. We should be set up and ready for action by two o'clock."

Andy continued his survey of the booths on the other side of the aisle. He was squatting down, petting the big female husky at Spader's Dogsledding and Yurts, when the phone on his hip vibrated. He stood and pulled it out.

"Yup, Andy here."

"Andy, it's Sonny."

"Hey, Sonny, what's up?"

"I think the big guy needs a little visit outside, if you know what I mean."

"I assume you're talking about Harald and not Thor. Be there in a min."

Andy headed over to the Hofdahl Farm Cheese booth. To reach it, he had to squeeze between boxes of wine bottles that were being unpacked by a couple of the guys from Boulder Creek Winery. Their stuff wasn't French or Californian quality, let alone Oregonian or Chilean. But they were good quaffs, and Ansel's Café featured Boulder Creek's Cabernet Franc and Frontenac Gris. Evidently, they and the Hofdahls were teaming up to share booth costs and promote each other's products.

Andy found Sonny placing shrink-wrapped cheese into a refrigerated display case. Thor was nowhere to be seen.

"Love your setup, Sonny. Wine and cheese united. Perfect. I wouldn't mind just hanging out here all day."

"Well, Andy," Sonny said, "when you go outside, make sure you hang onto Harald. I was just out to the truck, and I can tell you, the wind's really picked up. I'm betting on a pretty good blow this afternoon."

She handed Harald's leash to him, and the two headed for the conference center's main lobby, out by the big parking lot. They had just passed an essential oils display, its herbal scents wafting into the aisle, when they almost ran into a blonde with a pooch of her own. The woman, tall and striking in black leather pants and jacket, had hidden her eyes behind dark aviator sunglasses. She looked like some kind of rock star. Andy smiled at her.

Harald stopped in his tracks, his tail wagging, and peered expectantly at the other canine, who was brownish in color and clearly of mixed lineage—a mutt just like himself. But the other dog didn't have the least little interest in sociability, and neither did the woman. As they brushed by, the woman merely gave the duo a chilly up-and-down glance.

Andy and Harald watched them go, then turned to

see a nice-looking young woman in professional attire marching after the pair. Speaking intently into her phone, she didn't even seem to notice Andy and Harald as she walked by them.

"Well, Harald," Andy said, "I guess we're invisible. *C'est la vie*. But now on to the bidness at hand."

But before they got much farther, another woman came rushing up, panting as she lurched to a stop. Remarkably, she was dressed almost exactly the same as the magisterial blonde with the dog. All in black, but appearing rumpled rather than chic. Her aviator shades looked like cheap knockoffs, and her blonde hair, though cut in a similar cropped style, had dark roots showing. She was shorter and rounder and younger than the first woman.

A burly guy with shaggy hair, also in black duds, also rumpled, caught up with her. "The limo service just dropped her off outside," he said urgently. "What do you want to do?"

"We've got to talk to her, Bobby. We've got to clear up this situation."

And off they went up the aisle.

"Hmmm," Andy muttered, "what do you make of that, Harald? Kinda peculiar, huh?"

They proceeded unhindered through the conference center's lobby, then out the main door into the parking lot. Sonny sure hadn't been kidding about the wind. Man and dog both had to lean into it. It was definitely nippier than when they had arrived at the resort just a couple of hours ago.

Pushing into a biting cold breeze, they made their way to the far side of the parking lot, where the exhibitors had stashed their vans and trailers. A wooden fence separated the lot from one of the fairways of the Beaver Tail National Golf Links, which curled around the resort to the northwest. Caribou Creek, a popular trout stream, wended through the property on one of the far fairways. The golf-course architect had used it as a water hazard. In the winter, groomed cross-country ski trails were available for the resort's guests and the public.

Andy figured a fencepost would serve Harald's purpose, unless he had more in mind. It was always smart to carry a couple of plastic bags in the back pocket, just in case, but they weren't needed this time.

While Harald watered the post, Andy gazed back at the Conference Center, big and square and covered in dark-stained wood. Behind it, the main lodge loomed, all five stories of it. Extending off both sides of the main lodge were several smaller guest additions. A number of timeshare units sat out toward the clubhouse and first tee of the links. The whole complex was attached by enclosed walkways, a necessity in a winter climate. Not a huge fan of frigidity, Andy was all for anything that made life a little warmer in the dark months.

The morning's blue sky had gone gray, and some flakes were coming sideways, landing and making swirls of white on the black of the tarmac. Way off to the west, the gray had gone very dark, almost black. More ominously, Andy spied a flash or two of lightning. A winter thunderstorm was rare, but they did happen on the northern plains.

"That doesn't look real good, does it, Harald?" he said. "It maybe wouldn't be a bad idea to get an earlier start."

Harald looked at him as if to say: *Why don't we just leave now?* And he started dragging Andy toward the Silverado, parked a stone's throw away.

"Can't vamoose just yet," Andy laughed, struggling to pull the pooch back toward the conference center. "But I promise you, if there are no snafus, we'll be outta here before you know it."

Chapter Five

Back inside, Andy pulled out his phone and tapped the screen a few times. He listened to the message and then spoke.

"Hey there, Aunt Bev. I'm about halfway through talking to the exhibitors, and things are looking good. I should get the rest done in short order. And I was thinking I might bug out a bit earlier than planned this afternoon. You know, get ahead of the weather, in case it gets rough. Hope that's okay. Let me know."

Andy and Harald returned to Sonny Hofdahl's booth, where they found the cheese entrepreneur talking with a middle-aged woman who was wearing a red cardigan with a leaping white reindeer pattern across the top. The two were so wrapped up in conversation that it took Sonny half a minute to notice Andy and Harald.

"Oh, Andy," she beamed, "you have to meet this lady. She's an old, *old* friend of the family."

"Not *that* old," the woman said with mock outrage.

"This is Sage Mortenson. She was my youngest sister's best friend in high school. She and Betty were practically inseparable."

Sage nodded. "I probably spent more time at Sonny's house than ours. Of course, she was long gone by then, off to college and work in the big city. You wouldn't believe how much we looked up to her. So sophisticated and mature was Sonja. When she came home to visit, we couldn't hear enough about her adventures and the guys she was dating."

"And look where all that sophistication and hard work got me," Sonny laughed. "Milking goats for a living and married to an opinionated old coot. Sage, this is Andy Skyberg and King Harald."

Sage leaned over and gave Harald a pat. "Of course, I've read all about you two in the paper. How in the world did you guys get mixed up in those murder cases?"

Andy gave a dismal chuckle. "Put it down to bad luck. Harald and I were just in the wrong places at the wrong times."

"Wasn't it kind of scary, having your life threatened like that?"

Andy almost said something about being cool in the face of possible doom, but he decided to tell the truth. "Darn right it was. Still gives me the willies." He pretended to shiver.

"Sage works for Norske Knittery," Sonny explained. "They're right across the aisle there. She started out knitting for them at home, and then they hired her for sales. Isn't that terrific?"

Ah, thought Andy, that explained the Yule sweater. Norske Knittery sold hand-knit Norwegian and novelty-style sweaters all over the world. Andy had coveted a Norske cardigan for ages, but he just wasn't comfortable with the four-hundred-dollar price tag. It was a lot to pay for a sweater.

"Best job I've ever had," Sage said. "We go to these shows all over the Upper Midwest, but not so often here in the tri-county area, our home base. It's fun to see so many familiar faces around."

"Speaking of familiar faces, you haven't seen my Aunt Bev recently, have you?" Andy asked.

"She flew through here a few minutes ago with a big bundle of extension cords," Sonny said. "She was traveling in high gear, let me tell you. I've gotta get me some of whatever she has for breakfast. I could use a little of that rocket fuel first thing in the morning."

"Isn't that the truth?" Sage laughed. "Some mornings I can barely boil the water for my first cup of coffee. Pretty sad, huh?"

Andy didn't want to get caught up in one of those interminable discussions about aching joints and doctor visits that was typical of the baby boomer bunch. "I better get back to work, ladies. Thanks for looking after Harald, Sonny. And if my Aunt Bev should happen by, let her know I need to talk with her." He handed over Harald's leash and headed back to work.

More vendors were arriving, and Andy pitched in

wherever he could to help unload boxes. He was going back up the east aisle when he spotted Tim Fisher, Aunt Bev's boss, standing by one of the booths and talking with some guy. Maybe Tim knew where Aunt Bev was. But by the time Andy reached the booth, he had trotted off.

"Darn it," Andy blurted out. He looked around to see the man Tim had been talking with, eyeing him suspiciously. Andy gave him an embarrassed little wave and started looking at the display cases in the booth. They were full of jewelry—rings, bracelets, necklaces, and pins, in silver and gold and platinum. All of them were elegant, simple, and not cheap. Each had a card next to it with the price and the name "Grant Hamsden Designs."

One of them in particular caught Andy's eye. It was an exquisite opal-and-silver necklace—the type of thing he used to love to buy for Tracy, his ex. And that she loved to receive. Tracy had a graceful long neck, and he had delighted in putting her necklaces around it. And then kissing that neck and the soft skin of her shoulders below and...

Whoa, he thought, straightening up. Now is *not* the time or place for that kind of daydream. No siree! Nuh-huh. He shook his head, trying to dislodge the vivid memory of how great she used to feel and smell. Andy Skyberg was definitely way overdue for some female companionship.

"Are you shopping for anything in particular?" The man who had been watching him had a sharp, ascetic face and trim, brown hair. His suit looked like an Armani. Behind him, Andy noticed a handsome woman, impeccably dressed, arranging items in a teak display case. Her thick auburn hair was pulled back in a loose bun and she wore gold teardrop earrings, no doubt a Hamsden design.

"No, afraid not," Andy said, shoving his hands in his pockets. "Wish I was. No one to buy for at the moment."

The man finally smiled, his lips quite narrow, almost nonexistent. His gray eyes looked up at Andy from behind stylish metallic glasses.

"You must be Grant Hamsden," Andy said.

"Guilty as charged. And this is my sales manager, Stephanie Bukowski." He nodded toward the woman in the back of the booth, and she smiled at Andy. "Can we help you with anything, Mr.…?"

"Skyberg. Andy Skyberg. And I was about to ask you the same thing. I'm temping here this morning. Beverly Engebretson hired me to make sure all the vendors are in good shape and have everything they need."

"I do need something, actually," the jewelry designer said. "I have a special item that needs a special safe." He patted his chest, just over the heart. Andy could make out the outline of an object in the inside jacket pocket, something rectangular. Probably a jewelry case. And whatever was in it must be pretty pricey, if it required a special safe.

He felt a little flash of panic. "Hmm. I'm not exactly certain where we'd find you a safe at this late date."

"Oh, no, that's not what I meant. A unit's on the way up from the Cities. We'll soon have the item tucked away under lock and key. That's the plan, anyway. It was supposed to be here by now, but it hasn't arrived. I left a message with the safe company, but they haven't returned my call."

Glancing around the jeweler's booth, Andy noticed a framed, autographed photo sitting atop one of the displays. The woman's image looked slightly familiar. Then it clicked. It was the rude blonde who had brushed by Andy and Harald a little while ago, in front of the essential oils booth. The woman with the dog.

"Hey, I recognize her," he said.

The jeweler's thin-lipped smile appeared again. "Oh, you're a Kat Taggett fan?"

"Her name's Kat Taggett?"

Grant rolled his eyes. "Kat Taggett's a fictional character. The lady in the photo is her creator, Logan Kennedy. Surely you've heard of her. She's a regular on the *Times* bestseller list."

"Ahh, Logan Kennedy." In fact, Andy did recognize the name, but only because Aunt Bev had mentioned it earlier. She was the writer who was appearing at the resort tomorrow to launch a new book. But Andy had no idea what kind of books she wrote, except that they were evidently kind of raunchy. "Oh yeah, she writes those, umm…"

"Female assassin stories," Grant volunteered. "And she spent her formative years right here in the tri-county area. The author, that is. Not the assassin."

"Well, cool. I actually bumped into her and her dog a few minutes ago over in the other aisle."

"She decided to launch her new book here, because her mother still lives in Pinetop, and she's been ailing. That way Logan can kill two birds with one stone. Visit poor old mom and host her Kat Blast."

"Kat Blast?"

"That's what she calls her online media events. She'll be livestreaming from the ballroom."

"Super idea," Andy said, "to piggyback onto the Girls' Weekend Out. She'll have a captive audience here at the resort."

The jeweler sniffed. "Logan Kennedy has more than enough fans around here to fill the ballroom. I expect a few hundred will show up tomorrow afternoon. And there'll be thousands of people watching the Kat Blast online. Everyone's all excited about the big reveal Logan's promised them. She's told her fans she'll be giving away a prize. A *significant* prize. But no one knows what it is."

"So you know her personally?"

"Indeed. She's been a client of mine for many years." The jeweler absent-mindedly patted his coat pocket again. "She appreciates good design and crafts-manship, and she has the money to make it happen."

Andy was willing to bet that the item in Grant's pocket was a commission from the author. And maybe it was the big secret prize. But he really didn't care about

Logan Kennedy or her Kat Blast. Because in a few hours, he would be heading for his own Andy Blast down in the Cities. Having drinks and dinner with his old friends. Catching a b-ball game at the university. Reconnecting with a fine lady he hadn't seen in years. And topping it off with a Blitzers concert. Andy was psyched for a fantastic time.

"Well," he said, excusing himself, "Aunt Bev— I mean, Beverly Engebretson said that Logan's people were handling the event in the ballroom. But I'm sure if Logan needs any help with her super-secret big reveal, Beverly would be glad to lend a hand."

"Oh, Beverly doesn't know *any* of the details pertaining to the big reveal," Grant said. "Tim and Rosemary have been the only contacts here at the resort who do. They didn't think Beverly should be put on the need-to-know list. These older ladies like to gossip a lot, and this secret *cannot* leak out."

Another wimpy male dissing Aunt Bev, Andy thought with irritation. He debated saying something, but held his tongue.

The jewelry designer glanced again at the autographed photo. "All I can say is Logan's Kat Blast tomorrow better go off without a hitch. Otherwise, she'll be *furious*. And let me tell you, you don't want to piss off a woman who spends her days figuring out ways to assassinate people."

Chapter Six

It was almost eleven-thirty, and Andy was getting peckish. He hadn't eaten anything since breakfast, except for a few cheese-topped crackers at Sonny's booth.

Another Wi-Fi issue cropped up, and he called Butch Behr about getting the IT guy on it. Then he caught an earful from a chocolatier whose new catalogs had apparently arrived at the resort, according to the delivery company, but had somehow gone AWOL. The candy-maker said she had talked to Beverly Engebretson about it half an hour ago, but she hadn't heard anything more. She fumed that she had spent a lot on those catalogs, and they darn well better show up.

Andy quickly assured her that Aunt Bev would track them down. He didn't want any complaints about Aunt Bev to reach Tim Fisher's ears. He was still fuming about that snide remark Grant Hamsden had made about her—how these older gals couldn't be trusted with confidential info.

It was one thing for *Andy* to grouse about his aunt. And he had. On more than one occasion when her meddling somehow got him in a fix. He just didn't like it when others carped about her.

He was about to head over to the Hofdahl booth to see if Sonny and Thor wanted to catch a bite with him, when his phone ding-donged. Speak of the devil.

"Hey there, Aunt Bev."

"Hey there, yourself. Would you go tell the chocolate lady we found her catalogs? They got sent to the restaurant for some reason. They're on their way. And then could you lend a hand at Dillard Press? Marilyn Dillard just threw her back out and could use a bit of help. Okay? Gotta go."

She had spoken so quickly and hung up so fast that Andy didn't have a chance to ask about his early departure. He made a dash to L'Étoile Chocolatier, delivering the good news about the catalogs. In return, the owner rewarded him with a dark chocolate truffle that helped ease his hunger pangs.

At the Dillard Press booth, he found a woman sitting in a folding chair next to a table covered with books. She was scowling at two tall display units standing in the back of the booth.

"Marilyn Dillard?" he asked. "I'm Andy Skyberg. They told me you needed some muscle."

"I sure as hell do," she sighed. "Thanks for coming. I'll tell you, Andy, of all the days for a back spasm, it had to be today. There were supposed to be four of us here this weekend, but you know that stomach bug that's going around? Took down two of us, so it's just me and my son, Roger."

Wincing, the publisher slowly rose to her feet. She was tall and slender, with short, light brown hair. Back in the day, she might have been a fashion model, but right now she was noticeably crooked, shaped like a human apostrophe.

"Roger's getting more boxes out of the truck," she explained. "But if you want to start putting books up on those display shelves, that would be great. We're doing fiction on the left, non-fiction on the right."

She pointed to some boxes on the floor, and Andy got to work on the fiction shelf. He pulled out stacks of novels, usually a couple of copies of each title, and placed them where Marilyn told him to—some spines out, some covers out. Soon they were joined by her son Roger Dillard, who rolled in a handcart with four boxes stacked on it. A tall, slim fellow himself, he started tackling the non-fiction shelf.

Among the kids' books Andy was shelving was the Robbie Rocket series, which he remembered reading as a sprout. Robbie was a towheaded preteen who shot off rockets and thereby embroiled himself in adventures and mysteries. Andy loved those books and had even put up a Robbie Rocket poster in his bedroom.

"Excuse me."

It was Damian Powers. He had his shirtsleeves rolled up now, revealing swirls of Celtic symbols.

Andy wondered who tattooed the tattoo artist. Had Damian done his own?

"Do you happen to have Sigurd Nylund's *Wheat and Dust* trilogy in the boxed set? The hardcovers?"

Marilyn's face lit up. "*Wheat and Dust*? We do indeed."

Andy had been required to read one of the Nylund books in college, for what he had mistakenly thought would be an easy credit in Scandinavian studies. He recalled Norwegian settlers on the old prairie, battling unending drought, weeklong blizzards, and terminally gloomy personalities.

"I hope you don't mind me stopping in before you open. I'm Damian Powers. I own Written On Skin. We're over in the other aisle."

"So pleased to meet you, Damian. I'm Marilyn Dillard. This is Andy Skyberg."

"We met earlier," Andy said, nodding at the tattoo artist.

"And this is my son, Roger," Marilyn continued. "We're delighted that you stopped in. Have you read *Wheat and Dust* before?"

"I did two tours in Iraq, and the first book was in the camp library. *Prairie Dawn*. A beat-up paperback. Have to admit, it was kinda heavy going at first, but worth it. All that crap the Omdahls and Hanssens went through. Grasshopper plagues. Typhoid fever. Children dying. Made Camp Dreamland seem like a luxury resort. I always remember something Papa Omdahl said. 'You never leave your family behind, no matter how far you go. You carry them in your heart forever.' It really spoke to me, sitting over there in the desert."

Roger retrieved a shrink-wrapped trilogy set from one of the boxes and ran Damian's credit card through a gizmo attached to his phone. Damian thanked them, said he'd see them around the Holiday Faire, and took off with the box set under his arm.

"Robbie Rocket and Sigurd Nylund must be pretty good cash cows for you," Andy observed.

"Two of our top sources of revenue," Marilyn replied. "Our Pauline Peterson self-improvement books do really well, too."

"And, of course," Roger said, starting to put a new row of books on the shelf, "there's the big one that got away."

Andy raised his eyebrows. "Really? What's that?"

"Roger, I keep telling you, there's no point in bringing it up." Marilyn glared at her son. "It's ancient history." With a sigh of relief, she eased herself back down into her chair.

"You know, Mom, I was surprised you even signed up for this event, knowing that Logan Kennedy would be here."

"We should do nicely this weekend," Marilyn said. "I'm not letting that detestable woman get in our way. She's already cost us plenty."

Andy gave Marilyn a quizzical look. "She's 'cost you plenty'? What does she have to do with you guys, anyway? I figured she was with some big New York publisher."

Marilyn narrowed her eyes and sipped her coffee silently.

"Well, you see," Roger explained, "Logan submitted one of her early efforts at Kat Taggett to Dillard Press back in the mid-eighties. It had been rejected by quite a few agents by then. Action and suspense weren't really in our wheelhouse, but my folks saw a lot of potential in Kat."

"Logan knows how to spin a page-turner," Marilyn sniffed. "I'll give her that."

"Mom and Dad—especially Dad—worked with her on the manuscript," Roger continued, "for months. Evenings and weekends. Logan practically lived at our house. Back then, she was working as a teacher's aide at St. Magnus Prep."

"And she went by her real name, Laverna Klingelhoets," Marilyn put in. "Not as sexy as Logan Kennedy, is it?"

"I was just a little kid," Roger recalled. "But I remember her *very* well. She was around a lot. Then one day, she just stopped coming. Never returned calls. Nothing. Silence."

"Wow, that's kinda harsh, isn't it?" Andy said. "So what the heck happened?"

"One morning it was in the *Chronicle*," Roger recounted. "The headline said something like 'Local Woman Nabs Major Book Contract.' While my parents were helping her with her manuscript, Logan had sent it off to a big-shot Manhattan agent. He got her a hefty, multi-book contract."

Marilyn mumbled something that rhymed with "rich."

"The first book was as much Mom and Dad's work as hers. And you know the thanks they got?"

Sensing an unhappy ending, Andy shook his head.

"A fruit basket and a signed copy of the book. And we haven't had a word from her since then. Not a single word."

"Why didn't you take her to court?" Andy asked.

"It was a handshake deal," Marilyn said with a shrug. "We liked her and trusted her. Besides, Roger Senior just wanted the whole thing to go away. Truth be told, I think he had a bit of a crush on the woman."

"No, not true," Roger protested. "Dad never had eyes for anybody but you, Mom."

"After we heard the news about Logan, my husband seemed to lose some of his *joie de vivre*," Marilyn recalled. "I always wondered whether her betrayal had something to do with his heart attack. Kat Taggett has killed dozens of fictional bad guys. But my husband might have been her real-life victim."

Andy couldn't think of a good response. But based on what he'd heard about Logan Kennedy, she sounded radioactive—a cold, calculating piece of work.

"Well, anyway," Roger said, positioning the final books on the shelf, "we probably won't see her at all."

"I heard that she's doing some super secret give-away," Andy said. "All hush-hush."

Roger snorted. "You'd have to be comatose not to know what it is. Her publisher's giving away some pricey piece of jewelry as part of the launch of her new book."

"How'd you figure that out?" Andy asked.

"Kat Taggett likes her weapons lethal, her jewels priceless, and her sex steamy," Marilyn recited from her chair. "My husband came up with that tagline, back when he was helping *Laverna* shape the character."

"So," Roger said, "unless the publisher is planning to give away a sniper rifle or a night of hot sex—which I think might be illegal in Beaver Tail County—it's pretty safe to assume the secret giveaway will be a high-end necklace or bracelet." He grinned impishly. "Besides, we happen to have the straight scoop. Mom has a friend who collects Grant Hamsden pieces. And Grant told her about it but made her promise to keep her mouth shut."

Marilyn laughed. "Knowing Cecie Barnum, every-one in Hobartville will have heard about it by now."

Wishing the Dillards a successful Holiday Faire, Andy headed back to the Hofdahl Farm Cheese booth. It was a few minutes after noon now. He still wanted to track down Aunt Bev, but he figured he had better check on Harald to see if the mournful mutt needed any food or outdoor time.

When he got there, Sonny and Harald were all alone. The dog gave him a morose look.

"So, has he been down in the dumps since I left?" Andy asked.

"Oh, no," said Sonny. "Just when he sees you. People have been stopping by to pet him and fuss over him. That tail of his has been going like a windshield wiper."

"Ah-hah!" Andy said to Harald. "The Mr. Gloomy Pants routine was just an act." He turned back to Sonny. "So, where's Thor?"

"Beats me," she said, slamming a wedge of cheese down on the cutting board just a bit too hard. "I could've had my assistant here instead, you know. Now *she's* a hard worker. But Thorstein asked to come. And then he goes and wanders off just when I need him."

Andy knew that when Sonny called Thor by his full Christian name, she usually wasn't happy with him. He figured this would be a good time to take Harald off her hands for a bit. Saying so long, man and canine ambled out of the conference center hall and headed into the lobby, zigging and zagging among the guests. The place was starting to fill up.

Glancing out the broad front windows, Andy saw that it was snowing even harder than when he had taken Harald outside. He looked down at the dog. "Is this what you were trying to tell me? That a storm was coming our way?"

Harald gazed up woefully, and Andy could almost read his thoughts: *That is exactly right, you big dummy.*

It was early, though. If Andy left soon, he could still make it down to the Cities. But he needed to touch base with Aunt Bev and okay it with her. Where the heck was she? He pulled out his phone. As if by magic, the thing ding-donged and her number popped up.

"Hey, Aunt Bev, I've been looking for you…"

"Hello, Mayor Skyberg?" said a totally unexpected male voice.

Andy hesitated. "Umm, who is this?"

"Tim Fisher. General manager of the resort. We met earlier."

Andy could feel his heart begin to race a little. "How come you're on my aunt's phone?"

"Well, there's a bit of a situation here. I stepped into Beverly's cube to show her the *correct* way to fill out a temp requisition form. And suddenly she got light-headed and turned pale. Fact is, she almost keeled over. I suggest you get over here *immediately*."

Chapter Seven

Andy was relieved to find his aunt sitting upright, nibbling on what looked like a tuna salad sandwich and sipping from a bottle of Gatorade. It struck him, as it did sometimes, how small she actually was. Of course, to Andy, at six-four, lots of people seemed kind of small.

Inexplicably, Doris Schattenheimer, one of his aunt's best friends, hovered over her, earnestly encouraging further sandwich consumption. Andy wondered if Doris had been hired as a temp, too. Or was she here to attend the Girls' Weekend Out festivities? Whatever the reason, he was happy she was on the job. Tim Fisher was nowhere to be seen.

Harald, with his doggie ESP, whimpered when he saw Aunt Bev, padded over, and placed his chin on her knee, as if to comfort her.

"What a sweet ol' pooch." Aunt Bev put down her drink and petted Harald's dome. "You're worried about me, aren't you, Harald?"

"Him and me both," Andy said. "From what Tim

Fisher told me, I expected to see you sprawled out on a stretcher."

At the mention of her boss's name, Aunt Bev wrinkled her nose. "Tim tends to overreact. It was my own fault, just having that sprinkle donut for breakfast. And three or four cups of coffee the rest of the morning. And no lunch until this. Didn't fuel up properly."

She squinted at Andy. "You're not looking so great yourself. Have you had lunch yet?"

It was a pure Aunt Bev move, turning the tables so that *Andy* was the one who needed attention, rather than her. But he took it as a good sign. She must be feeling better.

"No, actually. Haven't eaten yet."

Aunt Bev gently pushed Harald away and grabbed her purse from beneath the desk. She pulled a twenty out of her wallet and thrust it at her friend. "Doris, hon, do me a favor, wouldja? Run out to the Lumberjack Café and get Anders a sandwich, okay? If he gets light-headed, it's a lot farther down for him than for me."

Andy protested that he could get his own lunch, but Doris scurried off, looking happy to have a mission.

"So what happened?" he asked, plopping down in the chair across from his aunt. "And how come Doris is here?"

"Well, she came up to Hobartville this morning for a dentist appointment. And afterwards, she popped in to say hi. Lucky for me. Tim was chewing me out about some darn form, and I suddenly felt all dizzy. Doris walked in on that, and claimed I was as white as a ghost and wavering in the breeze. She grabbed me before I could take a dive. Eased me down into the chair. She's a strong girl, Doris."

Andy smiled, remembering fundraisers around New Bergen for school and church activities, where Doris challenged all comers in arm wrestling. Buy a chance to vanquish Mrs. Schattenheimer, and you could win a prize. She had thoroughly trounced Andy on several occasions.

"Anyway," Aunt Bev continued, "Tim called you and, well, you know the rest." She took another nibble from her sandwich. "I'm sorry about this, Anders. I really am. It's just a lot of fuss about nothing."

"It is *not* nothing," snapped a voice from behind Andy. Tim Fisher had returned, a dark cloud shading his features.

"Beverly, we have not had one serious accident here since I started," the resort manager intoned. "What if you'd fallen over and hit your head on something and ended up with a concussion? That could be a big work-man's comp claim. Would that be fair to the corpora-tion? Do you think I want that on my tab?" He put his hands on his hips, his stern look suddenly morphing to fear. "You don't think it's the stomach bug, do you?" He backed up a couple of steps.

"No, Tim, I do not." Aunt Bev shot him that tight little smile she gave people she really didn't like. "The sandwich and sports drink are doing the trick. I think I'll maybe have myself a little power nap."

"Okay," he sniffed. "But you have to be out on the exhibition floor when the doors open at two. Understood?"

"Right." She nodded, looking at her desk clock. It was about twelve-thirty.

"I'm needed at the front desk," Tim said. "We're getting stranded travelers checking in. They're starting to close sections of the interstate up north. We may even have to break out the cots." His voice resonated with solemn and, Andy thought, phony concern. Then it brightened. "I bet we can fill up all those units out by the clubhouse." Again, darkness came over his face. Quite genuine this time, it seemed. "Oh, hell. They better not be giving people the off-season rates." Without another word, he scooted away at a half-jog.

"You know," Andy said, leaning toward his aunt, "I really don't like that guy."

"Tim's all right," she replied. "It's just that his people skills need a teensy bit more work. Oh, look, here comes Doris."

The New Bergen stalwart arrived bearing a hefty beef sandwich wrapped in cellophane. Andy thanked her and opened it. He pulled out some of the meat and fed it to Harald. Andy took a bite himself. It tasted delicious—tender beef, with mayo and lettuce, nestled in hearty whole wheat slices. Aunt Bev's instinct that he needed some chow had been right on. How did aunts and mothers always know these things?

"Now listen, kiddo," she said, "I got your message and I think it's fine for you to leave whenever you want to. You got that nice weekend planned down in the Cities, and if you take off now, you can beat the weather."

She stood up and, to Andy's dismay, wobbled. Noticeably. Doris grabbed her by the arm.

"I'm okay," Aunt Bev protested, though the look on her face wasn't reassuring. "It's nothing, it's nothing."

Andy's head had been momentarily flooded with happy visions. Of the packed basketball arena at the university. Of *pad see ew* at that hole-in-the-wall Thai joint. Of the Blitzers ripping up the stage. And, above all, of his date, Paula. Pretty, smart, funny, now-single Paula.

He had been looking forward to his big-city escape for weeks.

Which made it all the more painful to admit that Aunt Bev still looked shaky. A little nap was probably all she needed. But she had a tough job ahead of her, with Tim Fisher breathing down her neck. This was one situation where a spunky, full-speed-ahead gal might just need a lifeline.

Andy gave a big, silent sigh. "You know, Aunt Bev, I'm thinking I'll stick around a while longer. In case you guys need a utility infielder. Just to make sure everything's copacetic."

A brief look of relief flashed across her face. She tried to hide it. Then she shook her head firmly. "No, Anders. I can handle it. You just scram, before the snow gets any worse."

Andy could have taken her at her word—and driven off for his Friday evening fun. But he knew it would be wrong.

"Naw, I'll hang around a bit and get going by four or five. The Silverado's good in the snow."

Aunt Bev gave him a grateful little smile. "Are you sure, sweetie?"

"You betcha. It'll be fun." Taking a bite of roast beef, he hoped that last bit sounded like he actually meant it.

Just then Aunt Bev's phone rang. "Uh-huh," she said. "Uh-huh. Is it heavy? Okay, I have someone here who can do that. Just bring it to my cube."

"Wha' wa' tha' abou'?" Andy mumbled through the mouthful of sandwich.

"A box is coming that I need you to deliver to Logan Kennedy's suite."

"Oh, yeah," Andy said, wiping his mouth, "I met Grant Hamsden, the jeweler. He told me all about the Kat Blast."

"Oh, did he show you the necklace she's giving away? With that jeweled poison dart frog?"

Jeweled dart frog?! Andy thought. *No, he did not. But he did tell me that only a chosen few knew about it, not including Beverly Engebretson.*

"They're even bringing in a special safe just to keep the thing in when they roll it out onto the stage," Aunt Bev said. "Rosemary forgot to brief me on it before she left on her biking trip. I found the file about it on her desk when I was looking for my stapler. But don't tell anyone, Anders—it's top secret."

She stood on her tiptoes and gave Andy a peck on the cheek. He helped by leaning down a bit.

"Now I'm gonna go grab a little shut-eye before the Holiday Faire opens."

With that, she and Doris headed out of the office, arm in arm, like two schoolgirls making for the playground.

Andy looked down at King Harald and grinned. "Logan Kennedy's super-secret reveal has to be the worst-kept secret in the history of Beaver Tail County."

He pulled out his phone and a moment later was telling Phil that he might not arrive until nine or ten. It surprised him when his buddy encouraged him to wait until tomorrow. There were already reports, he said, of folks getting stranded in the snow, jack-knifed semis, the whole deal.

"Just sit tight and try to get down here in the morning," Phil advised.

Feeling a bit crestfallen about losing a chunk of weekend fun, Andy tried to sound upbeat. "Don't worry, buddy, I'll be there tomorrow, even if I have to hitch the mutt to a dogsled."

As he hung up, a guy from the front desk appeared with a medium-size cardboard box. "Special delivery for Logan Kennedy." With a thud, he put the box down on the desk. "Let me tell you what room she's in."

With the box under his right arm and Harald's leash in his left hand, Andy headed for the lobby, but realized he was thirsty. Earlier, he'd seen a water fountain down one of the corridors. A few feet from the fountain, there was an open office door and out of it came a distinctive voice.

"It's just not working."

Andy could hardly mistake Tim Fisher's sonorous, self-important tone.

"She's in way over her head. As soon as Rosemary's back, snip snip."

"Is it because she's so old?" a youngish female voice asked.

Tim laughed. "Now, now, now, you mustn't say that. You know as well as I do that we cannot fire someone just because they're *old*. That would be *illegal*." He chuckled again. "You need cause. And I have a feeling that Beverly will give us plenty of that this weekend."

Clearly, the guy had painted a target on Aunt Bev's back. Andy's first instinct was to tell her. But should he stick his nose in? His sister Kirsten—a veteran of the corporate world—had warned Aunt Bev that the workplace had gotten meaner since she had been a secretary at Lovely Lena Macaroni Corporation after high school. But, with that feisty outlook of hers, Aunt Bev had been determined to give it a try. She was a big girl, however short she might be.

In an even grumpier mood than before, Andy tiptoed away, hauling Harald behind. It wouldn't do for Tim to know he had been overheard. The two emerged into a lobby that was jammed with people—not only Girls' Weekend Out guests, Andy figured, but folks seeking shelter from the storm. As he wended his way through the crowd, he heard a voice call his name.

"Andy, hi!"

A grinning, parka-clad woman with a scruffy knit cap pulled down over her ears waved at him. It took him a second before he realized who it was.

"Well, Becky Reingold, howdy. I almost didn't recognize you with that cap on. You look just like some random dog musher."

She laughed. "It's an old hand-me-down from my dad's hunting days." She tugged off the blue cap to reveal a head of tousled dark hair. "It's the warmest thing I own. What brings you and Harald here?" She reached down and patted the dog's head.

"My aunt works at the resort and she needed a hand," Andy replied, shifting the box from his right arm to his left. "You come for the Girls' Weekend Out?"

"Yup, some of my co-workers from the hospital twisted my arm. Glad we got here when we did. If you don't want to get stuck here, you'd better hightail it back to New Bergen."

Andy explained that his aunt had just had a dizzy spell, so he wanted to stick around a bit longer and keep an eye on her.

Becky's face went serious. "Would you like me to look at her?"

Becky was a nurse practitioner at St. Luke's Hospital in Hobartville. Andy had originally met her through her great-aunt, a retired teacher whom he knew. He hated to impose on her, but a professional once-over couldn't hurt.

"You know, Becky, that'd be awful nice of you. She's taking a nap right now, but…"

Before he could finish the sentence, Andy did a double take. Steaming in their direction, looking bright and chipper, came the allegedly snoozing aunt.

"Aunt Bev," he sputtered, "you're supposed to be sleeping."

"I got an all-staff text that a Canadian hockey team was coming in," she said, stopping next to Andy and Becky. "Guess they can't get any farther north. So we have to find room for them."

Through the lobby windows, Andy saw a gray bus rolling up to the double front doors. Emblazoned on its side in bright red jagged script was *MOOSE JUNCTION BOLTS*. The vehicle, plastered with snow, lurched to a halt, and it almost immediately began disgorging bleary-eyed young men.

Andy turned back to Becky. "You know something? I think it's going to be a pretty wild weekend."

Chapter Eight

"Where the heck you gonna put 'em all?" Andy asked Aunt Bev, as the skaters of the Moose Junction Bolts trooped in through the lobby.

"Oh, that's in Tim's bandwidth. He's real good at envisioneering turn-key solutions."

Andy wasn't certain what that meant, but it sure sounded impressive. He watched as Tim and a female staffer consulted with a couple of tall, ruddy-looking men in winter overcoats—probably the team coaches or managers.

"Wonder if he's going to try to find another hotel for them," Andy said.

Aunt Bev shook her head. "Sounds like every room in town is taken. And Doris heard even the armory's starting to fill up. Anyway, someone told me they've got dozens of cots in storage for emergencies like this. They'll probably stick these kids in one of the conference rooms."

Even though it was just a minor league team, the

players in the lobby had already attracted plenty of attention from folks, including several young ladies. Andy speculated that some of the lads might find more pleasant accommodations tonight than cots in conference rooms.

Aunt Bev suddenly seemed to notice Becky standing next to him.

"And who is your friend, Anders?" she asked sweetly.

"Oh, sorry, forgot to introduce you. This is Becky Reingold. She's a nurse practitioner at St. Luke's. Becky, this is my favorite aunt, Beverly Engebretson."

The two women nodded at each other.

"I met Becky through her aunt, Cappy Briggs," Andy explained. "Remember? Cappy's the retired teacher who helped me track down that ebelskiver recipe." More recently, he had encountered Becky in the ER, the night he had clocked a murderer and messed up his right hand. He turned to her. "Aunt Bev works here at the resort. Like I said, she had kind of a dizzy spell earlier."

"Dizzy spell, huh?" Becky leaned in for a closer look at Aunt Bev. "How are you feeling now?"

"Oh, I'm perfectly fine," Aunt Bev answered firmly. "Just didn't eat enough this morning. Too gosh-darned busy. Had a sandwich and a Gatorade a little while ago, and it worked like a charm. Now tell me, Becky, does your husband work at St. Luke's, too?"

Andy shot Aunt Bev an irritated look. Talk about subtle.

But Becky didn't seem at all bothered by the question. "Actually, never been married."

Andy knew that look on his aunt's face. It was Beverly Engebretson's *Fitting-Up-Anders-for-a-Tux-and-Wedding-Ring* look. Anytime he went out with someone, he did his darnedest to keep both Aunt Bev and his mom in the dark. Learning that Andy was dating someone gave them both the vapors.

"Now Beverly, are you sure I can't give you a quick look-see?" Becky asked. "It'd only take a few minutes. We can go up to my room."

"No, no," Aunt Bev insisted, shaking her head. "I'm really fine."

"Well, I'm in Room 328 in the main lodge," said Becky. "In case you change your mind. Nice seeing you, Andy." She picked up her green canvas duffle and walked off in the direction of the main lodge elevators.

Aunt Bev smiled encouragingly at her nephew. "You could do a lot worse, you know."

"I've been around her like only three times," Andy protested.

"Well, I like the girl."

Andy liked her, too, but he wasn't going to tell his aunt that he did. "You know her even less than I do."

"I have good instincts when it comes to people, and that's a fact. And besides, how have sexy Finnish architects and bossy policewomen worked out for you lately?"

She had poked him right in one of his most tender

spots. "Ouch," he muttered darkly, frowning at the mention of his two most recent squeezes.

"Maybe you could use a nice, down-to-earth nurse."

"Nurse practitioner."

"Whatever. They make great wives, nurses. Ready to patch a husband up the minute he does something dumb. She's good-looking, too."

His aunt had a point there. But Andy definitely wanted to get off this particular subject.

"Listen, Aunt Bev, my friend Phil down in the Cities said I shouldn't try to get there tonight—too dangerous. So I'll hang around here a little while longer. Then I'll nip back down to New Bergen later. I'll drop off Harald with Uncle Frank tomorrow morning on my way out of town."

At the mention of his name, Harald—who had been calmly soaking in the hectic activity of the lobby— looked up and gave a quiet *woof*. It startled a few folks around them, but no one seemed to mind a canine presence. In fact, a little girl came running over to pet him, followed by her mom.

"That's not a bad idea, hon," Aunt Bev said, after the girl and mom left. "But if you need to, you and Harald can stay in my timeshare unit tonight." She blinked at the box Andy was holding. "That's for Logan Kennedy?"

"Yup, sure is," Andy answered. His shoulders were getting fatigued from holding the blasted thing.

"Well, you better go deliver it. And afterwards, you

can leave Harald in the timeshare while you help me with the Holiday Faire opening." With that, Aunt Bev headed back the way she had come.

Before he went up to Logan Kennedy's suite, Andy decided to make a quick pit stop in the resort's gift shop for a bite of dessert—a Nut Goodie. He bought the candy bar, set Logan's box down on top of a display case, and ripped the wrapper open. As he started to munch away, Harald peered up plaintively and made a tiny peep of a whine.

"Sorry, sport, chocolate isn't healthy for you." Andy dangled the wrapper in front of Harald. "See, it says right here. 'Do not eat if you have more than two legs.' It's the law."

Harald looked as if he wasn't buying it. As if he was perfectly willing to risk life and limb for a taste of the scrumptious morsel.

As Andy savored the concoction of chocolate, maple, and peanuts, the peculiar couple he had seen that morning in the conference center came clumping along. They planted themselves on the other side of a rack of sweatshirts not ten feet away, oblivious to Andy and Harald.

The woman was still in her monochromatic outfit, but she had at least removed her shades. She and her slouching male friend, who appeared to have combed his hair with an eggbeater, looked to be no older than their early thirties.

"If it weren't for Sara," the woman complained, "we could get through to Logan and explain things to her."

"Sara's nothing but a gatekeeper," the man muttered darkly. "I hate gatekeepers. They keep you outside the gate."

She gave him a sour look. "Well, duh, Bobby."

He shot her a goofy smile and shrugged.

"The problem is," the woman said, "we've maybe been a little too pushy. Bringing her the *cassoulet au canard* and the 1990 Petrus was a bit over the top."

"Big mistake."

The woman grimaced. "Yeah, big mistake. But I really thought Logan would appreciate the symbolism. I mean, surprising her with one of Kat's favorite meals— she eats it in almost every book."

"I guess turning up at her doorstep that last time kinda spooked her."

"Didn't think she'd threaten us with a restraining order, though. I really didn't. But she has to understand that we've learned our lesson, Bobby. We haven't approached her in like six months." Her expression hardened. "And she needs to appreciate how important my blog is to her. I've got thirty thousand Kat fans following me on Twitter. I bet I sell more of her books than all the advertising her publisher does."

"I wouldn't be surprised," Bobby nodded.

"Honeycakes, I just want her to respect me."

"But babe, she will. Because pretty soon you're gonna have the leverage. You know about what she did. And you can prove it. Logan'll never underestimate you again."

* * *

Man and dog took the main lodge elevator up to the fifth floor. Andy couldn't help thinking about the conversation he had just heard. The guy was called Bobby—aka Honeycakes—but he had no idea who the woman was. Should he share what he had heard with Logan Kennedy and her gatekeeper Sara? Or would it be better to keep his trap shut? He just wasn't sure.

As the elevator door opened into the fifth-floor hallway, Andy looked down to his right and saw a man emerge from a room at the far end of the corridor. An older man with gray hair, wearing old-fashioned horn-rimmed glasses. In a red flannel shirt and bib overalls. Looking suspiciously like Thor Hofdahl, purveyor of goat cheese.

Andy almost shouted out, but the guy took a quick turn and headed in the opposite direction, ducking into a stairwell.

Strange, Andy thought. Was that his and Sonny's room? Otherwise, who would Thor be visiting up here?

His question was answered when he and Harald arrived at the door Thor had emerged from. And what Andy discovered left him scratching his head.

It was Logan Kennedy's suite.

Chapter Nine

Andy stood outside Logan Kennedy's door, blinking and baffled. What kind of business could a crusty old socialist have with a glamorous, high-flying novelist? He knocked on the door, and a moment later it swung open.

A young, attractive woman with long dark hair and deep brown eyes regarded him, a phone plastered to her left ear. She was wearing the same conservative jacket and slacks she had been wearing when he ran into her and Logan down in the Holiday Faire. Glancing at him, she held up her right index finger. "Be with you in a sec," she mouthed to him.

"Good, good," she said into the phone. "I think we're pretty much set then. And it looks like the superfan books just arrived. Logan can start signing them after she gets out of the shower." She paused to listen. "Right, the livestream starts at five on the dot tomorrow." Another pause. "Grant said it's perfectly secure... No... No, she won't. I'll see to it."

As she spoke, the young woman reestablished eye

contact with Andy and pointed to the side table near the door. He figured she wanted him to put the box there, which he did, next to a big leather purse.

He snuck a quick peek at Logan Kennedy's suite. There was a living room and kitchenette, with two bedroom doors. Through one of the doors, Andy could hear the sound of a shower blasting energetically.

On the long, brown sofa, Logan's dog lounged languorously. It lifted its head for one look at Andy, another at Harald, then lay back down—the very picture of canine world-weariness. Harald's friendly body language and wagging tail had no effect on the animal, apparently. The big ginger mutt soon gave up, seeming a little miffed by such doggy indifference.

The young woman, still on her phone, went over to the purse, fished out a wallet, and extracted a banknote. She handed it to Andy. A five-dollar bill. She silently mouthed the words, "Thank you."

He realized she was giving him a tip.

"Now, Georgia," she said, "I've really gotta run. I'll get back to you tomorrow, okay?" The woman tapped the screen on her phone and turned to Andy. "Logan's publicity person. Wants an update on every blessed little thing."

"Listen," Andy said, thrusting the bill back at her, "I don't really work here. I shouldn't be taking this."

She raised her eyebrows. "Who are you then? Why are you delivering packages? And why do you have that dog with you?"

For a few seconds, Andy was flummoxed. Her questions struck him as somewhat existential and deep. Who *was* Andy Skyberg? Limo driver? Artist? Restaurant host? Reluctant politician? Apprehender of bad guys? Why, at age forty, *was* he doing menial labor for his Aunt Bev? Why did he always have Harald at his side? Did he need a therapy animal? A way to connect emotionally with others?

But, of course, this wasn't the occasion to delve into matters philosophical. "I'm Andy Skyberg," he blurted out, "and I'm the mayor of New Bergen."

Taking the bill back, she stared at him, a little wary—rather like Andy might have regarded someone walking down the street all alone, babbling nonsense to himself.

He tried to redeem the situation. "My aunt works at the resort and needed some help. As for Harald here, I'm on my way to stash him in my aunt's timeshare."

The woman looked a bit mollified, but not entirely. She leaned over, petted Harald, and straightened back up. "The mayor of New Bergen? *Really*?"

Andy gave the two-fingered Cub Scout salute. "At your service. It was kind of an accident, and I'm just the temporary mayor until the election next spring."

"*Ooookay*," she answered, "whatever you say." She went back to her purse, replaced the five note, pulled out a stainless-steel pocketknife, and zipped open the box.

"Copies of the new hardcover," she explained. "Logan needs to write a personal message in each of them for some local superfans. She's doing a book signing in the Holiday Faire tomorrow before the big Kat Blast at five. By the way, I'm Sara Blake, Logan's PA. Her personal assistant." She quickly offered her hand for Andy to shake, then pulled out the top book in the box. "Oh, it looks perfect. *Perfect.* Logan will be so pleased." She handed the book to Andy.

He examined it closely. The vividly colored title read *Dart Shot.* In the background, in silhouette, a sleek couple groped each other in a steamy embrace. Below the title, dominating the cover, floated the image of a brilliant blue frog with black markings. Excellent work by the illustrator.

"A poison dart frog," said Sara. "South American natives used its secretions to dip their arrows in. A single gram of the toxin could kill a thousand people. In the book, a rival assassin comes after Kat with poisoned darts."

So, thought Andy, this little blue guy must be what Grant Hamsden had used as a model for his necklace. What gems would recreate those vivid colors? Sapphires and black diamonds, maybe?

"You like Logan's books?" Sara asked.

"Never read any, actually. But maybe I'll give this one a try," he said, handing the book back. "That image of the frog is a knockout. Wouldn't surprise me if it jumped right off the dust jacket. I can't wait to see it on the…"

Andy suddenly caught himself. The frog necklace

was supposed to be top secret. Only a chosen few—*not* including Andy Skyberg—were supposed to know about it.

Sara stared at him. "See it on the *what*?"

"Ummm, on the poster," Andy improvised. "I imagine you're having some printed up for bookstores."

Sara seemed a little puzzled. "Well, yes, there's always promotional material. Now, if you don't mind, I have work to do."

"Oh, yeah, sure. Time for us to vamoose." Andy started to leave, but turned back. Ever since he arrived there, Andy had been wondering about that man he glimpsed when the elevator door opened. "Say, I thought I saw a friend of mine leaving the suite here just before I arrived. Old guy. Blue overalls and red flannel shirt."

Sara nodded. "He was in Logan's room for a while, before she took her shower."

"Door open or closed?" squeaked Andy.

She looked surprised at the question. "Closed." Then she shrugged. "Of course, it's none of my business what goes on in there."

Andy didn't like what she was implying. "No, you've got it wrong. Thor's like seventy years old and happily married." He laughed. "I can't imagine he'd be Logan's type."

She gave him a knowing look. "Oh, I can assure you, when it comes to men, all kinds of them are her type. And she particularly savors the happily married ones." She made air quotes when she said "happily."

Feeling a little unsettled, Andy turned to leave. Just as he was about to step out into the hallway, he heard a husky female voice.

"And who do we have here?"

He turned back and saw Logan Kennedy standing in her bedroom door, wearing a plush, white bathrobe, with a white towel wrapped around her head. She was rubbing her hands together, distributing some kind of skin cream.

"Haven't I seen you and your dog before?"

Andy smiled nervously. "Yeah, Harald and I almost bumped into you and your pooch earlier today. In the Holiday Faire."

"Well, I wouldn't have minded a good bump," said the author with something like a leer. "And Nikkie wouldn't have, either."

So, a female pooch. "What breed?"

"We ran her DNA. She's quite a mix. Golden retriever, boxer, black lab, fox terrier, and a few others. She's a mutt and a real sweetie. I named her Dominique, but we all call her Nikkie."

At the mention of her name, the dog climbed off the sofa and padded over to join her mistress.

"Nikkie id a compwete puddytat, idn't she?" Logan leaned over and kissed her on the top of the head.

"Logan," Sara said, "this is Andy Skyberg. He just delivered our books for the superfans. And he actually is the mayor of New Bergen."

The author looked at Andy with surprise. "Oh, my.

We're so important, they sent a mayor to deliver our books? Beaver Tail County really rolls out the red carpet."

She crossed her arms, moved closer, and looked him up and down, as if she were a judge in the livestock barn at the county fair and he were a prize bull. As if she were measuring the broadness of those shoulders, the girth of that chest, the straightness of the spine, the strength of that rump.

Oh, jeez, thought Andy. *How the heck do I get out of here?*

He blinked down at Harald for moral support. But Harald was sniffing Nikkie's posterior, and she was showing a certain interest in his.

"When I was a teenager, sixteen, seventeen years old," Logan said, "friends and I would drive down to New Bergen to Lasker's Bar. Remember Lasker's? On and off sales?"

Andy nodded. It had been on the north end of Skjegstad Street, near the interstate. They'd sell you booze to drink *on* the premises or *off*. "It's been closed fifteen years now," he noted.

"Well, in those days there was always a good chance they wouldn't card you at Lasker's."

Andy recalled that Lasker's patchy ID-checking was one of the things that had led to its demise.

"We'd get a twelve pack of whatever was cheapest, then go out to the county park and drink and party. Usually three of us girls and a couple of the boys.

Sometimes we'd go skinny-dipping. First time I got to examine the male anatomy up close and personal. A miracle no one got pregnant." She gave Andy a teasing smile. "So, I have kind of a soft spot for New Bergen."

Logan plopped onto the sofa and her bathrobe fell open to reveal some very shapely legs. Actually, amazing legs for a fifty-something, Andy thought.

"Andy is short for Andrew?"

"Actually, it's short for Anders."

"So, *Anders*, have you read my books?"

"Not yet. But I plan to grab a copy of this new one, for sure."

"A lot of men don't like them, you know. Because Kat Taggett is all about female empowerment. It's *her* sexual satisfaction that's paramount. The guys are just a means to an end."

She took the towel off her head and started to fluff her short damp hair. "Truth be told, I'm a bit sick of the woman. I mean, after fifteen books, who wouldn't be? But I'm contractually obligated to write one more Kat before I can take a break." She tilted her head suggestively. "She needs a new butler in the next book, you know."

Feeling like a mouse being toyed with by a cat, Andy confessed that he wasn't aware of this little fact.

"What would you think if I called her new butler, umm… Anders?"

Andy grinned nervously. He didn't want to be here anymore. "Well, uuuh, I, umm…"

"Kat's hideaway is in the Caymans, and her butler never wears anything more than a Speedo. Very often, less," Logan said coyly. "How does that sound, Sara? A butler called Anders?"

Andy caught a glimpse of Logan's PA. Sara looked no more amused than he was.

"What I think, Logan," she said in a firm, even tone, "is that you ought to start signing those books. And I'm sure Andy has other things he needs to get done."

"Oh, yeah, lots to do," Andy blurted. "The Holiday Faire's opening in a little while. They need me down there."

Andy and Harald started out of the suite, with Sara following them.

"Hope to see *more* of you soon, Anders," came Logan's husky voice from behind.

"Sorry about that," Sara whispered out in the hall-way. "Her cougar routine gets a little old, believe you me. But, hey, if you're here tomorrow, stop by the Kat Blast and I'll get you a comp copy of *Dart Shot*."

"That'd be great," answered Andy. But mentally he crossed every finger he had, hoping that by tomorrow afternoon he would be nowhere near the Beaver Tail Re-sort and Conference Center. Snow or no snow, he intended to make it down to the Cities for at least half a weekend of fun.

With a friendly nod, Sara went back into the suite and shut the door.

"You seemed to enjoy that more than I did," Andy

said, looking down at Harald. "So, Mr. Smooth, did Nikkie smell good?"

His pooch, the very ideal of discretion, said nothing.

"That Logan's a man-eater, Harald," Andy muttered as they headed toward the elevator. "I just wish I knew what Thor was doing with her."

The dog made a quiet *woof.*

Andy looked at Harald with alarm. "No, bud, no way. It couldn't be *that.*"

Chapter Ten

After he had fled Logan Kennedy's suite and left Harald with Doris Schattenheimer in Aunt Bev's time-share, Andy joined a cluster of folks watching the Weather Channel on the big lobby television. The meteorologist explained that the blizzard—for full-blown blizzard it had become—had taken an unexpected rightward swing, away from the border with Manitoba up north. Beaver Tail County sat right in the bull's-eye and could expect upwards of sixteen inches.

"Gotta say, I am real glad to be here," the guy standing next to him said.

Andy nodded. "Better than being in a ditch somewhere."

"No kidding. Nice bed. Restaurants and a bar. Cable TV. Great place to get stranded. And I hear there's a book signing with Logan Kennedy tomorrow. I've read a few of her stories. They really pull you in. I might actually try to get an autographed copy."

The guy was lanky and fit, in his fifties, with a full

head of salt-and-pepper hair and a trim silver beard. He was wearing a camo jacket and pants.

"Been hunting then?" Andy asked.

"Yeah. Pheasant. Over in South Dakota. Near Murdo."

"Do well?"

"Got my limit. They're field-dressed and out in the trunk, chilling down. You hunt?"

"When I was a kid," Andy answered. "Deer, ducks. Not my thing, really, sitting in blinds and stands, freezing my keister off. I like to fish, though."

The other guy did, too, and they compared recent fishing jaunts. In September the fellow had spent two weeks on a floatplane fishing trip up in the Northwest Territories. Andy was envious as heck—no way could he afford an expedition like that.

"Ready to get home, though," the man said. "Been on the road a week and a half. Before Murdo, I had some meetings in the Cities."

"What line are you in?"

"I farm and dabble a little in real estate. What about you?"

"I work in a restaurant down in New Bergen. And I…" Andy still found it a little awkward talking about his side job. "I'm mayor of the town. Actually, interim mayor, until the election next spring…"

He was saved from further blathering when his phone ding-donged. It was Aunt Bev, asking him to hurry over to the Holiday Faire. The doors were set to open in twenty minutes, and there were still a couple of vendors who needed help. Andy rushed over to pitch in, and by the time he glanced at his watch, he was surprised to see that it was already two-thirty. The Faire had only been open for half an hour, but it was packed.

People were milling around, talking and laughing and, more importantly, buying. All the vendors were busy swiping credit cards. A costumed quartet of strolling carolers added a dash of Victorian charm. But their "Good King Wenceslas" failed to lift Andy's spirits. That weather report had been a real bummer.

And the thing with Thor and Logan Kennedy was weighing on his mind, too. Andy had survived the experience of having a spouse cheat on him. No one deserved that kind of betrayal. He wanted to give Thor the benefit of the doubt—there may have been a good reason for him to be in Logan's bedroom with the door shut. But whatever was going on, Andy did not want to see Sonny Hofdahl get hurt.

He found the old boy at work in the Hofdahl Farm booth, busily describing to several attentive women the utter deliciousness that was Hofdahl Farm gouda in a grilled cheese sourdough sandwich. "Best grilled cheese in the known universe," he was saying. At the same time, the two guys from Boulder Creek Winery, who shared the booth with the Hofdahls, were rhapsodizing about their new vintage of Frontenac Gris. Sonny Hofdahl had just completed a sale when Andy caught her eye.

"How's everything going, Sonny?"

"I haven't had a chance to take a breath," she said, straightening a display of cheese. "With this weather, I thought maybe people might not show up. But I'm guessing half the folks who've come by aren't wearing GWO passes."

Andy knew that the guests who had registered for the Girls' Weekend Out had been issued lanyards with passes. They didn't need the passes to get into the Holiday Faire, but they would for the big smorgasbord and showing of *Sleepless in Seattle* that evening.

"Yeah, I've been wondering how many of these folks are staying at the resort and how many have to mush home later."

Sonny shook her head. "Sometimes people can be a little clueless about going out in this kind of weather. I just hope everyone gets home safe and sound."

"What about you guys? Gonna try to head home tonight?"

"Nope, wouldn't be safe. But we lucked out. Sage Mortenson said we could share her digs. Norske Knittery put her up in a nice suite. One of my girls is staying out at the farm to take care of the goats. How about you? Gonna try to make it home?"

"Yeah, gonna try. Aunt Bev said I could bunk with her if I can't get outta here. But hopefully it won't be necessary." He held up two pairs of crossed fingers.

As if on cue, he heard a very familiar voice. "Sonny, Anders. Any problems to report?"

Aunt Bev scooted toward them with that purposeful stride of hers. She seemed fully recovered from her recent wooziness. Behind her, like an overeager puppy, trotted Doris.

"Hi, Bev, Doris," Sonny greeted them. "No problems at all. You guys deserve a promotion for doing such a great job."

"Thanks, Sonny. Doris and I are on an errand of mercy. Vangie at the Cat House is working by herself, and she needs to use the litter box, if you catch my drift. We're going to spell her for a little bit." She peered up at her nephew. "Doris decided to spend the night here, Anders. Her husband didn't want her tackling the snow in her itty-bitty Mini. She'll be able to give me a hand if I need it. You should get out of here while the getting's good."

Andy grinned. "Best news I've heard all day."

After the two ladies bustled off, Andy glanced over at Thor.

"Himself there looks in good form." Andy nodded toward Thor, who was waving a circle of brie at his audience.

"When he's here," said Sonny, "he's Mr. Goat Cheese. But he's been taking too many long breaks. Won't tell me where he's been. I'm beginning to think he's probably buying me some fancy Christmas present and doesn't want me to catch him at it."

"Yeah, he probably doesn't want you to catch him at it," Andy said, squirming. He doubted that whatever

Thor was doing in Logan's bedroom had anything to do with Christmas presents. But fortunately, the conversation was interrupted by a customer who wanted to sample Sonny's chive chèvre.

Andy decided to pick up a cappuccino for his drive down to New Bergen. As the drink was being prepared, he decided to call his sister Kirsten—he hadn't talked to her all day. Stepping back from the counter, he pulled out his phone and tapped her number.

"Did you make it down to the Cities?" Kirsten asked, by way of greeting.

"Actually, I'm leaving for New Bergen in a few minutes. I'll take off for the Cities bright and early tomorrow."

"So you're still in Hobartville?"

"Yup. At the Girls' Weekend Out."

Kirsten hooted. "Well, sorry to be the bearer of bad news, but you're not going anywhere tonight. They just shut down the interstate all the way from New Bergen north to the state line."

"Oh hell!" Andy swore.

"We're even closing the restaurant early. You might as well kick back and have some fun with all your gal pals."

Andy groaned. "Yeah, I'm sure it'll be a riot." He said goodbye and stood there, stewing.

He had already given up his evening happy hour and New York strip at the steakhouse down in the Cities. Wasn't that enough? Now he wouldn't even be able to get to New Bergen tonight. And what if this was one of those storms that shut things down for days?

He felt a flash of panic about missing the Blitzers concert tomorrow night. He couldn't miss it. He wouldn't miss it. It would be a disaster. He'd been salivating over this show ever since Phil scored tickets. If Mother Nature herself had been standing there in front of him, in her green leafy robes, he would have flipped her off and said something very rude.

"Hey, Andy? Someone just die?" It was Roger Dillard. He was holding a scone and a cup of what smelled like spiced apple cider. "You look pretty down in the dumps."

"Hi, Roger. Yeah. Sounds like I'm stuck here tonight."

"Misery loves company. I didn't want to be here, either. But Mom thinks we can move a lot of excess inventory. She insisted we book a booth, even though she knew Logan Kennedy would be here. She despises that woman."

"She sure made that clear. How old were you when your parents worked with her?"

"About ten."

"And what did you think of her?"

Roger sighed. "Well, let me share a memory of a Christmastime long ago. I didn't see Mommy kissing Santa Claus. I saw Daddy kissing Logan Kennedy. In his office. They thought I was at hockey practice, but I came home early. Dad didn't see me. Logan did. She winked like it was a joke. I never told Mom, and I never will. I've only talked about it with my therapist."

"And you're telling me because?" Andy wasn't sure this was something he wanted to know.

"Sorry," Roger answered with an apologetic smile. "But you just have a sympathetic air about you. It's ancient history anyway—I've moved on. Maybe I'll catch you later." With that, he walked away.

What an awful thing for a kid to see, Andy thought. To carry that image around all these years. It wasn't the first time Andy had pondered the question, but why did people like Logan Kennedy have so much success, after they did such awful things? What the heck good was karma, then? He earnestly hoped he would have no further encounters with the woman while he was stuck there.

After he picked up his coffee, he decided to make another pass up and down the aisles. He spotted Aunt Bev in the Cat House booth and gave her the news. She said she'd call the front desk and have them make him a spare key card for her room. A moment later, ambling by the Written On Skin booth, he spotted a familiar face and stopped.

"Hey, Geraldine, planning on getting a tattoo?"

Geraldine Abbott, a solid, energetic blonde in fire engine-red glasses, offered her hand and shook Andy's with a firm grip. "Great to see you, Andy. And no tattoo for me. No siree. I get queasy at the sight of needles. I'm just waiting to have a few words with Damian. I've been trying to get him to join Tabby Dark. He's getting to be well known, and he'd be a great ambassador for us."

The dark-haired tattoo artist was busy inscribing what looked like a dove on a woman's upper arm, so there was no telling how long Geraldine would have to wait. Andy knew her as the Assistant Director of the Tri-County Area Business Economic Development and Revitalization Consortium—TABEDRC. Or "Tabby Dark," as locals translated the prodigious acronym. Part of Andy's mayoral duties was to represent New Bergen city government at the occasional Tabby Dark meeting. He had been to two, so far.

"Listen, Andy, I'm glad I ran into you," Geraldine said. "I was going to call your sister next week about a potential catering gig. But as long as you're here, you can pass it along. It's very tentative, but it could be lucrative and lots of fun."

"Okay, I'm all ears."

"Well," she said in a low, conspiratorial voice, "we've heard from the state film board, and they think Beaver Tail and Herkimer counties have a good shot at nabbing the location work for a new movie. I can't say what the story is or who's directing. But that person is a hot young property in indie filmmaking. If it happens, it'll be starting in late April. About a four-week shoot. Mostly exteriors."

"Wow!" exclaimed Andy. "That's fantastic."

"We're letting folks know that there may be parts of the production to bid on. Like the catering. So pass it on to Kirsten. I'll follow up when I know more."

"Will do, Geraldine." Andy's sister was always on the prowl for catering gigs, the bigger the better.

"And Andy, Tabby Dark is hosting a hospitality spread for the vendors after the Holiday Faire tonight. Why don't you pop in? It's some of the same chow that they're serving at the smorgasbord in the ballroom. It's in the Earl V. Sjolander Room. Festivities start at seven."

Andy, never averse to a free meal, said he'd love to come. "Okay if I bring Harald?"

"Absolutely. I mean, next to Logan Kennedy, he's the biggest celebrity here this weekend."

Chapter Eleven

Andy tossed his empty to-go cup into a trash can and glanced at his watch. It was only a little after three, and the Tabby Dark reception wouldn't start until seven. Four hours to kill before dinnertime. It was too early to start on the brewskies. What to do? Maybe some quality time with the pooch? And another thought struck him. He ought to check out one of Logan Kennedy's books. He liked a good action-suspense yarn, and now he was curious about Kat Taggett.

He strolled down the east aisle and popped into Copperfield's. The bookstore was hosting Logan's signing on Saturday, so naturally they had some of her paperbacks. He bought one that looked good—*Doom Shot*—and headed out of the conference center. After picking up the spare key card at the front desk, he found his way to the timeshare unit Aunt Bev was using. Harald, tail wagging, seemed happy to see him.

"So, bud," Andy said, tossing the book on the sofa, "you need a bathroom break?" He walked over to the sliding glass doors that led onto a small patio. Outside, the snow was swirling and seething, coming down heavily. Yup, the interstate was definitely no place to be right now. He unlocked and tugged open one of the doors, and frigid air blasted in, along with a few flakes. "Okay, Harald, you gotta go?" Then he realized something.

Harald's leash was nowhere to be seen.

"Now where did Doris put that stupid thing?" Andy searched around the timeshare, trying to spot it. Meanwhile, Harald hadn't budged and showed no sign of needing a couple minutes of outdoor time.

"Just as well," Andy said. "Don't know where your leash is at." He slid the door shut, hugged himself to warm up a little, and went to check the fridge, where he found a Diet Coke.

With Harald sprawled next to him on the sofa, snoring softly, Andy sipped his soda and started the novel. In *Doom Shot*, Kat Taggett had to infiltrate high levels of an Asian mega-conglomerate and knock off some scientist who was developing a super virus that could kill half the world. Along the way, Kat was infiltrated, so to speak, by a studly CIA operative with a six-pack and mucho mojo. Andy had read about ninety pages when he realized it was almost four-thirty. Yup, the woman could write a slick, sexy yarn.

It was enough of a page-turner that Andy wouldn't have minded continuing. But there were things he wanted to check out at the Holiday Faire. "I'll get you a couple burgers," he told Harald on his way out. "Rare, as usual, okay?"

On his way back to the Holiday Faire, he phoned Aunt Bev to see how things were going. She was helping set up the smorgasbord in the ballroom, where all the GWO gals would soon be chowing down. "Doris and I probably won't get back to the timeshare till after midnight, Anders," she said. "We're going to screen *Sleepless in Seattle* after the smorgasbord. You can just zonk out on the sofa whenever you feel like it. We'll try to be quiet coming in."

A few minutes later, Andy was standing in the Written On Skin booth. The tattoo artist was finishing up with a customer—apparently providing instructions on how to care for her epidermis in coming days.

"I figured you might be back," Damian said with a quick smile.

"Why do you say that?"

"When you came by this morning, you lingered. People who linger are usually experiencing some kind of inner turmoil. They want a tattoo, but they just haven't worked up to it yet. I see it all the time in the people who come into my shop. They look at the designs in my slide show and walk right out. But you'd be surprised how often they come back."

"Well, you've got good instincts there. I did want to ask you about something. I just wanted a recommendation," Andy said sheepishly, "about somewhere, umm, to go for a tattoo removal."

It was a deep, dark secret he had shared with few

others. Newly married, goo-goo-eyed Andy and his pretty wife Tracy had decided to get tattoos of each other's names. To cement their eternal bond through the infinity of time. Andy had gone ahead and done it. Tracy never did. The tattoo was in a well-hidden spot but had definitely been a sensitive issue for Cass Conlin, his former girlfriend. She snarked, repeatedly, how little she enjoyed seeing "Tracy" climbing into bed with them.

"There's a good dermatologist we send folks to down in the Cities." Damian handed Andy a business card. "You'll find the link on my website. As an alternative, I can cover it up with a new one. I could make a living just camouflaging the names of former lovers and spouses."

As Andy left Written On Skin, he noticed the pheasant hunter from the lobby standing there, watching the TV feature on Damian. Having ditched the hunting duds for tan corduroy slacks and a blue flannel shirt, the guy cleaned up nicely. He could have been a model in the L.L. Bean catalog.

"So, are you in the market for a tattoo?" Andy asked him.

"Heck no," the guy answered emphatically. "Fact is, I had one removed a few years ago."

"Did it hurt?" Andy had never been a big fan of pain.

"About as much as getting the tattoo in the first place. They can give you a topical anesthetic. But I went cold turkey."

"Brave of you. But I think I'll go for the anesthetic."

Leaving the hunter guy to chat with Damian Powers, Andy spotted the four T-shirt ladies examining the merchandise in Grant Hamsden's booth. While the other three milled around, Hot Pink appeared to be giving strong consideration to some bracelets on a tray. Grant's sales manager, Stephanie, was pushing the transaction along by draping several of the gold pieces over her own left wrist.

Andy was about to go over and say "Hi again" to the gals, when the lady in mint green—the short, stout one—toppled onto the floor with a muffled thud. It was as if he saw the whole thing happen in slow motion.

"Holy cow!" he exclaimed, watching the fiasco unfold. Two of the fallen woman's friends were fussing over her, and Stephanie rushed to help. Andy didn't want to get in the way, so he went and stood next to Hot Pink.

"How the heck did that happen?" he asked. "Did she trip or what?"

The woman looked peeved. "That darn Eileen! I told her at lunch that drinking three hot buttered rums was asking for trouble. She does this every trip. Tipples too much."

"Hope she didn't sprain her ankle or break anything."

"I'm sure she's okay. But she better ease up on the sauce tonight." She gave the tray of bracelets one last yearning look and joined her friends.

Andy moved on to Le Chocolatier, where he picked up a box of truffles for his mom. For his dad, he grabbed a bottle of Cabernet Franc at Boulder Creek Winery. For Kirsten, he bought the boxed set of Sigurd Nylund's *Wheat and Dust* Trilogy from Marilyn Dillard. His sister enjoyed grim Scandinavian literature, especially the dark, brutal crime stories. Then he got that pair of cobalt blue mugs for Phil and his wife—whom he would see tomorrow, if the weather and the highway department cooperated. And, as the young lady packed the mugs, he reminded himself he had to pick up Harald's dinner. A couple of big, juicy burgers should do it.

Just for the heck of it, he headed back to Norske Knittery to revisit a black-and-white Setesdal sweater that he had coveted earlier in the day. He *could* actually afford it, with some of that money his neighbor had given him—a thank you for saving her life. But he just felt too frugal to spend it on a pricey sweater. He spotted Sara Blake, her back to him, holding a blue cardigan in front of her. "Doing a little shopping?" he asked.

She dropped the sweater in a heap on the table next to her and turned around. He realized she had that blasted phone plastered to her ear. Again. And yet again, her index finger went up, silencing him in his tracks. She said a few words into the thing and disconnected.

"Not for myself," she finally replied. "Logan wanted me to grab a few items for some of the people on her Christmas list."

"Before you run off," Andy said, "I just wanted to mention something. About someone, actually."

She gave him a leery look. "I'm listening. Shoot."

"This morning, in the gift shop, I overheard a woman talking with a guy."

"Uh-huh?"

"She was, I don't know, about thirty. About yea high." Andy held his hand out at mid-chest. "A little doughy. Wore all black, like Logan. Had short blonde hair, like Logan. She had this tall, shambling sort of guy with her, also in black, whose name was…"

"Bobby?"

"So you know them?"

Sara's features went sour. "Oh, hell. The creep-o twins are here. I gotta tell Logan. She won't be happy."

"What are they, serial killers?" Andy's laugh died instantly when he saw the expression on Sara's face.

She shook her head dismally. "Justine Juveland's a blogger who's obsessed with Logan. She runs a popular Kat Taggett fan site and has tons of Twitter followers and Facebook friends. She was okay at first, but then she got a little extreme. Started shadowing Logan at events that weren't public. I mean, I've literally seen her hiding in the bushes, filming Logan. The final straw came when she and Bobby turned up unannounced on Logan's doorstep last spring. They came with a casserole and a bottle of wine, expecting to be invited in for dinner."

Andy whistled. "Whoa, major-league freaky, huh?"

"Logan was furious. She threatened Justine with a restraining order. And since then, she hasn't been so stalker-y. Did you hear what they were saying?"

"Well, Justine said she thought Logan didn't understand how much she, meaning Justine, had contributed to her success."

Sara rolled her eyes. "Yeah, heard that before. Can you spell narcissist?"

"And she mentioned something about having leverage over Logan. What's that about?"

"No idea," Sara snapped, pulling out her phone.

Something about her curt answer suggested otherwise, Andy thought.

"But I better warn Logan." And she charged off.

Sage Mortensen, who had been occupied helping a customer, came over. "I hope your friend didn't need me." That round, placid face of hers looked genuinely regretful.

"I don't think she wanted anything," Andy said. "And she's not really a friend. She works for Logan Kennedy. Personal assistant."

The look of regret on Sage's face barely changed, but just enough happened—the pale blue eyes opening wider, the un-lipsticked lips narrowing—to suggest that something shifted. What it was, Andy couldn't tell.

"Ah," said Sage, folding the sweater Sara had dropped, "I don't envy her that job. I knew Logan Kennedy once upon a time. When she was still Laverna Klingelhoets. We just called her Verna. She was a handful then, and I'm betting she still is."

"How'd you know her?"

"We were roommates in college. Best friends for a while. We got thrown together in the dorm freshman year, and then we shared an apartment sophomore year. Verna's mom still lives up in Herkimer, in assisted living. But Verna and I lost touch years ago."

"Well, you'll have to go to her book launch tomorrow and say hi. I bet you two will have a lot of catching up to do."

"Oh, you got that right, Andy." Sage's face had returned to its normal amiability. "After all these years, I'd love to have a chat with Verna. And let me tell you, I can hardly wait to see that jeweled frog she's giving away."

Chapter Twelve

Within seconds of the boss coming through the door, Harald could smell the meat.

It was cooked meat.

But that was okay.

He gladly accepted meat in any of its various and wonderful forms—raw, cooked, soft, chewy, tough, bland, gristly, hot, or cold. It made no difference to Harald. A lot better than that dry, crunchy stuff he ate most of the time.

"Brought you a couple of burgers, big guy. Grilled rare, just how you like 'em."

Lurching to his feet, Harald made a quiet *woof* and, tail wagging, ambled over to greet the boss. He sniffed the big bag first.

"Sorry, nothing in there but Christmas presents. And you don't drink wine or eat chocolate. This is the one you'll be wanting." The boss held out a small white bag.

Harald sniffed it. Yup, meat, glorious meat.

"Time to chow down. Geraldine said the Tabby Dark

reception starts at seven. That's just forty-five minutes from now. And we don't wanna be late, because your presence was particularly requested."

The boss refilled Harald's water bowl and put it on the hard floor. Then he dumped the meat into another bowl and placed it next to the water.

"Soup's on, pardner."

The meat smelled really good, and it was still a little warm. It took Harald a bit over a minute to gobble it all down. He looked up hopefully at the boss, who held his hands up in the air.

"Sorry, no more. Anyway, you just inhaled twenty dollars' worth of grass-fed beef. So that's it until breakfast."

Harald found the boss's palaver uninteresting. He trotted over to the sliding glass doors and made his intentions clear by lightly whining and slightly wiggling his posterior.

"Okay, so you're ready for your potty break." The boss walked toward the doors but stopped. "Oh, crap. I forgot about the leash. Where did Doris put it?" He walked around, looking here and there, muttering, then came back to the door. "All right, sport, here's the deal. When you go, *pleeeease* don't go too far, okay? I don't wanna have to come slogging through the snow after you. It's nasty out there."

He slid one of the doors open.

Harald stepped outside. He crossed the patio through the heavy snow, lifting his feet high before setting them down. Cold, wet flakes plopped onto his snout, beading up quickly. His coat was thick and coarse, so he didn't feel the chill very much. But the wind was strong and stung his nose and eyes. He found a shrub at the edge of the patio and lifted his leg.

When he was done, he turned around. The boss stood in the open door. "Okay, c'mon, pal. It's frickin' cold standing here."

But Harald didn't feel like going back in. It would be fun to have a look around and cavort a bit. He enjoyed cavorting in the snow. It was dark out, but the lights on the building and lampposts illuminated things nicely.

"Harald, where are you going?" came the boss's shout from behind him. "Harald!"

Harald, as he sometimes did, pretended not to hear the tone of exasperation in the boss's voice.

He tried heading off to the left, but the snow was too heavy. So he tramped along the side of the building in the other direction, one step at a time, looking in every sliding door as he passed. He only saw people a couple of times. Since running was not practical, Harald rolled in the snow for a minute or two. He caught a few flakes in his mouth, but they didn't taste like much.

He made his way toward the next building over. Someone else was out over there, playing in the snow— a person whose face Harald couldn't see. He watched intently as the person bent over next to a bush, brushed away the snow at its base, and stuck something in there.

Harald found the behavior puzzling. Was the person

playing a game? What was being hidden? Could it be *food*? That last thought nagged at Harald. He had just eaten, but he could always stand to eat some more. Eat as much as you can as often as you can—that was his philosophy.

Just as he was about to woof *Hello*, a brilliant flash lit the outdoors. Half a second later came a deafening *BOOM*.

Out of sheer terror Harald twirled around and bolted. But in the heavy snow, he couldn't charge more than a few dozen feet before he ground to a halt.

He growled at the thunder, then barked as fiercely as he could, two or three times. He hated thunder so much.

The worst part of it was that while he was running away and growling and barking, his potential playmate had vanished.

Still, Harald figured it wouldn't hurt to go have a sniff. In case it was food. He trudged over and found what the person had been fussing with—a plastic bag stuck behind the back of the bush. He smelled it.

Harald knew all about plastic bags, of course, because one of the boss's favorite things was putting Harald's droppings into them. But this didn't smell like doo-doo. Or food.

He stuck his snout down there, kind of sideways, and bit down on the plastic, then gave a tug. The plastic bag came out, clamped firmly in Harald's teeth. He dropped it in the snow and picked it up again, chewing lightly. There was something hard in the bag. *Definitely* not food.

Now what to do?

Harald could hear the boss calling for him, but he wasn't quite ready yet to return. He wanted to play some more.

Plastic bag gripped firmly in his jaw, Harald romped off through the snow.

Chapter Thirteen

"It's just darn lucky you found your way back," Andy scolded Harald. "People get lost in snowstorms all the time, you know. Dogs, too. When I was a kid, our neighbor's German shepherd wandered off in a blizzard and *was never seen again*." He glared at Harald as the two of them marched down a broad hallway, heading for the Tabby Dark reception.

"And then when you do finally show up, you're soaked to the bone. And *who* has to dry you off? That's right, your old pal Andy Skyberg. Good thing there was a blow dryer in the bathroom." He huffed a couple of times to emphasize how peeved he was. "At least I found the leash. Tell me, why in heck would Doris hang it in the closet underneath Aunt Bev's coat?"

Harald gazed up at Andy, as if he thought the boss was being a bit melodramatic.

Andy pointed a finger down at him. "Don't give me that look!"

But Harald was not buying it and gave a dismissive

woof that seemed to say: *Who's the idiot who let me out without a leash on?*

Walking into the Earl V. Sjolander Room—named for the late county commissioner who pushed through the resort project—Andy made a beeline for the bar in the near corner. "Got Biberschwanz?" he asked the young bartender. In his right hand, he held Harald's lead, and with his left, he pulled out his wallet.

"If it's not Biberschwanz, it's not beer," she sang, mimicking the old advertising jingle.

Andy grinned at the catchy ditty from the brewery's first incarnation back after WWII. "Well, then, I'll have a Dunkles, please."

She poured the dark lager and handed it to him. "Drinks tonight are compliments of Tabby Dark."

He thanked her, put his wallet away, and took the tall glass. Just as he savored his first sip, he heard Geraldine Abbott's voice.

"Andy, so glad you could make it."

"Hi again, Geraldine. Yeah, I was hoping to be partying tonight down in the Cities. But hey, your Tabby Dark shindig is the next best place to be."

She smiled at his obvious fib. "Well, at least you don't have to pick up the tab." Leaning over, she patted Harald on the head, then gave Andy a quizzical look. "A little damp, isn't he?"

Andy shrugged. "Playing in the snow. What're you gonna do?"

She laughed. "Understood. I have a golden retriever

at home. Now go grab a bite to eat." With that she flitted off to join Marilyn Dillard, who was sitting stiffly at a table in the corner. It looked like her back was still hurting. Roger Dillard was nowhere to be seen.

Andy surveyed the room. He recognized lots of faces from the Holiday Faire. At a table off to the right, Kurt Jesperson, a photographer, was yakking it up with Jill Tollefson of Tollefson's B&B.

The two owners of the Boulder Creek Winery shared a table with tattoo artist Damian Powers. But while the vintners were busy chowing down, Damian's attention was fixed on someone standing near the door. Andy looked in that direction and saw Sara Blake nibbling on cheese and crackers, with her ever-present smartphone in the other hand.

Oh, you poor guy, Andy thought, looking back at Damian's lustful stare. *She is so out of your league.* Sara struck Andy as a laser-guided career gal. No way would she—as she climbed the literary ladder in Manhattan—care to hook up with a mere tattoo artist from Flyoverland.

Andy caught sight of someone waving at him from a table on the other side of the room. It was Thor, sitting with Sage Mortenson. He headed over to join them.

"Greetings, young feller," proclaimed the old boy. "You look like you're in serious need of sustenance. Gimme the pooch and go grab some grub."

Andy put his beer down on the table and nodded at Sage, who gave him a little wave as she gobbled a spoonful of bread pudding.

"So where's Sonny?" Andy asked.

"Picked up one of her nasty headaches. She's sacked out in Sage's room. And I'm betting you're overnight-ing, too, huh?"

"No choice, really. Gonna try to head south in the morning."

"Better safe than sorry. Now go get some food."

As Andy heaped his plate with chow—smoked salm-on, Swedish meatballs, pickled herring, hardtack, and a Nordic-style potato salad full of dill and capers—he thought about bringing up the Logan Kennedy thing with Thor. But he had to figure out how to do it in a subtle, sneaky way. Back at the table, he speared one of the meatballs, put it on a paper napkin, and offered it to Harald, who promptly gobbled it down and, true to form, presented that Oliver Twist look of his: *More?*

"That's it, pal." Andy cut off a piece of salmon with his fork, laid it on a section of hardtack, and munched it down. "So, did you guys have a good day?" he queried between bites.

"Better than we expected," Sage said. "We sold a lot of mittens and scarves, probably because of the storm. Anyway, I just hope they clear the roads overnight, so we get a decent crowd tomorrow."

"Thee and me, Sage," Thor said. "But if there's much drifting, the plow boys are gonna have a hard time keeping things open."

"It gives me heartburn to think about it," Sage said,

patting her ample chest. "We need a good turnout tomorrow to make our costs." She grabbed her purse and began rummaging through it. "Darn, I left my antacid tablets back in my suitcase. Love this rich food, but it makes my acid reflux flare up. I'll be right back." She hopped to her feet, and threaded her way out of the room.

Sage's departure gave Andy a chance to be alone with Thor. He wanted to suss out what the old coot had been up to with Logan Kennedy. But he had to be sly about it.

"How long have you known Sage?" he asked, with an air of innocent curiosity.

"A long time. She came to our wedding with her folks. Was a teenager then. They gave us a Mr. Coffee."

"Remind me again. How long have you and Sonny been married?"

"Gonna celebrate our thirty-seventh next spring." Thor paused and scratched his chin. "Or is it the thirty-sixth?"

"Whichever it is, that's a heckuva long time to be able to put up with somebody else." Andy narrowed his eyes. "And not feel any need to *sample* the newer models."

Thor didn't appear to have felt any zing from Andy's subtle dig. He merely shrugged. "In certain cultures, having a mistress is accepted practice. Not in these parts, of course. That doesn't mean some folks hereabouts don't fool around. The human being is a randy animal, my friend."

Andy offered a weak grin. Not exactly the solid reassurance he was hoping for—given Thor's puzzling Logan Kennedy connection.

Just then, across the room, Sara Blake's phone rang. She put it to her ear, spoke briefly, and disconnected. She went over to the table where Geraldine Abbott was sitting. The Tabby Dark official listened to her, then Sara headed out the door. Geraldine stood and dinged her wine glass with a spoon. The room went silent and came to attention.

"People, we have a very special treat for you," she proclaimed. "It's no secret that tomorrow afternoon the Beaver Tail Resort and Conference Center is hosting a national event to officially launch the new Kat Taggett book. Readers from around the world will be watching the Kat Blast, live-streamed from the ballroom. *And no crummy blizzard is going to shut it down.*"

Folks around the room laughed and murmured their approval of Geraldine's defiance of Mother Nature. There was a light smattering of applause.

"The *Times*-bestselling author of that book has agreed to join us here tonight to say a few words and enjoy some great smorgasbord. Ladies and gentlemen, please welcome Herkimer County's own Logan Kennedy."

At that, Logan Kennedy swept into the room like royalty, followed obediently by Nikkie, her mixed breed, and Sara. She stood before the guests, her hands slipped casually into the pockets of cream-colored trousers. The black silk turtleneck she wore was minimally adorned with a multi-strand of pearls, perfectly matching the hue of the trousers. Her short blonde hair was swept back with effortless casualness. The woman, Andy had to admit, positively nailed that simple, elegant look.

The minute she had walked in, Thor straightened up in his chair and flashed the goofiest grin Andy had ever seen on him. Logan's eyes fell on Andy and Thor, and she gave them a little nod.

"As Geraldine just noted," Logan said, after the applause trailed off, "I grew up in Herkimer and Beaver Tail counties. I only left after I had sold my first Kat Taggett novel. Some of you may have heard of the lady. If you haven't, let me just hint that she might be heading to Hollywood."

There were oohs and aahs around the room. Andy stole a glance at Marilyn Dillard. Her lips were frozen in a sour pinch, and she was holding her wine glass so tightly it looked like it might shatter in her hand.

"I don't get back home very often," Logan continued. "But I wanted the launch of my newest novel, *Dart Shot*, to take place here. In honor of my mother, who still lives up in Pinetop. Now let me just tell you a bit about this fifteenth book in the series."

When her pitch for the new novel was over, Logan headed for Andy and Thor's table, with Nikkie and Sara in tow. As she was passing his table, Damian stood up and extended his hand. "Big fan," Andy heard him say.

"My name is Damian Powers, and I've been dying to meet you."

A quick flash of irritation registered on Logan's face, but then she caught herself. She gave him a faint smile and limply grasped his hand. "Thank you," she said, brushing past him with the deftness of someone used to briskly dispensing with annoying admirers.

Andy couldn't help but wonder if Damian had ever even read a Kat Taggett novel. More likely, he was smarming up to Logan to impress Sara. If that was his motive, it wasn't working—Sara seemed oblivious to him as she followed Logan back to Andy's table. After whispering a few words in her PA's ear, Logan sat down next to Thor. Nikkie squeezed between them. Harald attempted to worm his way toward the brownish mutt, but Thor's chair blocked him.

"Thorstein, Mr. Mayor, so good to see you both," Logan gushed.

"You two *know* each other?" Thor said, clearly surprised and, Andy thought, a bit annoyed.

"Anders and I met just this afternoon," she said with a honeyed tone. "He delivered a package to my suite, and we had a charming tête-à-tête, didn't we?"

"Yup, yeah," Andy muttered. "Guess we did." He looked pointedly at Thor. "And how do *you two* know each other?"

The answer was delayed when Sara returned with a plate of food and a glass of white wine for Logan. The author took a slow, appreciative sip.

"Thorstein is, for lack of a better term, my muse."

Andy was dumbfounded. He normally thought of muses as graceful beauties in diaphanous peignoirs who inspired poets and such. Curmudgeonly old Thor, who was sitting there in bib overalls and red flannel shirt, with that silly grin on his face, looked nothing like Andy's idea of a muse.

At that moment, Sage appeared with a full glass of red wine and eased down into her chair. Sipping from the wine, she turned to Logan. "Hello, Verna. Long time no see."

The smile on Logan's face evaporated instantly and her eyes widened. "What?"

"You don't recognize me, do you?" Sage seemed to be enjoying Logan's discomfort.

The author narrowed her eyes and studied Sage for a few seconds. "Oh my God. Sage? Is that you?"

"Thirty years older and with all the miles to show for it."

Logan's next question didn't bode well for a chummy reunion: "Why are you here?"

Sage smirked. "Oh, don't flatter yourself, Verna. I didn't come to see *you*. I'm working at the Holiday Faire." She took another sip. "But I do so hope we can have a little chat vis-à-vis the good old days. There are a few things I'd love to talk about."

It was pretty clear to Andy that the good old days Logan and Sage shared had not been so good. The situation was becoming uncomfortable and he figured a change of subject was in order. What, though? The weather was always safe to talk about with anyone— even old roommates who hated each other.

"You know," he blurted into the nervous silence, "I just let Harald outside for a little while and the wind was blowing so hard it nearly—" Andy stopped in mid-sentence and gaped at the strange apparition tottering straight for their table.

It was Grant Hamsden, the jeweler. He was limping along, pale as a sheet and clearly in pain. When he reached them, he slapped a hand down on the table to steady himself.

"It's gone," he panted, blinking at Logan. "It's *gone!*"

Andy felt his heart begin to race. The guy looked like he was about to collapse.

Logan's well-formed eyebrows went up. "Grant, get a grip on yourself. What *are* you talking about?"

The jewelry designer took a deep breath. "I was *attacked*. The necklace. The jeweled frog. It's been stolen."

Chapter Fourteen

"You *cannot* be serious," Logan hissed, rising up and leaning into Grant's face.

Tilting back from her, Grant jutted out his chin. "I most certainly am."

"What the heck happened?" Andy asked.

"I came back to my room a couple of hours ago. I remember slipping off my shoes. I went and had a look at the snow outside. I was about to put the necklace in the safe, when someone grabbed me from behind. I must have blacked out because the next thing I remember I was on the floor, tied up with tape. The bastard was pulling the necklace out of my pocket. I couldn't even shout because there was tape over my mouth."

He stood there for a moment, still wavering. Andy jumped up and eased him down onto a chair.

Sara, who had been sitting at a nearby table, rushed over to her boss's side. From what Andy could tell, most of the other people in the room hadn't yet fallen to the crisis in their midst. But he did notice a distinct look of curiosity on Marilyn Dillard's face as she rotated to take in the little scene.

"I rolled around, trying to get loose," Grant continued, sounding as though he might hyperventilate. "But all I managed to do was kick the bed." He looked down at his right foot. "I think I broke a couple of toes."

"Why wasn't the necklace already *in* the safe?" Logan demanded.

"Because the safe arrived a lot later than promised," Grant fired back. "You know, there's a blizzard out there. And I had to be in my booth all afternoon. You're not my only customer, after all. Anyway, I've carried valuable pieces on my person before and never had any trouble. I didn't think anything like this would happen. The darn thing's supposed to be a secret, isn't it?"

Andy figured that now was not the moment to mention all the people he had talked to who knew about the jeweled frog. Included among them was Sage, sipping her wine and smiling sweetly as she watched the little drama unfold.

"How did you get free?" Thor asked.

"Stephanie, my sales manager, came looking for me. I wasn't answering my phone, and she got worried. Thank goodness, I'd given her my extra key card."

Logan narrowed her eyes at Grant. "Does anyone else know?"

"Only Steph."

"Well, this is just wonderful." Logan slumped back down in her chair. "What the hell am I supposed to show all my fans tomorrow at the Kat Blast? You know, those *tens of thousands* watching on their smartphones and tablets? All those women hoping to win it?" She crossed her arms. "You damn well better have high-res photos of it."

Grant gave her an exasperated look. "Of course I do."

"How soon can you make another one?"

His chin was almost quivering. "I'll have to source the gems all over, which should take a couple of weeks. Then another few weeks to remake the thing."

Logan glared at him. "I'll hold you to that."

He glared right back. "By the way, thanks for all the sympathy."

"Shouldn't we call the police?" Sara had her phone at the ready, index finger poised.

"Good luck with that," put in Thor. "I guarantee you that every cop in Beaver Tail County is out in this blizzard, helping folks. They're not gonna have time tonight for an assault and theft. There are lives at stake. It can get brutal out there on the tundra."

"Yeah, Thor's probably right," Andy agreed. "For now, you're better off just working with hotel security. Anyway, I betcha whoever took it is still on the premises. Nobody's gonna get too far tonight."

"Anders, of course you're right," said Logan. She turned to her PA. "Sara, get on the phone right now and call the security office or the resort manager or whomever. And after that, call Georgia. This disaster could work to our advantage, publicity-wise." Her striking features brightened. "Perhaps it's a blessing in disguise.

Just think of the headlines. 'Logan Kennedy Book Launch Marred by Brutal Assault.' That'll grab a million pairs of eyeballs."

Grant looked outraged. "This is a *major* crime, Logan," he snapped. "I was *attacked* and held *captive*. I think I broke my toes!"

Logan was suddenly the very picture of concern and contrition. "Yes, of course, Grant, dear. What *was* I thinking? How insensitive of me. As soon as we talk to security, we'll see to your foot. I'm sure you'll be fine." She stood up. "Anders, Thorstein, Sage, I hope you'll keep this incident confidential, until we can get things straightened out."

With that, the author, the jewelry designer, and the PA wended their way out of the Earl V. Sjolander Room—Logan guiding Grant by the arm as he limped along. Of course, by now, most everyone in the room was watching the celebrity make her premature exit, and conversations died down to whispers. Andy suspected that "keeping this incident confidential" was probably not high on the list of probabilities.

"Too bad Verna wasn't the one who got her toes broken," Sage observed with a sour tone. She downed the last of her wine in a couple of long gulps and got up. "G'night, guys."

"Do you get the impression," Andy asked as she walked out the door, "that Sage isn't all that fond of Logan?"

"Uh-huh," responded Thor. "No love lost there, I

would say."

"Sonny's known Sage since Sage was a kid, right?"

"Yup. She was Betty's best friend in high school."

"Sonny's youngest sister?"

"Yeah, that's right. She lives in California. A school administrator."

"Sonny ever mention that Sage was Logan's roomie in college?"

"Nope, didn't know about that until tonight."

"And speaking of unrevealed relationships," Andy said, raising his eyebrows, "just how is it that you ended up as Logan Kennedy's so-called *muse*?"

Thor met Andy's skepticism head on. "You wouldn't be so surprised, if you paid a little more attention to my curriculum vitae."

Guilty as charged. Andy thought the world of Thor, but life was too short to keep up on all the guy's pet projects. Thor had recently sent Andy an electronic copy of his latest opus, an essay entitled "The Dialectical Essence of Technology in a Society Plagued by Income Inequality." It had put Andy to sleep in just a few pages.

"Thing is," Thor continued, "Logan is darned appreciative of the perspective I bring to—"

"Oh, Andy, Thor. I just saw Logan leave." Out of nowhere, Geraldine Abbott had appeared, sitting down in the chair recently occupied by the best-selling author. "She was taking Grant Hamsden out and he was limping. He looked really pale. Is there some *problem* related to…" She looked from one side of the room to the other.

"...the *F-R-O-G N-E-C-K-L-A-C-E?*"

Andy almost hooted. First, because Geraldine must not have appreciated that all the adults in the room probably knew how to spell. And second, because he was beginning to think that if he went out on the street and talked to any random person—not that he could get out in this bloody blizzard—she or he would be able to expound at length on the pricey little bauble. It had to be the worst kept secret in the tri-county area.

"Umm, Geraldine, how did you know about the necklace?" he asked.

"Kurt Jesperson told me all about it. When Grant finished the frog a few weeks ago, he brought it up to Kurt's studio for some photos. Kurt does all Grant's product shots. Kurt said the piece was just *stunning*. Exquisite. And, of course, *very* valuable."

Thor leaned toward her. "Logan asked that we keep this incident under wraps," he confided. "So we really shouldn't discuss it."

"Then something *did* happen!" the woman exclaimed.

"Can't say, Geraldine," reiterated Thor. "Just can't say. Sorry."

"Of course. I understand. Mum's the word. Well, gentlemen, help yourselves to some more food. There's plenty left."

She hurriedly went back to join Marilyn Dillard. Andy figured it wouldn't take more than a few minutes for everyone in the room to learn about the "incident."

Thor swirled what remained of his dark beer in the glass and observed that he maybe should go get another one, for the road. Or even two. "Don't have to drive anywhere tonight, do we?"

"Yeah, not a bad evening to get plowed," Andy agreed.

"You know, considering that the gendarmes aren't likely to get here real soon, maybe you could pitch in with the investigation. You've shown some aptitude for crime-busting."

"No siree, my friend," Andy declared, emphatically shaking his head. "I'll leave the detecting to the security guards. All I plan to do is hunker down on a tall stool in the Homesteader bar and catch the end of that Boston-Chicago game. I am no longer a temp employee of the Beaver Tail Resort and Conference Center. For the rest of the weekend, I am the boss of me."

Andy's phone ding-donged on his hip.

"Or not," he sighed, looking at it. "Helloooo, Aunt Bev. What's up?"

"I just heard from Tim Fisher, Anders, and we need some help."

Andy groaned. *Here we go again.* "Whadaya mean?"

"You know that nice nurse friend of yours that you introduced me to?"

"Nurse practitioner. Yeah. Becky."

"Grant Hamsden apparently broke some toes, and Tim thinks we should have someone check him out. He's in Tim's office, and he's in pain." She paused.

"Don't want a lawsuit, you know."

"But I have no idea where Becky is hanging out," Andy protested.

"If she's not in her room, you might want to start at the *Sleepless in Seattle* screening, over in the ballroom. It just got started. That's where most of the Girls' Weekend Out gals are at. If she isn't there, I'd check in the bar."

The last thing Andy wanted to do with his evening was crawl through a darkened ballroom, groping his way among dozens of women, hunting for Becky.

"It'd be a big favor, Anders."

Why was it so darn hard to say no to that woman? Andy supposed he could spare a few minutes to go track down Becky. But once he did, and brought her to Tim Fisher's office, that was it. He was going to hightail it to the Homesteader bar and turn off his phone. Then it was Biberschwanz and big-screen TV the rest of the night.

"Sure, okay," he sighed. "I'll see what I can do."

Chapter Fifteen

Andy tried Becky's room from the house phone in the lobby, but there was no answer. A quick walk-through of the bar by man and dog didn't locate her there, either. It was so noisy and crowded and lively and fun in there—the big flat screens blaring out several different b-ball and hockey games—that he wanted to linger.

But now he had to face that thing he dreaded most.

A ballroom full of raucous women. Hopped up on Pinot Grigio and Merlot. Watching a chick flick. In the dark. How the heck was he going to find Becky in there?

Still, he had to try. Opening one of the double doors into the ballroom, Andy stepped in among a congregation of women *oohing* and *aahing* as Tom Hanks told his son some heartstring-tweaking story.

Andy stood a moment and let his eyes adjust to the dim light. Bistro tables lined the sides of the ballroom, occupied by gals munching on popcorn and sipping drinks, as they raptly watched the show. A dozen rows of folding chairs, mostly filled, were arrayed across the back of the room. And in the front, sprawled on yoga mats spread across the dance floor, were more spectators. It looked like a big pajama party for grown-up girls.

Sitting by the doors in the back of the ballroom was Doris Schattenheimer, whom Aunt Bev had evidently deputized to check folks for proper Girls' Weekend Out credentials. Andy left Harald with her.

First, he worked the chairs in back, calling down each row. "I'm looking for Becky Reingold. Anybody know where she's at?"

"Not me," came a voice out of the dark. "But if you don't find her, I'm available."

A few titters followed.

"I'll definitely keep that in mind," Andy joshed back.

He went up and down the tables on both sides. The four T-shirt ladies, now in sweatshirts of their signature colors, were particularly insistent that he join them. He politely fended them off.

Finally, taking a deep breath, he tackled the gals on the yoga mats. Crouching as best he could—he hated to block anyone's view of the movie—he crept between the mats. "Becky Reingold here?" he whispered.

He was about to give up when, at the last table on the right, he saw Becky sitting down. He duck-walked over to her. She looked at him in surprise. "Well, Andy, hi. What're you doing here? I thought you'd be back in New Bergen by now."

He nodded at her two companions. "That was my

plan, but circumstances conspired. Anyway, I was sent to find you, 'cause there's no doctor in the house."

Becky's smile flattened, and she leaned toward him. "What's wrong?"

"Guy thinks he broke a couple of toes."

"There's not much I can do about it tonight but tape them. And I'd suggest the gentleman ice the toes and elevate them. But sure, I'll have a look." She lifted her plastic glass of white wine. "Okay if I bring my vino?"

* * *

Walking into Tim Fisher's office with Becky and Harald, Andy spotted Aunt Bev and a guy in a dark green uniform standing off to the left. One was short and one was tall, but both looked stern and authoritative, with arms crossed and legs slightly spread.

Behind the broad, dark wood desk, Tim Fisher had his phone up to his ear, speaking animatedly. Grant Hamsden sat in front of the desk, squirming as Nikkie inelegantly tried to sniff his crotch. Sara Blake was talking with someone on her smartphone, cradled between shoulder and ear, while trying to discourage the dog's brazen advances.

"So, we'll keep it on the QT for the moment," Tim was saying. "Seeing as how the cops are busy with the blizzard. They said we can't expect them till tomorrow morning at the earliest. Maybe even tomorrow afternoon. They asked that security staff here check into the matter."

"And Georgia," Sara was saying, "we need you to

get on the newsfeeds tomorrow at three eastern time. Have two releases ready. First one, an earnest item about the theft and how Logan's a trooper and nothing's going to interfere with her big Kat Blast. Not even a terrible mugging and loss of the frog. Second one, that the frog was stolen and recovered."

Logan, sitting next to Grant, nodded her approval, then looked over and shot Andy a bright smile. She almost seemed excited with the turn of events.

"Yes, Ms. Kennedy absolutely wants to keep a lid on it until the event tomorrow, and Mr. Hamsden's okay with that," Tim continued. "You don't share that with anybody but legal. Got it?"

"And make sure the release contains the URL for the event's stream," Sara told Georgia. "I mean, we might get tons more views *with* the damned frog stolen. That's breaking news." She paused and listened. "Yeah, we have photos of it. I'll get one to you."

"I can't promise very much in the way of an investigation," Tim went on. "I got just this one guy available. A second guy's guarding the Holiday Faire. My security chief and a few others are stuck off-site."

Sara nodded, having finally dragged Nikkie back to Logan's side. "Get us drafts of the releases by nine your time tomorrow morning, eight ours. Thanks, Georgia. Nighty-night."

"Yes, quite a profitable weekend, what with all the stranded travelers," Tim gloated. "They've got nowhere else to go."

Andy figured Tim was talking to someone at the corporate HQ. And Sara was evidently bringing Logan's PR person up to speed.

Aunt Bev sidled up to Andy and Becky. "Trained management in action," she said with admiration. "Interesting to watch Tim do his thing. He can be a pill sometimes, but he sure knows how to handle a crisis."

Andy remembered that part of the "thing" Tim would be doing soon might be firing Aunt Bev. As far as Andy was concerned, the guy was more louse than management star. But what good would it do to tell Aunt Bev right now?

"I'll keep you updated," Tim said and finally hung up the phone. He glanced at Becky and Andy. "Is this the doctor?"

"Nurse practitioner's the correct title, actually. I work at St. Luke's. My name's Becky Reingold." She nodded toward Grant. "Is this the gentleman who was injured?"

"Fourth and little toe on my right foot," moaned Grant, turning around to look at her. "And the damned things hurt. I think they've swollen up some. By the way, I'm Grant Hamsden."

Becky asked if there was somewhere she could take Grant for a look at the foot. "I could use a first aid kit, too. I'll need some surgical tape and scissors." She set her wine glass down on Tim's desk. "I think you'll be fine, Mr. Hamsden. And, with any luck, tomorrow we can get you to the hospital for x-rays."

Tim directed them to the office next door, and Grant limped out of the room, leaning on Becky's shoulder. Aunt Bev hurried out to find a first aid kit. Harald tried to follow Becky and Grant, but Andy reeled him back in.

"I gather the cops can't get here for a while," he said.

"After the dispatcher stopped laughing, she said no way would anyone get here tonight," Tim said. "I guess a stolen necklace and a couple of broken toes didn't sound too urgent to her. So Gilbey here is going to start collecting evidence. Right, Gilbey?"

The string bean of a security guard, who looked to be in his forties, gave a crisp nod. "Whatever you say, Tim. I'll canvas the area near Mr. Hamsden's room, and we'll see if there's any video that could be useful."

"We have a woman here who's practically a stalker," Sara put in. "I'd give her and her boyfriend a look. Her name is Justine Juveland."

"Now, Sara," Logan chided, "isn't that a little over the top? Justine may be a pest, but I don't think she'd stage a theft and an assault." The author looked at the resort manager. "You may not be aware of it, Tim, but we have an experienced sleuth in our midst."

Andy's heart went up into his throat. *Oh, please, no.*

Tim blinked at her. "We do?"

Logan twisted around and beamed up at Andy. "Anders here isn't just the mayor of New Bergen."

"Really?" said Tim, peering skeptically at Andy.

"Sara searched for him online, after we met this afternoon. It turns out he brought three murderers to book this past summer, at grave personal risk. A genuine hero, it seems." She looked as if she wanted to pin a medal on Andy's chest and then rip his shirt off.

"No, that's not quite correct," Andy stammered. He wanted to squelch this notion pronto. "I just did what anyone would have done. I'm no detective. I'd rather leave that stuff to the pros." He glanced pleadingly at Gilbey.

"It wouldn't hurt to have someone else working the case with me," Gilbey said. "I read about Mayor Skyberg and those killings, and he did some fine work, for an amateur."

Andy gave the guard a reluctant nod of gratitude. "I appreciate the compliment, Mr. Gilbey."

"Gilbey," said the guard. "Just call me Gilbey. Everyone does."

"Fact is, I'm really not qualified," Andy maintained. Besides, his intentions for the rest of the evening involved several tall glasses of beer and whatever game was showing up on the flat screen. He did *not* want to be running around with a magnifying glass, looking for clues.

Logan stood and came over to him, pulling Nikkie behind. "Anders, I would take it as a great personal favor if you did assist Gilbey. It would reflect so well upon Tim and your aunt if you could help a guest in such dire need."

Andy blinked at her. What a smooth operator. She had found his weak spot and knew how to prod it. If

Andy could help Aunt Bev hang onto her job by pitching in with the inquiry, he had no choice. He had to do it. Dammit.

"Okay then, I'm in," he sighed. "I'll do it as a personal favor to you, Logan."

"Thank you so much." She took his right hand and gave it a long squeeze, then turned to her PA. "Sara, exchange numbers with Anders." She looked back at him. "And why don't you leave King Harald with us? You can pick him up in my suite when you're done tonight. I'm a night owl, so don't worry about waking me."

"Then it's settled," said Tim, coming around from behind his desk. "You and Gilbey get to work. Just keep track of your hours, like you did earlier today, and we'll include the time on your temp agreement."

Aunt Bev came scurrying back through the door, almost breathless.

"I got that first aid kit to Becky, and she's checking out Grant right now," she panted. "Did I miss anything?"

Chapter Sixteen

It was a slow trek up to Grant's room, with the jeweler limping along in stocking foot between Andy and Gilbey. Becky had told him to ice the two taped toes and take some Tylenol.

"So, how long have you worked at the resort, Gilbey?" Andy asked.

"Well, I got laid off of the egg noodle line at Lovely Lena four years ago," Gilbey replied as they emerged from the back offices into the lobby, which was still bustling with guests. "Now I work two days a week at Jumbo Mart and three days here."

"What kind of stuff do you have to deal with?"

"Usually, we just walk around a lot, checkin' things. Doing the rounds outside in a pickup or golf cart. Working the video monitors. Occasionally, there's some excitement. I've had to bust up fights at wedding receptions and in the bar. And handle shoplifters in the gift shop. But this here is my first robbery with an assault. Pretty exciting."

Grant snorted. "Glad I could entertain you."

"Sorry, that's not what I meant, Mr. Hamsden," Gilbey apologized. "I feel really bad you got hurt."

The jewelry designer shrugged. "I don't mean to be prickly. But this was supposed to have been a big weekend for me. My work would have been seen around the world. Now all I've got is a few pictures of the jeweled frog and two broken toes." He winced again.

"It's perfectly understandable that you're feeling cranky," observed Andy. "But you never know. We might just find the necklace before the book launch." It didn't cost a penny to be optimistic, he figured, even though they probably didn't have a snowball's chance in hell of recovering the darn thing.

By now they had reached the timeshare building where Grant's unit was. The elevator doors opened, and they entered it. A young family of four hurried in after them. The parents and the little boy and girl were all clad in resort bathrobes, swimsuits, and flip-flops. A chlorine scent wafted off them.

The boy grinned up at the glum trio of men. "Have you guys been in the pool yet?"

Grant's expression soured, and Andy worried that a kid-inappropriate comment might be forthcoming.

"Nope," he quickly answered. "Was it fun?"

"*Awe*-some!" the boy proclaimed.

"It *really* is something," the mom said. "Paddling around in the warm water while snow's gusting outside those big windows." She tousled her son's wet hair.

The family, jabbering away, exited the elevator on the second floor. The three guys got off on the third.

As Grant hobbled into the corridor with Gilbey, Andy took a quick look out a nearby window. In the building lights, the whiteout made whirling patterns of impossible denseness and complexity. The wind wailed like a huge, angry banshee, and the snow pattered urgently against the glass.

Andy drew a big breath as he entered Grant's room. His entire crime-fighting career had mostly been the result of bad timing, with lots of help from Harald. The fact was that he had never, ever investigated the scene of a crime. "Gilbey, what do you suppose we should do?"

"For starters, let's ask Mr. Hamsden some questions, if that's okay." Gilbey pulled out a little spiral notebook and a pen. "I'd like to establish the timeline and the bullet points for the incident. Sound good, Andy?"

"Right, Gilbey." Andy was encouraged. The rent-a-cop seemed to know what he was doing.

Grant limped over to the bed and plopped down on it, leaning against the backboard. "Ask away. But first let me get a pillow under the foot. Becky said I should keep it elevated."

"You want me to get you some ice?" Andy asked.

Grant shook his head. "Maybe later."

"Now, Mr. Hamsden," Gilbey said, "can you describe how you came into the room?"

Grant scrunched up his face. "Okay. I walked in and turned on the table lamp."

"And what time was that?"

"A little before six. My feet were killing me, so I took my shoes off and went over to the window to look at the snow. Something about the way it swirled around gave me an idea for a bracelet—a blowing-snow motif."

"And you didn't notice anything unusual about the room?" Andy asked, thinking that *something* must have stood out.

Grant shook his head. "Not until he grabbed me from behind."

Gilbey raised an eyebrow. "How do you know it was a he?"

"Whoever mugged me was pretty strong. I tried to fight, but I was totally caught off-guard. If it was a woman, she was muscular and well trained. I think he, or she, might have been hiding in the closet."

"How'd the mugger grab you?" Gilbey asked.

"Well, from behind, obviously. Both arms around my head and shoulders, kind of strangling me. I couldn't breathe. Very scary. Thought this is it, I'm going to die. I blacked out."

"Sleeper hold," noted Andy, recalling all those pro wrestling shows he used to watch when he was a kid. He had even tried out for the wrestling team in high school, but decided that grappling with other sweaty young men definitely wasn't his thing.

"Huh?" said Gilbey.

"Somebody put him in a sleeper hold, like on TV wrestling. Only for real. Compressing the carotid arteries or the jugular veins. Do that to a guy, it causes temporary unconsciousness."

"When I came to," Grant continued, "I was face down, my hands and feet taped together, and there was a piece of tape across my mouth. Lucky my glasses didn't get broken."

"Hmm," the security guard said. "I've got a thought. Why don't we reenact the attack? Take some photos to show the police. Maybe even a video."

"Great idea," Grant said. "Let me be the DP."

Gilbey scratched his head. "DP?"

"Director of photography," explained Grant. "My iPhone takes good videos. Andy, since you know about sleeper holds, you can be the interloper. Gilbey can play me." He snaked a hand into his pocket and pulled out the phone.

Feeling a little ridiculous, Andy squeezed himself into the closet and closed the door halfway. He didn't really think these amateur theatrics would be helpful.

"And we are rolling," Grant said. Then his voice dropped a few tones. *"Our victim, Mr. Hamsden, walks into his room at about a quarter to six. He slips out of his shoes, and proceeds to the window to observe the snow."*

A silence ensued. Andy could hear the sound of heavy breathing. What was going on out there?

"Sorry about that," came Gilbey's voice. "I should have unlaced my shoes before we got started. They're kind of hard to take off unless I sit down."

Andy caught a few more grunts of labor, then Grant's narrative picked up again.

"Mr. Hamsden stands at the window, unaware that his attacker is sneaking up behind him."

That was Andy's cue. He crept out of the closet as quietly as possible and promptly tripped on Gilbey's shoes, nearly sprawling on his face.

"Sorry," he groaned. Coming up behind Gilbey, he did his best impression of the Duke of Doom putting one of his sleeper holds on his opponent. The security guy promptly slumped into his arms. Andy lowered him face down onto the floor by the bed, then mimicked putting tape around his arms and legs and across his mouth.

Grant's narration continued. *"Mr. Hamsden awakes, arms and legs duct-taped, mouth covered. The attacker is frisking him and locates the jeweled frog in his left inside pocket."*

Andy mimed some frisking of the prostrate Gilbey, feeling pretty silly doing it.

"After the interloper leaves, Mr. Hamsden flails about, trying to break free. In the process, his right foot whacks the bed's base, resulting in two fractured toes. He is discovered some time later, on toward seven-thirty, by his office manager, Stephanie Bukowski."

As if on cue, a phone rang. Saved by the bell, Andy thought. It was time to bring the curtain down on this goofy reenactment.

Gilbey, still sprawled on the floor, pulled his phone from his belt and looked at it.

"Oh, good," he said. "It's my boss. Wondered if he had any directions for us." He sat cross-legged and put the phone to his ear. "Hey Warren, what's shakin'?"

While Gilbey talked to Warren, Andy looked around the room. The safe sat in the corner, unopened and unused.

"Putting it in the safe was the next thing I was going to do," Grant said, following Andy's gaze. "We were going to wheel the thing out on stage tomorrow afternoon for the reveal of the frog. You know, for dramatic effect."

"How do you secure the jewelry you have down in the Holiday Faire?" Andy asked.

"We have our own safe that we bring," Grant explained. "For the more valuable pieces."

"I wonder if the guy thought you had already put the necklace in there," speculated Andy, nodding toward the safe. "He might have figured you wouldn't be here and he was planning to crack the safe. When he heard you come in, he hid in the closet."

"But why would he have duct tape on him, if he wasn't expecting to tape anyone up?"

"Beats me."

Grant rubbed his chin. "The whole deal is so weird because nobody knew about the necklace, except for a few staff here at the resort. And, of course, Logan's people."

Plus a couple dozen other folks, Andy thought, including some that Grant himself had evidently told. And they could all be suspects.

"Did the guy speak at all?" he asked.

"Not a word."

"Did you see anything distinctive—clothing or tattoos or a certain type of watch?"

"It was kind of dim in here, just that table lamp on over there. Maybe dark clothes is all. He had black gloves on, I'm pretty sure. Never saw his face. No distinctive smells, either."

"Right-o," Gilbey said into the phone. "I'll get on it." He tapped the screen, then, using the bed for support, heaved himself to his feet.

"Did your boss have any advice?" Andy asked.

"Yup. He said to be sure not to contaminate the crime scene."

Grant snickered. "Too late for that, gentlemen."

"He also thinks we ought to move Mr. Hamsden to another room, but I told him there isn't a single vacancy in the whole resort. And we definitely have to tell housekeeping to leave the room alone."

"You're not going to clean my room?" protested Grant. "I've got to stay here through Sunday afternoon."

"Well, we'll make sure you get fresh linens and towels. Just don't touch anything," Gilbey suggested helpfully.

"And how," Grant harrumphed, "do you propose I do that?"

"I'm wondering something," Andy interrupted. "You can't pick a lock that uses a key card. So, how'd the perp get in here?"

"I don't know, Andy," said Gilbey. "There might be ways to hack a lock like that."

"Good point," he replied, glad a pro was on the scene. "Who else would have a key card for this room?"

"A maid can open the door, of course," Gilbey said. "Or anyone with a master key card. Like managers and security staff."

"Of course, Stephanie has one," Grant put in.

Gilbey raised his eyebrows and looked at Andy.

"But don't even think about her," Grant said when he saw them exchanging glances. "She's been with me for years. Above reproach."

"But we still need to talk to her," Gilbey said.

"In the morning, please," Grant protested. "She's been on her feet all day, and she's probably in bed."

"Yeah, I guess it can wait," said Gilbey. "But in the meantime, I'm gonna head down to the security office and look at some video. Want to come, Andy?"

"I have one more question, actually." Andy turned to Grant. "What's the value of an item like this?"

The jeweler didn't look happy. "I insured it for eighty thousand."

"Wow," said Andy. "That's a tidy chunk of change."

"That it is. And now I'm worried my insurer might have issues with me carrying the necklace around in my pocket."

Andy could well imagine that Grant's insurance company might be irritated with their customer. "Do you have a picture?"

Grant swiped the screen on his phone and found the photo, holding it up for Andy and Gilbey to see.

Grant was a master craftsman, for sure, and a true artist. It was a striking piece, with its pattern of contrasting sapphires and black diamonds. Andy had expected something gaudy and ugly, but it was really very creative. It would be a shame if Logan Kennedy couldn't unveil it tomorrow at the Kat Blast.

Out in the hallway, the two investigators headed back to the elevator. Just before they reached it, Gilbey stopped in his tracks, laughed, and pointed upward. Andy followed the extended index finger with his eyes.

Mounted on the wall was a tiny video camera. And on the front of it, where there should have been the little dark circle of a lens, someone had slapped a square piece of duct tape.

"Well, how do you like that?" Gilbey said, shaking his head. "At least now we know why the perp had a roll of tape on him."

Chapter Seventeen

Harald had approached the other dog in the room once or twice, tail wagging, but she ignored him. He woofed at her, trying to get *some* response. But the only reaction was from the woman in the chair. She shook a finger at him and said, "No!" The boss used that word quite often, so Harald understood he had to cool it with the woofing.

"Logan Kennedy," the woman scolded, leaning down toward Harald, "does not tolerate barking. Especially in a hotel room. Do you understand, Harald? Barking is for the country house. Right, Nikkie?"

She petted Harald on the head, and he relaxed, relieved that she wasn't actually mad.

"I understand how boring this is for a big boy like you," she said. "So someone's coming to take you for a walk. Would you like to go for a walk, Harald?"

He recognized "walk" and his tail went into overdrive. The only words better than walk were "Frisbee," "ride in the truck," and, best of all, "meat stick."

Harald sat there, his tail thumping on the carpet, the other dog quite forgotten. Before long there came a knock on the door and another woman came in.

"Oh, Logan, thanks so much for calling me. I'm super, super honored that you asked me to give your dog a walk."

"Actually, he's not *my* dog, Samantha. An acquaintance needed to leave him for a while. Harald's a good boy, though. Aren't you, Harald? Just give him a nice leg stretch, okay? Don't be gone more than half an hour. I'm meeting someone for drinks later."

"Ab-so-*lutely*, Logan. Half an hour it is. But before we go, though, a quick selfie, if you don't mind. For Facebook."

"Of course, be my guest."

Harald watched the two women stand side by side. The new woman held up one of those shiny little objects like the boss had, and a harsh, bright light flooded the room. Harald winced at it but managed not to bark.

The first woman snapped on his leash, and the second woman took him out into the hallway and down the stairs, chattering all the way. About what, Harald had no idea. But she seemed friendly, and that was all that mattered. At the bottom of the stairs, Harald could see through a door into the swirling snow. He suddenly realized he needed to go outside for a minute, so he pulled the woman toward the door and whimpered.

"Okay, that's a look I know. I have a dog at home, and when he's gotta go, he's gotta go. I'm just gonna open this door, and you go out for a little tinkle, okay?"

Harald wagged his tail in agreement. She opened the door, and he slipped out as far as the leash allowed him. He shuffled to the right, by the wall, lifted his leg, and did what needed doing. Then he looked out into the tempest of snow and had the urge to go for a run in it. Maybe he could go get that treasure he had found.

He got about three feet before he was rudely yanked back by his leash and hauled through the door.

"Oh no you don't, mister!"

He looked up at the woman in surprise. Who did she think she was?

"I've seen that trick before, Harald, and you're not gonna get away with it."

He straightened himself up, attempting to regain his dignity, and vigorously shook off the snow still clinging to him.

"Now let's go on that walk."

And off they went, up and down long hallways and into wide spaces occupied by clumps of people. Along the way, they stopped and Harald got petted and stroked. He never minded receiving a little extra attention. They walked around some more and came into the big room with giant windows. The woman took him over to a place where wood was burning in a big hole in the wall. She looped his leash around the leg of a sofa.

"Now I'm just going to go get some pop, Harald. I'll be back in a wink."

He watched her walk away and wondered if he was

going to be left alone for long. Not that there was anything wrong with that.

"Here, let's sit here."

Two people walked up and sat down on the sofa.
Harald was ready to get petted again.

"It's gone."

"What?"

"It's *gone*. I hid it outside and it vanished."

"*Vanished*?"

"I know just where I left it. Right under that bush.
It's not there anymore. I dug around in the snow for like
ten minutes, practically got frostbite. Someone must
have found it."

"That's impossible!"

"Yeah, well, the impossible just happened."

"Shit!"

Harald tried to slump down. Angry, he thought. They
sounded like how the boss sometimes sounded when he
was angry.

"I know, I know. I just wonder if our friend got a
little greedy and snatched it. I'd love to get my hands on
the thief."

One of them turned and caught sight of Harald
slouching there, eyeing them. He tried to shrink down a
little more.

"Umm, he's been listening to our conversation."

"Well, I don't think he's going to squeal on us. Are
you, poochie?"

Harald wagged his tail, glad for a friendly word—

just as it ought to be.

The people talked some more, then left. A moment later Harald's walker returned, carrying a paper cup. "You poor doggie, you. Stuck here with all these silly people. Let's get you back to the room and you can play with Nikkie."

But Harald wasn't listening. He was looking all around, wondering when he would see the boss again.

Chapter Eighteen

To get to the security office, Andy and Gilbey had to go through the maze of cubicles where Aunt Bev worked and down a dim, gloomy alley of a hallway near the loading docks. When they got there, they found Tim Fisher and Butch Behr, the facilities manager, huddled in front of the LCD monitors. From a speakerphone, someone seemed to be issuing marching orders.

"…and you need to have Gilbey go through the other feeds for that time frame in the areas around the building where the incident occurred. Could be we'll find some footage of those people before they managed to disable the cameras. I want you to account for every master key card in the place. And I'm gonna call some of my contacts and see if there've been any other thefts like this recently around the region."

"That's Warren on the horn," Gilbey whispered. "Our security chief."

"We need to try to clean this up internally," the disembodied voice continued. "Because word *will* get out. We don't want guests thinking the resort isn't safe. If we can find the mugger before the cops get involved, we're gonna look a heckuva lot better. Call me if anything changes."

Tim clicked the phone off and looked up at Andy and Gilbey. "Did Grant Hamsden give us anything more to work with?" he asked.

"Not much more than he already had," answered Gilbey. "So what did you guys see on the video?"

"We looked at the feeds of both cameras in that area," Butch said. "The one near the elevator and the one in the stairwell. And basically all we saw was a black-gloved hand coming up and slapping tape over the lens. The one by the elevator first, then a minute later the one in the stairwell. The one by the elevator stayed black until Andy there removed the tape."

"And you couldn't see anyone at all?" Andy asked.

"Nope, afraid not. He or she knew the blind spots."

"And there's the key card." Tim massaged his temples with both hands. "Heck, everyone who works in housekeeping has access to one, and so does most management. That's a lot of people we need to talk to."

"There's also the possibility," Andy put in, "that a card was stolen or the lock was hacked with some kinda computer geekery."

"Andy's right," Gilbey said. "It's not necessarily an inside job."

At the mention of an "inside job," Tim groaned. "My neck will be on the line if it is."

"Okay, what do we do now?" Gilbey asked.

"Grab yourself a tall cup of java," Butch instructed. "Then plant your butt in this chair. Warren said to review all the other cameras. Maybe we can spot the crook on his way up to the third floor."

"So, you don't need me anymore?" Andy asked hopefully.

Tim Fisher shook his head. "Not until morning. I'd like you and Gilbey to start interviewing people as early as you can tomorrow. Hamsden's assistant, other people on that corridor, folks who knew about the necklace, whoever else you think might be worthwhile. Go catch yourself some Z's, Mr. Mayor. You've earned them."

Since he seemed to be in Tim Fisher's good graces at the moment, Andy decided to do a little public relations. "Before I go," he said, "I just wanted to thank you for bringing my Aunt Bev on board here. She's really excited about the job."

Tim's face tightened. "You should be thanking Rosemary. She's the one who hired Beverly. I had nothing to do with it."

Feeling no particular reassurance about Aunt Bev's future employment status, Andy said goodnight. But he had no intention of sacking out just yet. He made a beeline for the Homesteader bar. He intended to kill at least a couple of Biberschwanzes before beddy-bye time and, if he was lucky, catch some hockey or hoops. Thus fortified, he would go to Logan Kennedy's suite and retrieve Harald. She had said she was a night owl and would be up waiting for him. He had an ominous feeling she might want to try to debrief him, one way or another.

The blizzard was still swirling and howling outside, but the resort's main lobby felt quiet and cozy, with its twinkling Christmas lights, warm piney wood, and holiday decorations hung all around. That feeling of peace and serenity ended the instant Andy walked into the Homesteader bar.

The place was hopping, crammed to the gills, standing room only. There wasn't an empty stool in sight. All Andy could do was wade into the mob, grab a beer, and position himself in front of one of the flat screens. It looked like the Rangers/Sharks game was well under way, the score New York 2, San Jose 1. He had just taken his second sip of beer when he felt someone tap his shoulder. He turned around and found Becky Reingold grinning at him. "Why don't you come and sit with us?" she hollered above the din.

A minority of Andy wanted to watch the game, but it was quickly outvoted by the sensible majority of him. Hockey game versus hangin' with a really nice lady? Easy choice.

They shouldered their way across the bar room. It was impossible not to bump into people, and Andy had to excuse himself several times. He held his glass with both hands, guarding every precious drop.

Becky slid into a booth and patted the empty space next to her. "Have a seat."

"Delighted to." He plopped down. "Thanks for the

invite."

He smiled at the two women sitting on the other side of the booth—one a blonde, the other with streaks of pink in her dark hair. Both looked considerably younger than Becky.

"These two characters work with me at St. Luke's," Becky said. "Shannon is an admitting clerk in the ER."

The gal with the pink streaks said hello to Andy.

"And Jade's a radiology tech."

The blonde reached across the table and shook his hand.

"Andy works at Ansel's Café in New Bergen," Becky explained. "And he's also the mayor of the town."

The two young women tried to pretend that they were impressed, but Andy could tell they really weren't interested. In fact, Shannon, sitting opposite him, kept looking past him, out into the crowd—as if he were invisible.

Andy was going to thank Becky again for tending to Grant Hamsden's broken toes, but his phone ding-donged, filling him with a sense of dread. *Please, please, please don't be Aunt Bev*, he thought, looking at the screen. Feeling relief, he put the phone up to his ear and said, "Hi, Phil. How are things down in the tropics?" He plugged his other ear with a finger, so he could hear clearly.

His friend hooted. "Hey, good buddy, the whole gang is sitting here at Fitzgerald's, crying in our beers because you're not with us."

"I'm not dead, you know. Just stranded in a snowstorm."

"Yeah, and from the noise I hear in the background, sounds like your misery's got plenty of company. Probably some of those ladies from the Girls' Weekend Out, huh?"

"Actually, yeah. In fact, three of them invited me to join them for a drink. So, being the gentleman that I am, I couldn't refuse." Andy winked at Becky, who gave him a quizzical look.

"Well, just remember, we're counting on you to get down here tomorrow for the game and concert. And that new Thai place, you'll love it. By the way, Paula said to say hi. She reminded me about those venison pot stickers you and Tracy made that year we all were hosting progressive dinners."

Andy laughed. Tracy had thought he was nuts when he suggested the dish, but it was a big hit. Those were the good days of the marriage, before things went sideways. Andy sure missed them.

"Tell Paula I still have the recipe, if she wants it. And, rest assured, Andy Skyberg will be there for the Blitzers."

As soon as he hung up, Becky grabbed his arm and squeezed hard. "Omigosh! You scored Blitzers tickets? That's the toughest ticket of the year. How in the world did you manage that?"

"Well, my friend Phil knew somebody who knew somebody."

"You lucky duck, you! I'm a Blitzers fan from way back. I have every CD, and I've seen them live like nine times. Still have my posters from the dorm. I tried to get tickets for one of the shows this weekend, but they both sold out in minutes. I really, really wanted to see Dusty again. He's a genius on that Telecaster of his."

Andy puffed himself up a little bit. "Well, I happen to count Dusty Newell as an acquaintance, practically a friend. I worked for him a few times. Hope to catch him backstage tomorrow night."

Becky's eyes widened. "You're pulling my leg."

"Nope. I used to drive him when he came to the Cities. I even hauled him up here one time because he wanted to see New Bergen. Brought him to meet my folks and my mom made us breakfast. Waffles and sausage."

Becky slumped back into the booth. "That. Is. Amazing."

"I am so psyched. They're doing a whole set of their acoustic tunes. And just playing small venues. No arenas. That's why they're calling it the 'Pretty Little Thing Tour.'"

Becky sat up again, shut her eyes, and began to sing and strum air guitar.

"You're a pretty little thing with a heart of ice.
I wanna love you, babe, but can't pay the price.
You're so cold, so cold
The way you freeze me out.

So cruel, so cruel
The way you leave no doubt."

Grinning like a fool, Andy played drums with the tips of his fingers on the table, then joined in the vocalizing. He leaned toward Becky and she toward him and they touched shoulders.

"Can't feel my eyes, can't feel my nose.
Can't feel my legs, can't feel my toes.
Wanna feel your cheeks, wanna feel your lips,
Wanna feel your waist, right down to your hips."

They burst out laughing, then Andy noticed Jade watching them. He couldn't tell if she was amused or horrified.

"Wow," she said, "you two must love the Blitzers even more than my parents do."

Ouch, he thought, feeling the sting of the generation gap.

Shannon suddenly slapped her hands on the table. "That was *so* rude."

All three of her companions stared at her. "I don't think we sounded *that* bad," Becky said.

"No, that's not what I meant. It's just that those two guys over there are staring at us. It's getting kind of irritating."

Andy twisted around in the booth and spotted two of the Moose Junction Bolts hockey players leaning on one of the tall tables with their beers and a nacho plate. They both looked down as soon as they saw Andy eyeing them—like guilty teenagers.

"Oh my heavens!" Becky exclaimed with exaggerated alarm. "You're being ogled! Call the gendarmes!"

"You want me to ask them to knock it off?" Andy offered, feeling chivalrous.

Shannon blinked at him as if he were an idiot. "We are perfectly capable of taking care of ourselves. Right, Jade? I think we should go over and give them a piece of our minds."

"Darn right," Jade affirmed. "First just let me freshen up my lipstick." She pulled a tube from her purse.

"Oh, great idea," Becky said. "Bright red. That'll scare 'em away."

Ignoring Becky's gibe, the two young women slid out of the booth and sallied forth to make their assault on the ogling hockey players—who looked eager to surrender.

"It's entirely possible," speculated Becky, "that we won't see those two again tonight."

"Entirely possible," Andy agreed.

Chapter Nineteen

Andy didn't mind being left alone with Becky. After this long, bizarre day, he just wanted to wind down and relax before hitting the sack. And Becky seemed like an easy, comfy person to relax with.

"Can I get you another wine?" he asked, noticing that her glass was almost empty. "My treat."

"Why, thank you, kind sir. Another house Merlot would definitely hit the spot. But the waitress seems to have disappeared."

"In this zoo, it's hardly surprising." Andy looked around the packed joint but couldn't spot a server. He figured it would be quicker to head for the bar and grab the vino himself.

"Be back in a jiff." He heaved himself out of the booth and wended his way through the crowd toward the bar, bumping shoulders again and again. He caught the eye of the bartender, who said it would be a few minutes. As Andy leaned against the bar, he noticed his pheasant-hunting friend on the stool next to him, working on a rocks martini.

"That looks awful tasty," Andy observed.

"Oh, hi again," the man said. "Yeah, it sure is."

"Vodka or gin?"

"Beefeater's. Only way to fly, in my humble opinion. I might have a couple more. I could use a little self-medication tonight."

"You okay?"

"More or less. Just feeling morose is all."

Andy didn't want to get into a discussion with a stranger about his problems. He had enough travails of his own. So he defaulted to small talk. "Where is it you farm?"

"Just south of Milton Mills."

Andy nodded. "Ahh, the garden spot of Solberg County."

The man chuckled. "We like to think so."

The bartender returned and asked Andy what he wanted.

"A glass of the house Merlot, please. No, make that a half-carafe." More wine, Andy figured, meant a longer conversation with Becky. "And while you're at it, I'll have me one of those." He pointed at the martini, then turned back to the guy. "So, been farmin' long?"

"It's the home place, actually. I'd been working mostly overseas since after college. I'm a structural en-gineer. But my pop passed away about seven, eight years ago. Mom was kind of a basket case. And neither my brother nor sister wanted to farm, so I came home."

"And you said you dabbled in real estate. By the way, I'm Andy."

"And I'm Ross." The man offered his hand, and Andy shook it.

"I've been buying farmland around Milton Mills. As they say, they're not makin' black dirt anymore. I'm also looking at a couple of other projects."

"Like flipping houses?"

The guy thought it over. "Yeah, like flipping houses."

"Do any of your kids plan to farm when you retire?"

"Nope, never had any kids. I was married a couple of times. Divorced a couple of times. My work had me going all over the world. I didn't want to commit to having kids until I knew I could be there to help raise them. It just never happened. Wish it had been different. How about you?"

"No kids," Andy answered. "I always figured I'd be a dad some day, but my wife wanted to wait. Then she left me."

Ross gave him a sympathetic look. "Well, we're a couple sad sacks, aren't we?"

"Guess so," Andy laughed.

The bartender arrived with the half carafe and martini. Andy paid for them and wished Ross a pleasant evening. To avoid plowing through the crowd again, he took another route back, around the perimeter of the tavern. Booths lined the walls, most of them packed.

In the booth just before the big eight-seater in the

corner, he spotted Logan Kennedy talking to someone. She had on, of all things, a light gray St. Magnus College hoodie, and she seemed to have removed her makeup. Andy almost didn't recognize her. An empty highball glass sat before her. She was holding some man's well-weathered hands. The wedding ring he wore looked ominously familiar.

As Andy turned the corner, he glanced back to check out Logan's pal.

Oh, hell! It was Thor.

What the heck was up with him? He was the one friend Andy trusted to be rock-solid. And here he was, looking like some infatuated teenager. Andy picked up his pace and headed back to the booth. The last thing he wanted right now was for Logan or Thor to see him.

"No fool like an old fool," he muttered as he sat down across from Becky.

She gave him a look of concern. "Anything wrong?"

"Nah, I'm okay." He shrugged. "It's just that I saw someone I know holding hands with someone he definitely shouldn't be holding hands with."

She looked a bit confused, then wrinkled her nose. "That sounds like a sticky situation. Do you know the party with whom the hand-holder *should* be holding hands?"

"Uh-huh, I do. And she's a real honey."

"Are you going to talk to the offending hand-holder?"

Andy shook his head. "I'd rather not, actually."

"Don't blame you. Unfortunately, that kind of thing is way outside my professional skill set. Give me a broken toe over a broken heart any day."

Suddenly it struck Andy that before he sacked out, he had to go retrieve Harald from Logan's room. And he *did not* want to have to deal to that woman anymore tonight. "Becky, would you mind if I made a quick call?"

"Not at all," she said, topping off her glass from the half-carafe. "I have Monsieur Merlot here to keep me company."

Andy tapped Aunt Bev's number, got her immediately, and asked if she could pick up Harald and take him back to the timeshare. He gave her Sara Blake's number and said the PA should be able to hand off Harald. Aunt Bev said she would have Doris fetch the pooch pronto.

"So," Becky said as Andy tucked his phone away, "Grant told me, on the down low, that a very expensive necklace was taken when he was attacked. He said it was going to be the big scene-stealer at Logan Kennedy's book launch tomorrow."

Andy groaned. Grant needed to keep his trap shut, or everyone in the resort would know about the theft before Andy and Gilbey could do a single interview. But as long as Grant had already spilled the beans to Becky, he figured it couldn't hurt to fill her in.

"I saw photos of the thing, and I can tell you, it's amazing. A gorgeous piece. Evidently, the frog's poison plays a big role in the latest Kat Taggett escapade. You ever read any of her books?"

"Just one. It was okay, I guess."

"Now that's damning with faint praise," he said.

"I have to admit, after dealing with real gunshot wounds in the ER, assassin stories just aren't my thing."

"Understood. I met Logan this afternoon, and somehow she found out about my misadventures in crime. And she's asked me to make some preliminary inquiries with Gilbey. He's a security guard."

"I'm curious," Becky said. "Was Grant keeping any of his other jewelry in his room?"

"Nope. He told us the rest of his stuff is in a safe down in his booth. The safe in Grant's room was just for the single item. They were going to roll it onstage at the Kat Blast and pull out the dart frog necklace. You know, make it the grand finale."

Becky pursed her lips. "So the robber was only going after that necklace. But who'd want the thing? It's really unique. Any buyer would know it's hot."

"It's still worth something. Maybe they just plan to pry the gems off and sell them. Anyway, I'm wondering if the theft maybe isn't about the money."

Becky shot him a quizzical look. "Go on."

"What if Grant messed with someone and that person wants to get back at him?"

"But he seems like such a nice guy. I can't imagine him ruffling anyone's feathers."

"True. But remember, he's an artist, too. And artists

can have big egos. You never know with that type."
Andy took a final swig of his beer. "Or maybe somebody's out to get Logan Kennedy. Ruin her big book
launch. I've heard enough to know that the woman isn't
universally beloved."

"Or it could be an obsessed fan." Becky's voice
darkened dramatically. "Someone whose dreary exis-
tence is only made tolerable by escaping into Kat
Taggett's world. She owns all the books. Every edition.
She even made a skin-tight black outfit just like Kat's.
Above all, she wants to actually be Kat. And that necklace belongs to her." She narrowed her eyes. "And *her*
alone. *Boo-hah-hah-hah!*"

Andy grinned. "Actually, it's not a bad theory. In
fact, there's this blogger, Justine. She was Logan's self-
proclaimed greatest fan, and almost earned herself a
restraining order. Like a stalker. And she actually does
dress like Kat."

"She's here? Ooh, the plot thickens. Is she big
enough to mug a guy Grant's size?"

"She's kind of short. But she's here with her boyfriend, who's a fairly big guy. So I guess he could have
provided the muscle."

"But how would she have even known about the
necklace?" Becky asked. "Grant said only a few folks
were even aware it had been commissioned."

Andy couldn't help laughing. "If you assembled all
the people who told me they knew about it, you could
fill up the ballroom. And, believe me, a few of them are

not Logan Kennedy fans."

"Like who, for instance?"

"To start with, Marilyn Dillard and her son Roger. They own Dillard Press. Marilyn and her husband spent a lot of time working with Logan when she was starting out. Then she slapped them in the face when she took an offer from a big New York publisher. Reneged on a handshake deal."

"Tacky, for sure. But was it traumatic enough for the Dillards that they still hold it against her? That's a long time to nurse a grudge."

"Oh yeah, they hold a grudge. Marilyn thinks her husband died prematurely because of Logan's betrayal. Her son thinks so, too, and he's certainly a big enough guy to take down Grant."

Andy was not going to mention that Roger Dillard had walked in on his dad and Logan in the midst of a passionate clinch. But he made a mental note to talk with Roger about where he had been that evening about six o'clock, when Grant was mugged.

"And we also have Sage Mortenson. She works for Norske Knittery. There's definitely some bad blood between her and Logan."

"How does she know Logan?"

"They were roommates in college. Had some kind of falling out. They ran into each other at the reception to-night and it wasn't exactly hugs and kisses."

"Looks like there's no shortage of good suspects." Becky shook her head. "Almost makes your noggin hurt, doesn't it?"

"You can say that again. The cynic in me even wonders if Logan is behind it herself. What if it's a PR stunt she concocted? Who knows, maybe Grant was in on it from the start. The broken toes might have just been an accident."

Out of the crowd, the harried, long-vanished waitress materialized. "Either of you folks ready for a refill?"

"Thanks, but I'll just finish this martini here." Andy turned to Becky. "You good?"

"More than enough Merlot here, thanks."

The waitress left and they talked a while longer—but about more pleasant topics.

Becky reported that her Aunt Cappy was doing great, for an "old dame" living in the woods all by herself. The job at St. Luke's was even better than Becky had hoped. Andy told her about the groundbreaking for the Nordic Deli and his role in the project. And, best of all, how his old neighbor—since moved to warmer climes—had gifted him with "a nice piece of change."

The beer and the martini and the long day were finally taking their toll. Andy felt absolutely bone tired. But he still had something he wanted to ask Becky.

"Could I, um, maybe get your number?"

Her face lit up. "Absolutely."

When they finished tapping on their phones, Andy couldn't help yawning. "I think I've hit my wall. I'm gonna go crash. Lucky I scored the sofa in my aunt's timeshare. Lotsa folks are stuck on cots tonight."

Becky tilted her head slightly. "Not meaning to be forward *at all*. But I have a king-size in my room. You're welcome to half of it. It'd be a lot comfier than a sofa, for a tall guy like you. And I promise not to get fresh."

Through the fog of the beer and the martini and his fatigue, Andy pondered the meaning of Becky's proposal. He wasn't quite certain what his acceptance would signify. But he knew for sure that it was the best offer he had received all day.

Chapter Twenty

Andy awoke to the warmth of someone's breath on his face.

Struggling to clear his slightly hungover head, he remembered Becky and how she had invited him to share her bed. He didn't need to open his eyes to know that *he*, at least, wasn't naked. But what about *her*?

The sudden slobbery lick of a large wet tongue on his cheek brought him instantly awake. He pushed himself upright on the sofa in Aunt Bev's room, blinking through blurry eyes as Harald backed away, tail wagging expectantly.

"Well, at least it wasn't a French kiss," Andy croaked, looking down at his eager hound. "But good morning to you, too, sir."

Disentangling himself from the blanket, he stood and wobbled a few seconds, until his feet felt firmly centered beneath him. Aunt Bev and Doris were nowhere to be seen. Stumbling over to the sliding doors, he threw open the curtains.

Outside, the snow was still coming down, though not as heavily. He figured there must be sixteen, eighteen inches on the ground. The wind was gusting sharply. In the distance, he could hear the din of snow-blowers and the scrape of a plow blade on blacktop. The resort was trying to make a dent in all that white stuff. He knew it could be long hours, though, before roads were clear enough for travel. He wasn't departing any-time soon, that was for sure.

Clipping the leash on Harald, Andy slid the patio door open a bit and let the dog out, holding tight against any more canine rambles. The breeze was cutting, not too comfortable for a barefoot guy in his skivvies. It raised goose bumps all over him. At the same time, he was reminded of how much beer he had guzzled the night before.

As soon as Harald was back inside, Andy sprinted for the bathroom. When he was finished, he picked up his Timex from the countertop and put it on. It was seven-thirty. A folded piece of paper with his name on it lay under one of those plastic-wrapped, freebie hotel toothbrushes.

Morning, sweetie, the note began. *Thought you might need a toothbrush. Feel free to use my toothpaste. Call me when you get up. Aunt Bev.*

First things first, Andy thought, stripping down. Just a couple of minutes under the hot blast of the shower-head revived him nicely. He dried off, dressed, and brushed his teeth. He wouldn't be able to shave, unless he bought a cheap razor at the gift shop. The five o'clock shadow look would have to do.

It had been a bizarre twenty-four hours. Assuming the plows got the interstate open by noon, he could still make it down to the Cities for dinner and the Blitzers. But no way would he catch the hoops game at the university.

And what a story he'd have to tell the guys down there. About his encounter with a bestselling, man-eating author. About being paired up with a security guard to investigate a necklace heist. About his delightful nightcap with Becky and her invitation to share her king-size bed.

Well, he probably shouldn't recount that last little nugget. Especially if Paula was present.

Andy had been anticipating his reunion with Paula all week. Like Andy, she had survived the trauma of divorce. He felt they were a good match, and he hoped for something more than just a single date.

But what was the deal with Becky? Andy frequently struggled, often unsuccessfully, to figure out what women really meant when they said certain ambiguous things. Had Becky merely intended to be generous to a tall guy who only had a sofa to curl up on? Was she a little tipsy and just being overly friendly? Or was there more?

He had enjoyed hanging out with her last night, no doubt about that. She had a great sense of humor, which he found really attractive. And she was certainly pleasing to the eye, in a grown-up tomboyish way. He hoped he hadn't hurt her feelings by declining her offer— whatever the intent. But the timing was all off for Andy. He was primed for Paula, not Becky. He didn't want to get all confused and flustered, juggling two women at the same time. Some guys could handle that. But Andy couldn't.

He glanced at his watch again. It was about ten to eight and he was getting hungry. Time to scrounge up some breakfast. But first he needed to call Aunt Bev.

"Anders, they say the snow is winding down," she said by way of answering.

"Maybe so. But it doesn't look so great out the window."

"I just talked to your Uncle Frank. He's got the driveway snow-blown, but the plow hasn't been down our street yet. Guess there are lots of cars in the ditch on the interstate and some jackknifed semis. So even if they get that cleared off, it's still going to be slow-going for a while."

Andy made a mental calculation. He could leave the resort as late as five and still make it in time for the concert. Maybe dinner, too, if he was lucky. He would call Phil after breakfast and give him a status report.

"So I guess you won't be able to take those buses down to New Bergen for shopping and lunch at Ansel's," he said. "Too bad Kirsten's going to lose the business."

"That remains to be seen. I just talked with her. She

said if the interstate gets cleared, we could bring a bus or two down for dinner instead. A lot of the stores are staying open tonight, so that'd work out nicely. By the way, Tim says to remind you that he wants you and Gilbey to keep on investigating."

"You got any theories about the heist, Aunt Bev?"

She sniffed. "No, I do not. But I think some people didn't to their due diligence—including Tim and Rosemary. If I'd been in charge, I would have insisted Grant put that necklace in the resort safe the minute he got here. And he has that safe in the booth. Why the heck didn't he just put it in there with his other jewelry? The night guard would have kept an eye on it."

"Yeah, pretty dumb," Andy agreed. But then Grant assumed no one outside a small circle of people even knew the necklace existed.

"Just one last thing, Anders. Would you mind making a final sweep through the Faire when it opens at nine? Just to see that everything is tickety-boo?"

"So, what are you up to this morning?" he asked.

"Doris and I spent a lot of time last night trying to figure out how to keep these GWO gals entertained, since they're marooned here. We came up with free cross-country skiing and snowshoeing on the golf course. And a couple of our chefs are going to improvise demonstrations—appetizers for Christmas and stuff like that. The ballroom isn't needed for the Kat Blast until midafternoon. So we're showing another movie, with free coffee and cookies. I suggested a game of broomball, but the pond ice isn't thick enough."

Andy was impressed with his aunt's resourcefulness. But then she always was a great ad-libber.

"Listen, Aunt Bev," he said, "I'm going to catch breakfast and try to scrounge up some chow for Harald. Then I'll connect with Gilbey and check in on all our vendor friends."

"Let me have Doris take care of Harald. Just leave him in the room. And hon, I almost forgot. Tim wants you to go update Logan Kennedy on developments. She's expecting you in her suite about eleven. Baseline her on your findings and samepage Tim on how it went."

Andy smiled at her business jargon, in spite of himself. He really did not want another encounter with Logan Kennedy. But for Aunt Bev he'd do it.

"Okay, I'll baseline Logan and samepage Tim."

* * *

The Lumberjack Café was jam-packed and hopping. There was hardly an open spot anywhere, even to share a table or booth. But Andy saw a woman getting up from a seat at the counter, busily swiping her smart phone. He scurried over to claim the spot. As she turned around and came toward him, he realized it was Sara Blake.

"Well, hey there, Sara," he said as they met.

She looked up from her ever-present Samsung and seemed startled to see him—almost as if she didn't know him. "Sorry, I can't talk now, umm... Mayor. I've got a million details to take care of before the Kat Blast tonight." She hurried out of the bustling eatery, leaving

Andy shivering a bit from her cool response.

Taking the stool she had vacated, he realized that she had been sitting next to Damian Powers, who was just finishing some buckwheat flapjacks. The tattoo artist gave him a much warmer reception.

"Hello, again. You look well rested. Must have gotten a good night's sleep, huh?"

"Let's just say the sleeping was easier than the waking up. So, Damian, do you know Sara Blake?" Andy recalled the guy eyeing her the night before, and wondered if he had made any headway.

Damian furrowed his eyebrows. "Sara Blake?"

"Yeah. The young woman who was sitting here before I arrived."

"Oh, her." Damian smiled slyly. "Nice looking lady. And I wouldn't mind getting to know her a little better. But, for some reason, she isn't falling for my natural charisma. You ever have that problem?"

"Me? Are you kidding?" Andy joked. "Never. Have to fight them off with a stick."

The two men grinned at each other and yakked a little about the Holiday Faire until Damian left. Andy was ravenous and it didn't take him long to demolish his eggs over-easy, rye toast, and bacon. The coffee tasted especially good this morning.

After breakfast, he phoned Gilbey and arranged to meet him in the Holiday Faire. Out in the main lobby lots of people were milling around and chatting. The resort had become a kind of small town during the blizzard, with everybody getting to know everyone else. Andy joined the folks standing in front of the big TV, watching the weather. The reporter, up to his knees in snow, was saying that though the storm was slowing down, drifting and blowing snow would be a problem the rest of the day. The interstate from the Dakota line down to New Bergen was still closed. Authorities were having trouble clearing a big rig jackknifed in the southbound lanes near the Flèche Droite Nation Casino.

Andy headed over to the Holiday Faire where he found Gilbey standing in front of Grant Hamsden's booth, head bent, eyes focused on his smartphone. At the back of the booth, Stephanie Bukowski was pulling jewelry trays out of a safe and placing them on top of the display cases.

Gilbey looked up and said hi.

"Hi to you, too," Andy said. "So, did you spot anything on the video feeds?"

"I was up till one o'clock looking at the damn things. But all I saw were some guests and one of the housekeeping staff. I really doubt they're the culprits."

"So a dead end, huh?"

"Yup, that's about right. Ms. Bukowski said she can give us five or ten minutes, then she's gotta get things set up. And don't worry, I've got this. I've been rehearsing questions."

"Fine with me."

But Andy had actually been doing the same thing and was a little disappointed to not conduct the interview. He flattered himself to think that maybe he could figure out "whodunit," as he had twice last summer. This time, to his relief, no dead bodies had turned up, though, of course, the day was still young.

Gilbey waved at Stephanie and she came over. "Thanks for talking to us, Ms. Bukowski."

"Happy to help. What happened to Grant was deplorable, beyond the pale. You don't expect that sort of thing in our little corner of the world."

Gilbey took out his notebook and pen and cleared his throat. "Basically, ma'am, we'd just like you to tell us the chain of events last night, leading up to your finding Mr. Hamsden. If you don't mind, begin with when you phoned him the first time."

"Okay, let me see," Stephanie said. "It was around a quarter after five, and Grant decided to rest up before the reception. He told me he'd meet me back here about seven and help put our stock back in the safe. But he didn't show up, which isn't like him *at all*. He's usually very prompt. I called him, but there was no pick-up. So I left a voicemail. I had to put everything back in the safe by myself. Then I called him again. Still no response, so I decided I'd better pop up to his room and see if he was okay. He always gives me a copy of his keycard at shows like this, in case he's busy and needs me to fetch something."

"Did you see anyone on the elevator or in the hallway on your way to his room?" Gilbey asked. "Anyone who looked suspicious?"

She pondered that a moment. "Well, I can't remember in detail, but I saw some women from the Girls' Weekend Out. I could tell because they wear those lanyards. Also, I saw an older couple. The wife smelled like she'd fallen into a bottle of cheap perfume." She waved her hand in front of her nose, as if she were still sniffing the noxious aroma.

"And when you entered Mr. Hamsden's room, ma'am, did you notice anything unusual?"

Stephanie shot Gilbey a narrow-lidded look. "Other than my boss lying on the floor all wrapped up in duct tape? Nope."

Andy almost laughed out loud, but stifled it.

"After you unwrapped him," the security guard continued, his cheeks turning a little pink, "what did you do?"

"Grant insisted that Logan be informed immediately, even before we called hotel security. I helped him limp down to the elevator. He knew Logan would be at the Tabby Dark reception, and he wanted to tell her in person. I went back to my room and called our insurance agent with the bad news, as Grant asked. I ordered room service and just zonked out the rest of the evening."

Gilbey nodded. "Can you think of anyone who might have a grudge against your boss?"

"No, not all," she said. "Once in a while a customer's not happy. Just like any business. But as long as I've worked with Grant—almost since the beginning—we've never had a dispute that rises to such hostility. Most customers are super happy with their Hamsden creations. Including, I might add, Logan Kennedy. She owns a number of them."

Gilbey put notebook and pen back in his pocket and nodded at Andy. "All done, I think. Thank you, Ms. Bukowski."

But Andy had a question, too. "One last thing, if you don't mind. Did you notice anything that seemed peculiar here yesterday? Anyone acting oddly?"

Stephanie shook her head, then paused. "Well, now that you mention it, there was this strange woman dressed in black. I caught her checking out the safe we have in the booth. She stuck out like a sore thumb. She had short, pale blonde hair and wore aviator glasses."

Andy had heard all he needed to know. Justine Juveland had been casing Hamsden Creations.

Chapter Twenty-One

Gilbey headed upstairs to canvas the guests in the rooms near Grant Hamsden's. He planned to ask if anyone had seen anything suspicious the prior evening—for example, a short blonde in dark glasses lurking in the hallway. He promised to give Andy a call once he had finished. Then he needed to head off to shovel out cars in the parking lots. Tim Fisher had called for all hands on deck to help with the snow removal.

Talk about great customer service, Andy thought. It ought to net the resort some nice Yelp reviews. But it left Andy to report to Logan Kennedy all by his lonesome.

He embarked on what he hoped would be his final Holiday Faire rounds. One thing he knew for sure—he had heard enough Christmas carols to last the entire season. Maybe the next few seasons. Whether they came out of the PA system or from that quartet of carolers in their green and red Victorian outfits, they did not warm the Christmasy cockles of his heart. They made him want to scream. At least at Ansel's, Kirsten had the good taste to play stuff like Vivaldi and Handel and Bach during the holidays—music that didn't make you want to scream after you listened to it umpteen times.

Most of the vendors told him they were pleased with their Friday sales and hopeful that new customers would show up later on Saturday, as the roads were cleared. The only pressing issue he ran into on the show floor was a malfunctioning power strip in the booth occupied by Fuzzy Snugglies, a maker of cozy flannel PJs decorated with campy, colorful designs.

Pulling out his phone, he called Butch Behr, who was just over on the other side of the conference center. The facilities manager showed up half a minute later clad in dark work pants and an olive-drab T-shirt. He was glistening with sweat. "What's the problem, Andy?"

"Bad power strip in the Fuzzy Snugglies booth."

"Well, let's go see if we can find a replacement."

They made their way out of the Holiday Faire. "Dressed a little light for a blizzard, aren't you?" Andy said, grinning.

Butch pulled out the bottom of his T-shirt and flapped it around a bit. "Jeez, I'm sweating like a stupid pig. I was out wrestling with a snowblower. Guess I'm a little out of shape. Only the first week in December and I'm already sick of winter."

"You from around here?"

"Naw, I'm from Iowa originally," Butch said as they entered the main lobby. "Moved around a lot into my thirties. When I was living in California, I met a girl from Herkimer County who was waitressing in a restaurant in Pomona. She went out to LA to try acting, and you know how that usually turns out. Anyway, one date and I was hooked. I couldn't get her out of my head."

"Yeah, falling in love really sucks," Andy joked. But, of course, he sure wouldn't mind giving it another try. "So I'm guessing her connections here brought you back."

"We had a baby girl, and Heather didn't want to raise her in California. Wanted to live near her own family. I can understand that. So back east we came. Been here now about eleven years. Two more kids came along and we're doing fine. She works in the office at the paper mill in Hilltop. But she still acts in community theater. She's in the new production of *Blithe Spirit*."

They marched through the cubicles behind the check-in to a supply room not far from Tim Fisher's office. Butch made a beeline for a shelf unit in the back corner.

"Dammit," he said, "I thought there were a few left here. They gotta be in this room somewhere."

Andy trailed behind him as he hunted high and low for the elusive power strips. The facilities manager went up on his tiptoes, peeking over a high shelf. "Nope, not here." He went around to another shelf and began hunting through it.

"Anyway," he said as he pawed through a pile of cords, "I was surprised how much I liked this area. I enjoy hunting and fishing, so that's all good. I even like my in-laws. We live on an acreage just this side of the county line, near the interstate. The kids and dogs have lotsa room to roam. I've got a great shop in the old barn. Got me a '58 Chevy Impala I'm restoring. The wife has a huge garden. The winters get a little long, though. Not crazy about the ice and sub-zeroes and whatnot."

He squatted down to hunt through a low shelf. As he did, his T-shirt pulled up and his pants headed south, revealing the very top inch of the classic plumber's crack. Andy grimaced. Not what he wanted to see early in the morning, and he tried not to look. He was intrigued, however, by an odd circular tattoo that revealed itself a bit above the right cheek. It looked like a clock face with Arabic numerals, about three inches wide. He leaned in for a closer look, but couldn't see any hands. No minute hand. No hour hand.

"Interesting tattoo you got there," he observed.

"Whoops," Butch laughed, tugging his T-shirt down. He twisted around and looked up at Andy. "Guess I'm giving you more of a view than you probably want. The wife says I need to start wearing suspenders." He turned back around and kept digging.

"Finally!" He reached to the very back of the bottom shelf and pulled something out. He stood up, tattoo and crack disappearing, holding the power strip like an angler showing off a big fat walleye. "Here you go, Andy. Need any help installing it?"

"Nope, Butch, I can take it from here."

* * *

Andy replaced the defective power strip in the Fuzzy Snugglies booth and flipped it on. The retail light boxes came to life, illuminating oversize transparencies of folks cozying up in various types of Fuzzy Snugglies attire. Andy thought a snuggle in comfy flannels looked awfully nice—if only he had someone to cuddle with. And that reminded him of Paula, whom he hoped to see tonight. He had better call Phil, though, to see how things were looking down in the Cities.

The Faire was open now, but there weren't many shoppers in sight. He decided he could take a few minutes for a coffee break. Stopping at the Coffee Hut, he ordered a cappuccino and gave Phil a call while it was being made.

"Andy," a groggy voice answered, "what the hell time is it?"

"Time for you to be up and at 'em, buddy. You must have partied hearty last night."

Phil coughed and cleared a phlegmy throat. "A few of us ended up over at Mitch and Nicole's condo, sipping Cognac. We really missed you. They're right on the river, ten floors up. You can see all of downtown from their windows. Man, that skyline was gorgeous, with all those Christmas lights on."

Andy tamped down a surge of jealousy. He wished he could have been there. "Did you guys get much snow?"

"Only about an inch."

"Well, I'm gonna get out of this joint as soon as I'm sure the interstate is clear. But I think I'll be a no-show for the game. Timing's just too tight."

Cappuccino in hand, he headed to the Hofdahl Farm booth. He had been mulling it over all morning and finally made a decision. He *had* to say something to Thor about his furtive meetings with Logan Kennedy. Even if the old boy took offense. The future of the Hofdahl marriage might depend on it.

Walking down the aisle, he spotted Justine Juveland and her hulking male companion exiting the Dillard Press booth. They were deep in conversation. Andy almost reversed course, so they wouldn't see him. But that was silly, since they had no idea who he was. He waited a minute until they were out of sight, then proceeded. Marilyn Dillard and her son Roger were both on duty.

"Thought I'd see how you guys were doing," Andy said, taking a sip of his cappuccino.

Marilyn, sitting in a chair with a pillow behind her back, had a tall coffee of her own. "My back still hurts, but we did okay yesterday. I was pretty worried that we might lose a small bundle, thanks to that darn storm out there. The only downside is we're surrounded by Logan Kennedy worshippers. They keep stopping in to ask if we carry her books. It's all I can do to keep my mouth shut."

"You knew Logan was going to be here, Mom," sighed Roger, leaning hipshot against one of the bookshelves. "What did you expect?"

"I know. I know," Marilyn grumbled. "You keep telling me that. But if I ever come face to face with that conniving bitch, I intend to give her my nastiest stink eye." She demonstrated by screwing up her face and glaring at Andy.

He burst out laughing. "Sorry, Marilyn, but you're not making my spine turn to jelly."

She made a wry little smile. "Needs work, huh?"

"I'm curious about something," he said, shifting gears. "I just saw two people come out of your booth. The couple in black. I'm wondering what they wanted."

"Oh, those two." Marilyn rolled her eyes. "Justine Juveland and Bobby Wakely."

"Are they suspects in the necklace theft?" Roger asked, perking up.

Andy sighed. "Nobody is supposed to know about the necklace *or* the theft."

Roger snorted. "It's probably on Twitter by now."

Just then, a gray-haired woman came into the booth and asked about buying a complete set of the Robbie Rocket books for her grandson. Roger steered her over to the appropriate display and began to assemble the dozen or so books in the series.

"The young woman and her boyfriend run some sort of blog about Logan Kennedy and Kat Taggett," Marilyn explained. "She's working on an unauthorized biography of Logan and wondered if she could interview me. Since I was one of Logan's first mentors." She shook her head. "As much as I despise Logan, I'm not sure I want to go on record about her. She's litigious as hell if you cross her."

"Sounds like the kind of book that could sell a lot of copies, given how famous Logan is. I'd imagine there are plenty of publishers who wouldn't mind having a look at it."

"Oh, Justine wondered if *we* were interested in publishing it. She hinted at a big scoop." Marilyn shrugged. "Yeah, that kind of book could sell well, for sure. But after all Logan has put us through, I wouldn't touch the manuscript with a barge pole."

As she made her viewpoint crystal clear, Andy noticed Roger—still working on the Robbie Rocket books—giving her a disapproving look. Was he afraid there might be Logan fans within earshot?

"Pardon me," a young woman interrupted, "but do you have Anita Wirtanen's *New World Finnish Cuisine*? My mom wore out her copy, and I need a new one."

"Sure, let me grab it for you. Hardcover okay?" Marilyn rose slowly to her feet. But before she hobbled off, still looking a little crooked, she turned back to Andy.

"I told Justine good luck and goodbye. That woman is in for it, if she means to tangle with Logan Kennedy."

Chapter Twenty-Two

Andy had wanted to ask Roger where he had been the previous evening, but mother and son were both occupied with customers. So he headed for the Hofdahl Farm booth. He wished he had never witnessed that cozy little scene between Thor and Logan in the darkened corner of the bar. Somehow he had to figure out what the heck was going on.

But, of course, Thor had company. Sonny was in the booth, too, loading cheese into a box while her husband jawed with one of the winery guys. As soon as he caught sight of Andy, he motioned for him to come over.

"Sounds like you might be able to escape Hobartville this afternoon," Thor said. "Gonna depend on the inter-state, though."

"Guess so."

"Where's Harald?"

"Left him in Aunt Bev's room. I can't be hauling him around when I'm working." Andy wanted to dis-pense with the small talk and move onto the issue of

Thor and Logan, but he couldn't figure out how. This whole situation made him feel edgy.

"Well, if you like," Thor said, "bring him here and we'll keep an eye on him. Fact is, he draws folks to the booth. People notice him and come in to pet him. Then I move in with some cheese samples and make a pitch. We kind of double-team them. Don't ask me why, but that mutt has charisma."

Thor didn't seem to notice Andy's unease. Before the conversation could continue, Sonny walked up to them, carrying the cardboard box she had been filling.

"Honey, can I steal Andy for a minute?"

"All yours." The crusty septuagenarian turned his attention back to the wine guy.

"Hi, Sonny," said Andy, "what for can I do you?"

"Would you be a sweetheart and take this over to the Voyageur restaurant? They're offering a holiday appetizers demo for the Girls' Weekend Out gals. And they're making some goodies using our cheeses."

"No problemo. Give it here."

Andy had some time to kill before his eleven o'clock appointment with Logan Kennedy. So first, he'd drop off the cheese, then run over to Aunt Bev's timeshare unit and liberate Harald.

"Andy, one more thing," Sonny said, handing him the box.

Her big blue eyes almost looked as though they were about to tear up. *Good lord,* Andy thought, *does she know about Thor and Logan?*

"It's just that Thor... " She paused, looking downcast.

"Uh-huh?" Andy said, feeling even more nervous.

"Well, he mentioned that there was a little scene between Logan and Sage at the Tabby Dark reception last night. Sage still seemed upset about it when I talked with her this morning. And I just wanted to clear up some things for you. You know, since you're investigating the theft and Sage could be a natural suspect."

Andy figured that Sonny had heard about the theft from Thor. And Thor must have heard about Andy's role in the case during his late-evening rendezvous with Logan. In fact, Andy *had* wondered about Sage. But he had a hard time believing that she was capable of perpetrating the mugging itself.

"Yeah, I have to admit Sage did cross my mind. She made it pretty clear she has a beef with Logan. Something going back to college."

"Sage had a pretty good reason to hate Logan's guts, I can tell you. As they say, 'Hell hath no fury like a woman scorned.'"

Andy's eyebrows shot up. "Sage and Logan were an item?"

Sonny burst out laughing. "Oh, heavens no. They were both of them boy crazy back then. I guess I'd better start at the beginning. But, Andy, that woman has suffered enough over this. You can't say a thing about it to anyone. Promise?"

"Absolutely. Mum's the word." Andy crossed his heart with an index finger.

Sonny drew a deep breath. "Sage and Logan were roommates in the dorm their freshman year. And they both hated the dorm, so they agreed to find a cheap apartment to share the next fall. Well, during her sophomore year, Sage met this really nice guy. My sister Betty said he was quite the dish. Athletic, good looking. A small-town boy. Innocent in the ways of the world. Sage fell head over heels for him. She was even making wedding plans. Didn't want to wait until they graduated."

"Uh-oh," Andy said. "I think I see where this story's going."

Sonny made a single, somber nod. "They'd been dating for about four, five months, when Sage went home for a weekend visit. Her boyfriend stopped by the apartment to pick up a textbook he'd forgotten. Logan was there, and one thing led to another. When Sage got back two days later, the boyfriend told her it was over."

"And Sage didn't take it well."

"That's putting it mildly. She plunged into a deep, black depression. Her family pulled her out of school. Spent some time in a psych ward. Started using drugs. A really, *really* bad scene."

Andy suddenly felt for Sage. Except in its extremity, her reaction wasn't much different than what he had gone through after Tracy left him. He drank too much, slept too much, ate too much junk food, isolated himself. He was a mess when he arrived back home in New Bergen. But thank goodness, he had forgiven Tracy and moved on. He couldn't imagine carrying that kind of anger in his heart for thirty years, as Sage evidently had.

"It sounds like Logan screwed up Sage's life pretty good," he said. "Enough that Sage would have plenty of motive for getting even. Logan stole Sage's man, so Sage finally gets her revenge by stealing something precious to Logan. The jeweled frog."

The goat cheese guru shook her head emphatically. "No. Absolutely not. The Sage I know wouldn't do anything violent. She wouldn't attack Grant Hamsden. Not in a million years. She might indulge in a bit of schadenfreude, but who wouldn't in her situation?"

Andy wasn't so sure. "Do you have any idea where Sage was about six last night? That's when Grant was mugged."

"I assume she was still at the Holiday Faire. I was up in her room laid out with a miserable headache. But I'm sure someone else could vouch for her."

Andy suspected Sonny was right. But he still needed to talk with Sage, as uncomfortable as it might be for both of them.

"Sage went through hell, Andy. She deserves a chance to be happy and have a normal life." Sonny glanced over at her husband—still talking with the wine guy. "I'll tell you, if some woman tried to steal Thor, I'd rip her face off." She smiled. "But you know, I don't think I have to worry. I mean, *really*. I love Thor to pieces, but he's not exactly a chick magnet."

Andy gave a nervous little laugh. "Oh, yeah, just

look at him." But in his head Andy kept seeing the old man and the glamorous author holding hands, whispering sweet nothings. "Well, listen, I better go deliver your cheese. See you later."

He started toward the exit that led to the resort's main lobby, cradling the cheese box in his arms. The aisle was blocked up ahead, so he headed back down and up the east aisle. Along the way, he spotted Becky and her pink-haired friend Shannon, just outside Damian Powers's tattoo booth.

"Hey, ladies," Andy said, "how you doin'?"

"We are doing okay," Becky said, looking happy to see him. "But will you please help me talk some sense into this girl?"

Shannon gave Andy a wide-eyed, innocent look and shrugged.

"Why?" Andy asked. "What's up?"

"Shannon wants to get a tattoo."

"Well, she looks to be of legal age and of sound mind and body."

"Maybe the first part of that statement is true," Becky agreed. "But she doesn't want a flower or a butterfly. She wants a red maple leaf."

"Maple leaf?" Andy was puzzled by the choice, but then it hit him. "Ah, I get it. The Canuck hockey player you met last night."

"He's a defenseman," Shannon informed him. "Rookie of the year last year. His name's Pascal, and he has the sexiest French accent. When we were in bed last night, he—"

"Whoa, whoa!" Becky made the time-out T sign with her hands. "Please, no details. I'm just saying it's a really bad idea to get something permanent like a tattoo after only one night with a hottie."

"It's not just one night," Shannon protested with a pout. "I have his cell number and his e-mail address and his Twitter handle. It's only six hours to Moose Junction from here, and we're definitely getting together for the holidays."

"Shannon, look at that," Becky said. She pointed at the nearby flat screen that was showing examples of Damian's work. Featured at that moment was the photo of a woman's upper back and neck, where a flight of larks soared upward, ending near a birthmark.

"That's way prettier than some red maple leaf," Becky enthused. "Why don't you get something like that instead?"

Shannon groaned. "It's a bunch of birds. What do they have to do with hockey?"

Andy turned and saw Damian Powers coming toward them.

"So," the dark-eyed tattoo artist said, "which of you lovely ladies is interested in the maple leaf?"

"That would be me." Shannon gave him a flirty little smile. "I'd like it on my right shoulder."

Damian had switched his long-sleeved black shirt for a black tee, revealing well-sculpted arm muscles beneath all that ink. "Fantastic." He turned back to Andy. "Any news on the stolen necklace? I hear that you're investigating."

Andy sighed. "Well, if there *is* any news, everyone in this joint will probably hear about it before I do."

"Yeah, well, there was a lot of chatter about it after you and Logan left the reception last night. Man, I feel for her. Must be a total bummer to have the thing gone right before her big Kat Blast."

Andy figured Damian's concern for Logan had less to do with the stolen necklace than it did with her fine-looking young PA. But from what Andy had seen, Sara showed no sign of reciprocating. Still, a guy could always dream.

"A quick question, Damian, you being a tattoo expert."

"Is it about the tat you want removed?" Damian asked.

Becky gave Andy a curious look, and he hoped she wouldn't follow it up with a question of her own. He didn't want to explain having "Tracy" inscribed on his person in a very private place.

"No, not that. I saw a tattoo design, and I wondered if it has some secret meaning."

"I'm pretty well versed on the symbology of tattoos. What was it?"

"A clock face without hands. No minute hand, no hour hand."

Damian pondered the question. "Interesting. I've seen clock tattoos, but not that particular one. I'd imagine it could mean different things to different people. Where'd you see it?"

No way was Andy going to admit that he had been staring at Butch Behr's butt. "On someone's arm," he lied.

"Wish I could help you, but that one doesn't ring any bells. Now if you'll excuse me, I've got a maple leaf to create." He gestured for Shannon to follow him, and, with a giggle, she trailed after.

"So where are you headed now?" Andy asked Becky as they left Written on Skin. "More shopping?"

"Actually, I'm meeting Jade, and we're going snowshoeing. This morning, all the Girls' Weekend Out participants had flyers left outside our doors, listing a whole new schedule of events for today. Someone must've been up all night pulling it together."

"That'd be my Aunt Bev," Andy explained, wondering if Tim Fisher understood how hard she was working. He held the door for Becky as they left the conference center.

"Well, thank her for me. Gotta say, I dreaded being cooped up in this place all day. I'd signed up for the shopping trip down to New Bergen, with lunch at Ansel's. Your sister's place, right? But I guess there's still a chance of that happening. Just later in the day."

"That's what I understand. And if it doesn't, let me extend you a personal invite. You come down to Ansel's any old time, and I'll buy you lunch and a glass of Merlot. Take you on the cook's tour of Skjegstad Street, too."

They emerged into the resort's main lobby which, as usual, had clusters of stranded guests standing around yakking, drinking coffee, and watching the Weather Channel.

"You know," Becky said, "I've never spent much time in New Bergen. So a little exploration is definitely in order."

"Was your move up here spontaneous? Or something you planned for a while?"

"Truth be told, I was getting tired of Chicago. And I'd broken up with my boyfriend."

"How long were you two together?"

"Eight years."

"Wow, that's almost as long as I was married."

"Yeah, there were times it felt like we *were* really married. Josh is a surgeon and we met at work. We share a lot of interests. Adventure travel, especially. But somehow along the way we just got bored with each other."

"It happens."

"About that time, Aunt Cappy had a bad bout of pneumonia. I came up to check on her, and that's when I decided this was where I wanted to live. The lakes, the woods, the prairie. It's just so beautiful. I dropped in at St. Luke's. And I started to say I was a nurse practition-er, but before I could finish the sentence, they said, when can you start? All I had to do was get my state license. So, here I be—lacking romance, but happy otherwise."

Andy laughed. "Speaking of romance, how long do

you think Shannon and Pascal's immortal affair will last?"

Becky shook her head. "Given Shannon's attention span, I'd say about until the tattoo heals."

"Yeah, I noticed her giving Damian quite the flirty look."

"Well, he's not too hard on the eyes. He kind of has a bad-boy vibe going. Oh, that reminds me, Andy. You were talking about the tattoo of a clock face without hands."

"Uh-huh."

"I know one thing it could mean."

"You do?"

Becky suddenly looked a little grim. "Back in Chicago, we had patients come into the ER all the time with gunshot or stab wounds. And I saw that tattoo on a few of them. They were ex-cons, felons. Some were actually under arrest and getting patched up."

"Okay, you've got me in suspense, Becky. What does it mean?"

"It's a prison symbol. It means you're in stir for a long, long stretch. So, no hands on the clock because time is meaningless. Right? You've done a major crime, like murder or manslaughter. To wear that clock, at least from my experience, you've got to be a pretty bad dude."

Chapter Twenty-Three

Becky headed off to meet her friend Jade for their snowshoe outing on the golf course. Before she left, Andy made her promise that she would take him up on his invitation to lunch at Ansel's one day soon.

Next, Andy had to deliver Sonny's cheese box to the kitchen. But after that, he was going to do a little bit of sleuthing. Becky had put her finger on something that felt like an important clue. Had Butch Behr been in prison? If so, what was the conviction for? It must have been something pretty serious, if the clock tattoo symbolized a lengthy stretch in jail. Having a record didn't necessarily implicate him in the jeweled frog heist. But it would definitely land him high on the list of suspects.

If Butch Behr had served a term in the slammer, it ought to be on his job application. After Andy dropped off Sonny's cheese, he would track down Gilbey to see if there was any way to access Butch's employment records.

Tramping through the lobby, Andy spied the couple

he had met on the elevator the night before. Their two kids were nowhere to be seen. The parents were looking out the broad front windows of the main lodge onto the white scene outside, pointing and laughing. For the moment the snow had stopped, but the wind was still gusting strongly in the unprotected areas. The sky remained a solid slate gray, but it seemed to Andy that it had lightened.

Andy came up behind the couple to see what was so entertaining. About a dozen little kids, all in colorful winter parkas, were making snowmen out on the big oval patch of ground inside the circular drop-off drive. And right in the midst of them, supervising like a cop directing traffic, stood Aunt Bev in her own cranberry-colored parka. She was going bareheaded, as she always did in even the coldest weather, her henna dye job popping out against all that white.

"Looks like they're having a blast," Andy observed.

The pair swiveled around.

"Oh, hi again," the mom said. "Definitely a blast. We're from Arkansas, and we hardly ever get a snow that's good enough to build snowmen."

"The lady that put this together for the kids is a hoot," the dad gushed, nodding in Aunt Bev's direction. "She's terrific, a real live-wire."

Andy remembered all the snowman competitions that Aunt Bev used to organize when he was growing up. He had won a few of them himself, back in the day. Of course, so did the other kids. Everyone got a prize, even if it was just a box of Cracker Jack.

"So what brings you guys this far north?"

"Came up to visit my dad and stepmom," the young mother said. "Dad was in the Navy for thirty years, so I grew up all over the place. But when he retired, he decided to come back to his boyhood haunts. He loves it here." She turned and looked out the window and made a little gasp. "Oh, look, look. Kyle's going to stick a carrot in, for the nose. Oh, is that cute or what, Donnie? Quick, make a video!"

Andy slipped away from the doting parents and made for the Voyageur restaurant. In the kitchen, a prep cook directed him to a meeting room at the back of the main dining room, where the impromptu cooking class would take place. One of the chefs was consulting with Doris Schattenheimer, who seemed to be suggesting a different spot for a stainless-steel worktable. Geraldine Abbott, the assistant director of Tabby Dark, was setting up chairs in a semi-circle.

"Hey, Geraldine," Andy said, "whatcha doin' here?"

"Well, I ran into your aunt and asked if I could help with anything, since she's had to throw a whole new schedule together because of the snow. She put me with Doris here, to help organize the *hors d'oeuvres* demonstration. It should be lots of fun—I know I'm always looking for easy appetizer recipes. What's in your box?"

"Sonny Hofdahl sent over some of her goat cheese for the cooking demo."

Geraldine took the box from him. "Oooh, I adore

Sonny's cheeses. I love putting her chèvre on a cracker with just a dollop of garlic jelly on top."

"Sounds delicious. I'll have to try that."

"Can I ask you a question, Andy?" She was hugging the cheese box like it was a treasure chest.

"Sure, shoot."

"The Tabby Dark board has been talking about hiring a part-time events coordinator. And I was wondering if you think maybe, possibly, your aunt would be interested. I mean, I'm just super impressed seeing Beverly in action these last couple days, what with the storm and her boss Rosemary out of commission. She's really picked up the pieces and made the proverbial lemonade."

Andy didn't think Geraldine got that figure of speech exactly right, but he knew what she meant. And she was on the mark—Aunt Bev would be a great addition to the Tabby Dark staff. Considering how little respect Tim Fisher had for her, she would be wise to explore some other options.

"It couldn't hurt to ask her," he said. "She's a real booster for the Tri-Counties—always excited when a new business opens up in the area."

Geraldine gave him a conspiratorial look. "Want to hear some interesting business gossip?"

"I'm all ears."

"I met a fellow at breakfast this morning. The diner was so crowded, he asked if he could share my table. Nice looking man. A silver fox, if you get my drift. If I weren't married…" She winked at Andy. "He was coming home from a hunting trip."

Andy smiled. "Yeah, I think I know who you mean. Name is Ross. Chatted with him in the bar last night. He told me he farms up by Milton Mills. Also flips houses and whatnot. I think he said he was a structural engineer."

"Well, you know the old Aalberg Hotel on Third Street?"

Andy nodded. It was considered an Art Deco landmark in the area. Four stories tall, which passed for a skyscraper in Hobartville. It had gone from being the county's premier hotel to cheap apartments to a flophouse, before the bank foreclosed on it. It had sat empty and unused for years.

"This gentleman is evidently thinking about buying it and converting it into condos."

"Whoa," Andy exclaimed. "That's way more ambitious than flipping some bungalow or split-level. He's gonna need really serious dough. Gotta cost a million or two."

"I know. But apparently, he thinks he can get his hands on that kind of financing."

* * *

Andy went back into the lobby and phoned Gilbey. "Andy here," he said. "I'm wondering if we could rendezvous and discuss something."

"You betcha," the security guard answered. "Ten minutes, say? Employee canteen? Know where it is?"

"Around the corner from my aunt's cube?"

"That's it. Just one quick thing before you go," Gilbey said. "I wanted to give you a heads-up about something my boss Warren is checking into. He's stuck out on his acreage, you know. But he's been in touch with law enforcement contacts around the region. And he came up with a cluster of jewelry store thefts in South Dakota a couple weeks ago. And then a week ago, a rash of them on a single day down in the Cities. There might be a gang operating, but he didn't have any details."

"And he thinks the guy who mugged Grant Hamsden might be connected with this gang?" Andy asked dubiously.

"I'll admit the MO doesn't sound the same, but who knows? He figures it's worth following up on."

Ten minutes later, Andy walked into the staff canteen, a drab room painted institutional green. Vending machines and microwaves lined one wall, and on the opposite side, a half-dozen cots were set up, no doubt for employees who couldn't make it home the previous night. A couple of the housekeeping staff sat off in a corner, yakking over cups of coffee.

Andy spotted Gilbey at one of the tables, blowing on a cup of hot tea, and went over to join him.

"So, Gilbey," he said, sitting down, "what can you tell me about Butch Behr? Background, reputation, whatever."

"Butch? He's a good guy. Hard worker. Been an employee for about nine, ten years, from what I know. I think he started as part-time on the maintenance crew. A janitor basically. Worked his way up the ladder."

"What kind of security check would they have done for a position like that back then?"

Gilbey shrugged. "Probably just verified his references and had him do a drug test. It's not real easy finding guys like him who are jacks-of-all-trades. There isn't a thing in this place he can't fix. They probably wouldn't have gone too deeply, vetting him. But why are you so interested in him?"

Andy glanced around to make sure there was no one within earshot. "I think he may have spent some time in chokey."

Gilbey's eyes widened. "Butch? In prison? Naw, I don't buy that. He's a straight shooter. And you couldn't find a more devoted husband and dad."

Andy paused a second. He knew Gilbey wouldn't like his next request. "I really need to know if Butch listed any felony convictions on his job application. I saw a tattoo of a handless clock on his—um, on his back. And a friend of mine thinks he could have gotten it in prison." He drew a deep breath. "Any chance you could access the resort's personnel records and pull up his file?"

Gilbey sat back and crossed his arms over his chest. "No can do, Andy. Sorry. Number one, I don't want to lose my job, which I most certainly would if I even tried to get into that file. And number two, I wouldn't know how to do it without a password. Do I look like a computer geek to you?"

Andy couldn't blame him for refusing. If Butch's background needed checking, Tim Fisher would have to authorize it. But Andy didn't want to go that route. He wasn't going to drop Butch in the doo-doo on a misguided hunch. Even if the guy had lied about being a felon, he didn't deserve firing. Andy didn't want to be responsible for that.

"There *is* one thing we could do," Gilbey said, leaning toward Andy. "Butch's locker is next to mine, and he never locks it. He says he never leaves anything valuable in there and if someone wants to steal his lunch, they're welcome to it. We could sneak a peek and see if there's anything unusual in it. Like black gloves or a black ski mask."

It was a long shot, but Andy agreed it was worth a look. Gilbey led him back into the men's locker room, and the two of them stood in front of Butch's locker, No. 28. Even though they had been given the okay by Tim Fisher to search anywhere on the property, Andy could sense that the security guard was reluctant to open the door.

"There's probably no evidence in there," Andy said. "I mean, I understand my tattoo theory is awful circumstantial."

"Pretty weak soup," Gilbey agreed. "Butch could've just gotten the thing for the heck of it."

"Maybe," Andy said. "But we still ought to have a look." And with a sharp clanking sound, he pulled up the handle and opened the narrow door.

He pawed through the contents as Gilbey watched. There was a winter coat with gloves in the pockets, a stocking cap, a pair of work boots, a couple of car magazines. No stolen jeweled frog. No black ski mask. No roll of duct tape. No evidence or clues of any kind.

They looked at each other, relieved.

"Well," Andy said, "maybe we can cross Butch off the list after all."

"Cross me off what list?"

The two men spun around to face Butch Behr scowling at them, his face red with anger.

Chapter Twenty-Four

Butch Behr was almost as tall as Andy and built like a tank. He did not have the look of someone you'd want to mess with. Caught in the act, Andy was only able to mumble a few incoherent syllables. Gilbey, fortunately, kept his cool.

"Hey, Butch," the security guard said, "we're just eliminating staff from our list of suspects. You know, so the police don't have to question everyone. We went through your locker to confirm that, nope, nothing in there to link you to the crime."

It was a good save, Andy thought, but Butch didn't look like he was buying it.

"I don't appreciate being considered a suspect." He glared at them, jamming his hands in his pockets.

"Jeez, Big Behr, we just searched *my* locker a couple minutes ago," Gilbey lied, sounding offended. "We figure whoever stole the thing maybe had some inside help. How else could they have beaten the cameras? And we're gonna do Tim's office, too. Right Andy?"

Andy nodded. "Absolutely. No one gets a pass."

He had seen plenty of TV detectives who misled suspects, feeding them inaccurate info to trick them into confessions. Andy felt kind of mean, treating Butch like that. But he needed to find out if the guy had a record. Maybe a more direct approach was called for.

"You know that I saw your tattoo, Butch. The clock without hands. On your backside, when you were digging out that power strip."

Butch leaned toward him in a pugnacious posture. "Yeah, so what? Lots of people have tattoos."

"I think that's a prison tattoo, Butch. I think it means you did time. Lots of time. I talked to a prison tattoo expert about it." Another lie, Andy thought, but a harmless one.

To his relief, Butch backed off a few inches. "Naw, I saw the design someplace years ago and thought it looked cool. That's all. Nothing to do with prison."

"I don't know, Butch." Andy said. "Someone put a sleeper hold on Grant Hamsden. You look like you might have been a wrestler."

"He was, actually," Gilbey put in. "Told me so himself. Back in high school in Iowa. Heavyweight."

Butch looked desperately at Gilbey but didn't deny what he said.

"So you could've wrapped the poor guy in duct tape and filched the necklace out of his pocket," Andy continued. "You saw a score worth tens of thousands."

Butch blinked a few times. "I didn't take anything,

guys. I swear. Really, I didn't hurt anyone."

Andy narrowed his eyes at Butch, trying to look resolute.

Suddenly, Butch's mask of defiance crumbled. "Okay, okay. I'll admit it. I'm an ex-con."

Bingo, thought Andy, feeling pretty smug about his little gambit.

Beads of sweat were forming on Butch's forehead. "I lied about it on my job application. I was desperate to get a job after we moved back here. I'd learned the hard way that when I was upfront about my time inside, I never got hired. So when I applied here, I just didn't tick that box. Nobody asked and I didn't tell."

"Holy crap, Butch, you could get fired over that," Gilbey said, sounding genuinely concerned.

"Only if you guys rat me out." Butch shook his head. "I was planning to get that damned tattoo removed," he muttered. "Wish I would have gotten around to it sooner."

The plaintive look on his face got to Andy, who always tended to give a fellow a second chance. It made him a soft touch sometimes, but better that than going through life as a hard ass. Still, much as he'd like to believe him, Butch might be lying about the robbery. Andy needed to get him in front of Grant Hamsden. The jeweler wouldn't be able to identify him from his face, since the attacker had been masked. But Grant might sense something familiar in Butch's bulk—his form, his movement, his manner, even his smell.

"I won't say anything for now," Andy said. "And if there's really no connection between you and the robbery, I'm willing to keep it a secret. How about you, Gilbey?"

The security guard nodded fiercely. "Heck, you think I want to get Butch in hot water for no reason? Everybody around here likes you, man. And you do a great job. Nobody wants to mess that up for you."

The relief that washed over Butch's face was almost comical. "Thanks, Gilbey, Andy. I really appreciate it. This would've destroyed me, if it got out." He gave a nervous laugh. "Now if you'll excuse me." Reaching into his open locker, he pulled out his coat and cap. "Some bozo decided to try to escape this loony bin before the main entrance got cleared. I gotta go help get him unstuck."

Andy glanced at his watch and was surprised to see that it was nearly eleven. "I need to get moving, too. I'm supposed to brief Logan Kennedy in just a few minutes. Gilbey, I'll check in with you when I'm done, okay?"

After a quick hike through the office and the lobby, and a torturously slow ride on a packed elevator that stopped at every floor, Andy finally arrived at the door of Logan's suite. He stood for a moment to catch his breath, then rapped on it. He heard movement inside, and the door swung open.

Standing there, phone in hand, was Sara Blake, with a cross, impatient look on her face. Her early-morning frostiness had not melted. But even wearing a frown, she was a pretty woman. Andy wondered what kind of dreams she had. He couldn't imagine that being Logan's personal assistant was easy. It was never much fun working for super egos.

She stepped out into the hallway with Andy. "You're late."

He looked at his watch. "Just three minutes."

"Late nonetheless. The author…" Sara nodded back inside, where Andy could see Logan slumped down, petting Nikkie listlessly. "She's in a blue funk this morning."

"Do you know why?"

Sara's tone went down to a whisper. "She gets in these moods sometimes. All I know is that last night she was going to meet someone in the Homesteader bar."

Andy knew exactly who it was that Logan had met in the bar. He had seen Thor holding her hand. But what in heck would Thor have said that could have depressed her? Bored her to tears, maybe, but sending her into the pits of despair? Or had she met someone else, too?

"I really don't have time to coddle her this morning," Sara groused. "The producer for the Kat Blast was going to fly up from the Cities, but the flights coming into Hobartville are delayed. I don't know what I'll do if he doesn't make it. Anyway, you better come in and tell her what you know about the theft."

"Fine by me," he said. "By the way, I saw you sitting next to Damian Powers in the café this morning. Really nice fellow." Andy liked Damian and figured it couldn't hurt to put in a good word for him.

"The tattoo guy?" she sniffed. "I barely talked to him, so I wouldn't know."

Sara clearly had no interest in him. Still, with his good looks and "bad-boy vibe," as Becky described it, Damian shouldn't lack for feminine companionship.

As they walked into the suite, Logan looked up, her face a mask of fatigue and despondency. "Hello, Anders. Come, sit beside me." She patted the sofa cushion next to her. Her cougar act was nowhere to be seen.

Andy eased himself down, positioning his long legs so as not to displace Logan's dog Nikkie, who looked up at him with a morose expression that mirrored Logan's. Nikkie was very much a different sort of canine than Harald. Like her mistress, she was a little inscrutable. Not unfriendly, but not nearly as gregarious as Harald.

"So, Anders," Logan said, straightening up a bit, "have you made any progress?"

"Well, not to the point of finding your necklace, unfortunately."

Andy described how they had reenacted the crime in Grant's room. Looked at security footage and found nothing. Interviewed folks in rooms nearby who might have seen something. Checked into similar thefts in the area. There was one person of interest on staff, he told her, but he took care not to reveal Butch's identity. He didn't want Logan jumping the gun and calling Tim Fisher about it.

Rather than showing any curiosity, Logan seemed

indifferent. When Andy finally finished, she looked over at her PA. "Sara, would you go track down a green smoothie for me? Or the closest facsimile?"

After Sara left, Logan stood and began to pace back and forth. She almost acted as if Andy weren't even there. Nikkie got to her feet and trailed after her.

"I knew it wouldn't be easy, coming home," Logan said, standing in front of the window, looking out at the white landscape and gusting snow. "I only decided to launch the new Kat book here because of my mother. She's not in the best shape, and I don't know if she'll be around very long. I just wanted to try again to make her understand how well I've done."

"She must be awfully proud of you," Andy said.

Logan gave a hollow laugh. "You'd think so, wouldn't you? Mom never really approved of the path I took. She's very straight-laced. Lived all her life in a small town, where everyone knew everyone else's business. And judged it. Appearances mean everything to her. Having a daughter who earned her celebrity writing about a promiscuous female assassin wasn't exactly something to boast about. Ever been called a blasphemer? I have."

Andy could offer no words of advice. He had been blessed with loving, supportive parents. Dean and Susie Skyberg never expressed disappointment in his career choices—even when he was driving a limo while his sister Kirsten was climbing high on the corporate ladder in Silicon Valley.

"Well, none of us gets to pick our parents." Not the cleverest comment, but Andy felt uncomfortable being made privy to Logan's personal angst.

She eased herself down next to him, with Nikkie reclaiming her spot in front of the sofa. The three of them sat there silently. Andy was about to excuse himself, when Logan finally spoke.

"It's not just family, you know. There are ghosts from the past coming out of nowhere. Coming out of the woodwork, it seems."

Of course, she meant Sage Mortenson and the Dillards, Andy figured. The old roommate—the embittered third corner of that college-era triangle—and the former mentor Logan had betrayed back in the day. He wasn't going to reveal that he knew about them. But he wondered if some of her distress was due to the guilt she felt for what she had done all those years ago. And how did Thor fit into all this?

"I didn't think it would be this hard coming back."

Andy had no idea *why* Logan was confiding in him. But he had learned long ago that when a woman—any woman—wanted to unload emotionally, the best thing to do was to sit back and provide a sympathetic ear.

"I've done some things that hurt people, Anders. Things I'm not proud of." She sighed. "But that's ancient history. What's past is past." She turned to look at him, and Andy detected a hint of anger in her eyes. "Why can't people understand that? Why can't people get beyond it? Why can't they just leave me alone?"

The cavalry arrived when Sara returned with Logan's smoothie. It allowed Andy to make a graceful exit before the author revealed anything more.

Riding down in the elevator, he remembered he needed to fetch Harald, for his promotional gig with Thor and Sonny. But before that, it was vital to get back to Grant Hamsden's booth. When he arrived, he exchanged a few quick words with the jewelry designer, then phoned Butch Behr.

"Hey there, Big Behr," Andy said when Butch answered. From the growl he received, he knew he had made a mistake. The ex-con apparently didn't want to hear that nickname from someone he hardly knew.

"I'm at the Hamsden Designs booth," Andy said, recovering quickly. "And another one of those power strips is giving us trouble. Could you grab a replacement and come over?"

In truth, Grant Hamsden hadn't had any trouble with either of his power strips, until Andy made a slight modification to one. The point was to compel Butch Behr to pop by, so that Grant could eyeball him. Did Butch, in stature and manner, resemble the thief who had mugged the jeweler?

Butch arrived about ten minutes later with the power strip in hand and quickly crawled under a table to get at the "defective" one. When he came back up, Grant stood next to him as they examined the neutered power strip. Andy could see Grant casting furtive glances at Butch's hands and arms, as if doing mental calculations comparing them to the criminal's.

"So?" Andy said to Grant, after Butch left. "Could he be the guy?"

The jeweler threw his hands up. "I don't know. He's big enough, for sure. But then so is that guy over there." He nodded down and across the aisle, where a beefy fellow was gnawing on a sample in the venison sausage and jerky booth. "Or that guy."

Andy looked in the direction he was pointing. Tramping toward them came Bobby, Justine Juveland's slouching, oversize boyfriend.

"Guess I'm not a very good witness," Grant apologized. "Sorry."

But Andy was barely listening, as he watched black-clad Bobby disappear down the aisle.

Justine, by all accounts, was totally obsessed with Logan. Earlier that morning Stephanie Bukowski had described someone like her casing the safe in Grant's booth. Had her compulsion led her to steal the thing? Sara Blake had suggested as much last night, but no one had taken her seriously. Justine's boyfriend Bobby seemed like a doofus, but it wouldn't hurt to find out if he knew how to administer a sleeper hold.

But how in the world would Andy be able to do *that*?

Chapter Twenty-Five

Andy would have liked to follow Bobby and ask him a few questions. But he had another matter to attend to.

When he fetched Harald from Aunt Bev's timeshare, the dog was so happy to see him that he nearly knocked him over. The two headed back to the Hofdahl Farm booth, where Andy found Thor chatting with Ross, the structural engineer-turned-farmer he had met yesterday. Ross had to be the guy Geraldine had talked about—the one who wanted to rehab the old Aalberg Hotel as condos.

Thor beamed as Andy and Harald approached. "Well, there's the mutt and his manservant."

Ross laughed and so did Andy. Truth be told, that's the way it felt sometimes.

"Do you know Ross here?" Thor asked.

"Yeah, I do," Andy said. "Think you'll be able to mush out of here today, Ross?"

"I've been following the DOT reports," he replied, "and it sounds like they're making progress. I'm thinking a late-afternoon departure is a good possibility." He picked up a small paper bag from the display counter. "Well, got a few more things I want to grab. Christmas gifts, you know. Catch you later." Ross nodded at the two of them and ambled away down the aisle.

"Hey, thanks for bringing his royal highness," Thor said. "Business has been slow this morning, and he's sure to attract some tasters." Thor looped the leash around a chair. "You stay here, big fella. No meandering for you."

Okay, Andy thought, *Sonny is nowhere to be seen. Time to talk turkey with the old boy.* He took a deep breath. It had to be done. It was the only way to save Thor from his baser instincts.

"Thor, there's a little matter I'd like to discuss with you."

Thor pushed his horn-rimmed glasses back up his nose and tilted his head. "My goodness, that sounds ominous."

"Thing is this, Thor. Yesterday I caught sight of you..." Andy struggled to come up with the right verb. "...*sneaking* around."

Thor's bushy gray eyebrows shot up and his pale blue eyes widened. "Sneaking around?"

"Yup," Andy continued with a curt nod. "Sneaking around. Slipping out of Logan Kennedy's suite. And from what I've been told, you two had been in her bedroom. *With the door closed.*"

Thor looked thunderstruck. "Andy, I—"

"Let me finish, Thor. Then last night in the bar, I spotted you two holding hands. And it sure as heck looked like you were whispering sweet nothings to her."

"Andy, you got the wrong—"

"And Sonny told me you keep disappearing, leaving her with all the work here." Andy wasn't exactly enjoying this, but once he got started, the words kept rolling out. "I don't know exactly what you and Logan are up to, but, as they say, the optics are not good."

"Listen, this is just a—"

"You and Sonny are my most favorite old couple, apart from my folks, and Aunt Bev and Uncle Frank. I mean, you're role models in the marriage department. And the idea that you'd go and get the thirty-seven year itch, or whatever the heck it is, and do something—"

"Will you please just shut up for a minute?" Thor snapped. "For Pete's sake, let me get a word in edgewise." But instead of looking angry, the old geezer looked unaccountably amused.

Andy crossed his arms. "Okay then, talk."

"I suppose I ought to be flattered. You think I still have enough juice left for a torrid affair."

Thor and Logan rolling around together in the hay wasn't an image Andy wanted living in his head. "That's not the point."

"As a matter of fact, I do have enough zip," Thor boasted. "My get-up-and-go hasn't gotten up and went. Not yet, anyway. But I got me a hot mama already who I'm crazy about. I don't need to go sneaking around with anyone else."

"So you're saying you and Logan aren't having a fling?"

"Absotively, posilutely not. It's kind of a compliment, I suppose, you hooking me up with Logan. But did you consider that I might be hanging out with her for reasons other than steamy illicit sex?"

"Like what?" Andy demanded. "What reason could you possibly have to be holding her hand in a dark corner of a crowded bar?"

Thor sighed. "The lady was having a tough evening, okay? She needed a shoulder to cry on. Her silly jeweled frog had just gotten ripped off. And then she had some kind of encounter with someone from her past."

"That had to be Sage," Andy said. "At the Tabby Dark reception. Logan looked like she was going to have a cow when she recognized Sage. Sonny told me about their feud back in college. Sounds like Logan stole Sage's one true love right out from under her—so to speak. If Logan was upset, maybe she was feeling a twinge of conscience for what she did all those years ago."

"I couldn't say. A few tears trailed down. Then I got her talking about her new book. She writes a darned good thriller, let me tell you."

Two women—they looked like sisters—came into the booth, and one of them asked if there was any of Sonny's gouda left. Thor sold them each a one-pound wheel of the rich, Dutch-style cheese.

"But how do you even know Logan?" Andy asked, after the women left. "She called you her *muse*, after all. How did that happen?"

"Actually, this is only the second time we've met in person. But I've known her for quite a while. We're e-mail buddies. I sent her a long fan letter years ago. She was kind enough to respond, and now she calls me one of her favorite superfans."

"I didn't even think guys read her books."

"Logan says ten to fifteen percent of her readers are male. Ross—he's the guy who just left—he's a fan, too. He was in the bar last night and even managed to talk with Logan a little bit before she met me. He told me he took book number ten—that's *Last Shot*—to South Dakota with him. Guess he was out there hunting pheasant with a gang of his buddies. Anyway, Logan considers me part of her team, as it were."

Andy had never thought of Thor as a fanboy, but the man had always had the capacity to surprise. "Wow. She must really value your opinions."

"Well, I do offer some special perspective that she needs. She found out that I did two tours in Nam. Turns out her dad, gone now, served there, too. In fact, he and I were in some of the same quote-unquote 'garden spots' at about the same time. She's writing a book about him, and she interviewed me on the phone a few months ago, and yesterday in her bedroom. Top-secret project. So, you see, Andy, she values me for more than just my pretty face."

"Does Sonny know about all this?" Andy asked, narrowing his eyes.

Thor jutted out his chin defiantly. "Of course she knows I know Logan. And she knows I met with Logan this weekend. But I think she's a teeny bit annoyed I haven't been around the booth as much as she'd like."

"Do you blame her?"

Thor gave Andy a bittersweet smile. "No, guess not. But you gotta realize that when you get to be a guy my age, the accolades don't come so often. I guess I'm just saying that having the attention of someone like Logan gives a guy's ego a boost."

Thor had a point. Praise and admiration were addictive. But there was something Thor had said a few minutes ago that floated back up in Andy's head. The words "gang" and "South Dakota" lit a light bulb. Hadn't Gilbey talked about a gang of jewel thieves from South Dakota hitting stores down in the Cities? And hadn't Ross said something to Andy about being in the Cities recently?

"Thor, did Ross happen to mention his last name?"

"As it turns out, he did. I remember it because one of my all-time favorite writers has the same surname. Ueland. Brenda Ueland. Now her book on—"

"How do you spell that?" Andy grabbed a piece of paper from a table.

"U-e-l-a-n-d. Norske, of course. Why do you want to know?"

"The guy's maybe going to convert the old Aalberg

Hotel into condos," Andy said as he scribbled. "I'd like to Google him and see if he's legit. I mean, that's a big project."

"Oh, yeah," Thor agreed. "A million buck budget, at least. Now if you haven't ever read anything by Brenda Ueland, you ought to, because she's—"

"Thanks, Thor, I'll do that," Andy said, cutting him off. "But right now, I've gotta run."

Andy shoved the piece of paper into his pocket and took off. He knew it seemed kind of farfetched, but he wanted to see if Gilbey's boss could track down any info on Ross. He was so engrossed in his theory that he bumped right into a woman who was balancing two bird-houses built like little log cabins. She almost dropped one of them, but Andy helped her catch it.

"Oh, gosh, I'm sorry," he apologized, passing the birdhouse back to her.

"No worries," she panted. "These things are bulkier than they look. One's for me and one's for my daughter. I'm meeting her at the Coffee Hut."

"Here, let me have that one back and I'll carry it." Andy accompanied her to the coffee spot, where her daughter was waiting. As he turned to leave, he stopped short. There, within spitting distance, sat Roger Dillard and Justine Juveland, deep in conversation. Justine was doing most of the talking, with Roger nodding occasion-ally as he sipped.

Andy went over to them. "Hey, Roger, hi again."

"Oh, hi, Andy." The publisher looked a little uncomfortable. "This is Justine Juveland. And this is Andy Skyberg, Justine. He's here helping out with the Holiday Faire. He's the mayor of New Bergen, and he's also investigating the theft."

"I hope you're not telling everyone about the incident, Roger," cautioned Andy. "The security people here think it's best to keep the details under wraps."

Justine hooted. "A little late for that," she said, pulling out her smartphone. She tapped and swiped, then held it up for Andy.

The headline, from a CNN story, popped into focus: **LOGAN KENNEDY BLIZZARD BLOW—PROMOTIONAL PRIZE PILFERED**.

"Her PR agent Georgia put out a series of tweets a little while ago," Justine explained, putting her phone away. "They urged everybody to tune into the live stream of the Kat Blast for the latest news. And as you can see, it's starting to get traction in the media." She took her phone back and stood up. "Since you're investigating, let me give you *my* theory."

"Uh-huh?" Andy said, feeling blindsided. Why hadn't Logan told him about this? He felt like a fool in front of Justine and Roger.

"I think this whole robbery was a setup by our favorite author and her press agent," Justine said. "I think it was the plan all along." She took a sip of her coffee. "Something like this happened a few years ago. An anonymous party sent Logan threatening e-mails, demanding she stop publication of one of her books, because there was supposedly some thinly disguised real person in it. Logan went public with the threats. The police never did track down the extortionist, but the publicity boosted sales."

Andy had entertained the same notion about Logan setting up the theft. "So maybe Grant Hamsden was in on it. But would he have broken his toes on purpose?"

"Well, who knows?" Justine shrugged. "That was probably just an accident. But I'll bet you Logan is making it worth his while."

Andy considered that scenario for a few seconds. "I don't know. I've spent some time with Grant, and he just doesn't strike me as a person who'd take that kind of risk."

Justine gave him a withering look. "You evidently have *no* idea of how persuasive Logan can be."

The woman's attitude was beginning to annoy Andy. "Can I ask you a question? Where were you and your boyfriend last evening? About six o'clock?"

"You're not a cop," she smirked. "Bring me a real cop, and I'll answer the question." Looking very pleased with herself, she sauntered off.

Andy turned back to Roger Dillard. "I thought you and your mom decided not to have anything to do with her."

"*Mom* decided not to," Roger responded. "But I own half the business, and I'm interested in Justine's bio of Logan. She gave me a proposal and sample chapters. After I closed the booth at quitting time yesterday, I grabbed a sandwich and spent the evening reading it. Actually, it's an appealing project."

That explained why Roger hadn't been at the Tabby Dark reception. And if he had stayed at the Holiday Faire until it closed at seven, he had a pretty airtight alibi for the time of the theft. Andy figured he could cross the Dillards off his list of suspects.

"You're considering publishing Justine's book?" Andy asked. "Even if your mother's against it?"

Roger sighed. "To tell you the truth, Dillard Press revenues have been stagnant. We've been thinking about putting the company on the market, and we could really use something to boost our bottom line. If Justine's book is any good—and I think it could be—that would mean sales north of fifty thousand copies. In hardcover alone."

"So if you sell the firm, would you be looking to find another job in the publishing biz?"

"Not a chance," Roger snorted. "You wouldn't believe how bloody sick I am of writers. They're nothing but a bunch of needy, whiny little dweebs."

Chapter Twenty-Six

Harald always felt a little pang when the boss handed him over to somebody else. It was probably because his first boss had handed him over and not come back. Harald had been afraid that he would never have a boss again, but that's about when the new boss turned up. And it had been great ever since.

Harald liked the old man that the boss had just left him with. But it was kind of boring, being tied to a table. He tried to get away, but he couldn't budge the thing. Once in a while, someone came over to pet him and say friendly words, so that was all good. He could never have too much petting. But it was still pretty tedious, until a woman he recognized came by. She bent over and petted him. Then she turned to the old man.

"Thor, how about I take King Harald for a walk? I'm on break, and he looks like he could use some exercise. And I could, too."

"Sure, Sage, why not? Things going well this morning?"

"They are indeed. A woman came in and bought five of the same sweater in different sizes. You know, that blue-and-white snowflake design. She's going to put everybody in them for the family Christmas card."

The old man whistled. "That's a nice fat sale." He disentangled Harald's leash and handed it to her. "By the way, if you want a friend forever, buy this fellow a meat stick."

Harald's ears perked up. Those last two sounds were *very* nice.

The woman gently tugged him out of the booth. They went up the aisle and into a corridor, walking for a while until they ended up in a place with food and lots of other things. Harald saw the woman grab a meat stick off a shelf. The crinkly sound of the wrapping in her hand was pure bliss. He hoped to get it in his mouth immediately, but she had other ideas.

She bent the meat stick in two, put it in her pocket, and took Harald to a bench that looked out on the snow. She sat and he plopped down facing her, tail wagging in anticipation of something tasty.

Lots of people were looking at a tall tree near the door. Harald thought it odd to see a tree this big growing inside. But it was extremely interesting, with all sorts of sparkly things hanging on it.

"Hey there, you two."

Harald stood up, his heart racing. It was the boss.

"Oh, hi Andy. Thor said it would be okay if I took Harald for a walk."

"Absolutely, Sage. It's been a pretty boring week-end for the pooch there. Is he behaving himself?"

"Oh, yeah. Good as gold. You wouldn't consider let-ting me adopt him, would you?"

The boss smiled. "You're not the first person to ask. He kinda has that effect on people. Everybody wants to hang with Harald."

The woman gave Harald a shoulder rub. "I under-stand perfectly. Bakken, my black lab, passed a few months ago. Just old age. But you wouldn't believe the hole he left."

"Oh, that's tough. I'm so sorry. Don't know what I'd do without this guy."

All of a sudden, the boss sneezed. A sneeze that seemed to require a reply. Harald woofed, though not as loudly as he might normally have done.

The boss laughed, and so did the woman. The boss reached into his pocket and pulled out two pieces of paper. One he put up to his nose and blew into. The other fluttered to the floor. The woman reached down to pick it up. She stared at it for a few seconds, then handed it back to the boss.

"Tell me, Andy, what do you think of Verna? I mean, Logan?"

The boss looked a little uneasy, and Harald could sense that he didn't want to be there anymore. "Well, I just met her and we've gotten along okay. But I under-stand that you had some issues with her."

"Issues, right. That's a polite way of putting it."

"Yeah, there's an awfully big ego working there, huh?"

"You don't know the half of it, Andy. What Verna wants, Verna gets. She's always been like that. Just steamrolls anyone standing in her way."

"Umm, Sage, could I ask you a question?"

"Sure, why not?"

"Could you tell me where you were last night at about six?"

The woman chuckled. "If you think I stole Verna's damned necklace, Andy, I've got to disappoint you. I was in the booth until seven, and my two gals will confirm that."

"Sorry, Sage, but I had to ask. Wish I could talk some more, but I really got to run."

"Of course, Andy. I'll maybe see you later."

It was disappointing when the boss went off, but Harald forgot all about him the instant the woman pulled out the meat stick. He caught its aroma and it smelled wonderful.

"Bakken was a very good listener," she said, petting Harald's head.

He eyed the meat stick in her hand.

"If Bakken were still around, I'd tell him that I really thought I was over Verna. She practically destroyed me. I took drugs for a long time, to numb the pain. I almost OD'd. But I thought I'd finally put the bitch behind me."

Harald looked her in the eye, wondering *when* he would get his treat.

"Ohhh, look at that concerned expression on your face," she said, lifting up his snout. "You're such a good boy to be worried about me. And I'm sure you understand that I can never forgive that woman."

The thought of the meat stick was driving Harald nuts. But the woman was staring out the window now, as if he wasn't even there.

"I wonder what she's been telling Andy about me." She had a cold, dark tone in her voice. "Verna probably said I was a mental case. Probably accused me of stealing that stupid necklace."

She gazed back down at Harald. "Is this the face of a jewel thief? This plain, bland face? You never can tell, Harald. There's nothing more invisible than a middle-aged woman—we can do all sorts of things unnoticed."

She sat silently for a moment. Harald was feeling desperate.

"Just between you and me, Harald, Verna's book signing this afternoon may not be the triumphant return she's expecting. I could make it very awkward for her. Do you think I should, Harald?"

Meat stick, thought Harald. *Meat stick!* He gave an impatient woof.

"Good boy, Harald. I'm glad you approve. You've earned your reward."

She pulled the meaty treat out of its wrapper and gave it to Harald.

Chapter Twenty-Seven

Andy hated to judge anybody on the basis of just an encounter or two, but he couldn't escape the impression that Sage Mortenson was obsessed with her ancient grudge against Logan. Thirty years ought to have been plenty of time for old wounds to heal. The way she had prodded Andy to reveal what he thought about "Verna" made it clear she was still carrying heavy emotional baggage. Andy wondered if, as unlikely as it seemed, Sage's hatred for Logan had pushed her to the point of committing a crime. Even with an alibi, she could still have had an accomplice.

After he left Sage and Harald, he phoned Gilbey. Andy wanted to mention his suspicions about Ross Ueland—probably a long shot, but worth a look. The security guard, though, didn't pick up. So before he caught a quick bite, Andy decided to head back to the offices. Maybe Gilbey was there.

As he was walking past the Homesteader bar, Andy spotted Justine Juveland and her boyfriend Bobby sitting at one of the tall cocktail tables. The black-clad couple was deep in conversation over burgers and fries. Andy kept walking but then stopped. He still had unfinished business with Justine. She had avoided answering his questions earlier, but this time he wasn't going to let her off the hook.

He did an about-face and headed for her table.

"Uh-oh," Justine said, when she saw him approaching. "Here comes the fuzz, Bobby. You better tape this. You know, in case of police brutality."

Bobby pulled out his phone, tapped it, and shoved it in Andy's direction.

"Okay, bubba," he smirked. "You're on video."

"Bubba?" Andy groaned. "That's the best burn you can come up with?" He climbed up on one of the tall chairs. "Mind if I join you? And I'm not the fuzz. I'm the mayor. Of New Bergen."

Bobby looked confused. "Who is this character, babe?"

"Some guy the resort hired to look into the jewel theft. He wanted to know if we have alibis for six o'clock last night. Guess that's when the frog thing went down."

Bobby's face lit up. "You mean we're suspects? Cool! But seriously, dude, we couldn't have done it. We were—"

"Bobby, will you shut up!" Justine glared at him. "We're not saying anything, okay?"

He scrunched up his features and nodded. "Okay,

gotcha. Stonewalling. Understood." He picked up his beer in his very large right paw and took a long, slow slurp, staring at Andy while keeping the phone aimed in his direction.

Andy looked at the beefy boyfriend and said, "Bet a guy like you was on the wrestling team in school. Bet you even know how to do a sleeper hold."

Justine snorted. "Not exactly a smooth interviewer, are you?"

Andy turned to her. "Well, if you won't let Bobby speak, maybe you can tell me why you were in Grant Hamsden's booth yesterday casing the safe."

Justine just shook her head. "You may as well pack up and go harass someone else. 'Cause you're getting bupkis from us."

Andy took a few seconds to consider his next move. "Listen, I think we got off on the wrong foot. Let's try again." He offered his hand to Bobby. "Andy Skyberg."

Bobby looked at his girlfriend, as if he didn't know what to do.

She just rolled her eyes. "Go ahead and shake it. He's not contagious."

That little formality seemed to put Bobby at ease, but Justine was still scowling at Andy. He needed to turn on the charm.

"I'm helping out because the cops couldn't get here last night or this morning," he explained. "Lots of folks stranded in cars, you know. So one of the security people here and I have been gathering evidence while it's still fresh." He tried to summon up a sincere smile.

"Still not telling you anything," Justine snipped.

"Okay, fine." There had to be another way to crack that tough-broad veneer, Andy thought. Maybe a little flattery would do the trick.

"I was just talking with Roger Dillard. He told me he was *seriously* considering your proposed biography of Logan."

Justine's expression changed ever so subtly. A glimmer of curiosity flitted across her face. "Is that so?"

"He said he thinks it has the potential to sell fifty thousand copies."

"Fifty thousand?" Justine grinned at Bobby and backhanded his arm.

"In hardcover. Trade paperback would add a lot to that." Andy made up the last bit, but it sounded legit.

Justine's face turned inscrutable again. "Well, that's all very flattering, but there's no contract yet. Still, Roger's one of the first people to take my project seriously." She dipped a fry in ketchup and munched on it. "Fact is, I'm a proper reporter and biographer. I've published articles on Logan and Kat in scholarly journals. Every *true* Kat Taggett fan reads my blog. No one's done more to promote Kat and Logan than me."

"And how does she reward you?" Bobby huffed. "She threatens you with a stupid restraining order. Just because you approached her a few too many times." He turned to Andy. "I mean, Justine would never hurt Logan. That's just nuts. Logan's lucky to have such a Kat freak on her side."

Yeah, Andy thought. On her side, in front of her, behind her, above her, below her, and out hiding in the bushes.

"Thank you, honey pie," Justine murmured, tossing an affectionate glance Bobby's way. "Thing is, Andy, Logan's a bit upset with me, and it's not just because I've been allegedly *stalking* her. You see, I have a manuscript of one of her early, unpublished books. It was written before she worked with the Dillards. She wants me to give it to her, but I won't."

"How'd you get hold of it?" Andy asked.

"Can't tell you. But it's fascinating to see Kat Taggett in her early form—before Logan had a good editor to work with. She wants it back so she can destroy it. She's offered good money for it, but I won't sell."

"That burglary we had," Bobby interjected. "That was probably someone looking for it. Wouldn't put it past Logan. She can be as ruthless as Kat." He turned to Andy. "That's why Justine was looking at the safe. We figure we have to upgrade our security."

Justine glared at him. "Too much information, Bobby."

Andy found it hard to believe that Logan would commission a burglary. That was awfully risky. Wasn't it enough that Justine would be in deep legal doo-doo if she published the complete manuscript? After all, Logan owned the copyright. That was hers, from the moment she put words on page.

A waitress came up and asked if Andy wanted anything. He ordered a clubhouse sandwich on rye, fries, and a Diet Coke. The waitress scurried off.

"So, you're going to quote the manuscript in your biography?" he asked.

"Absolutely. Fair use law lets me use excerpts."

"What other juicy tidbits are going to be in your book?" Andy gave Justine a hopeful look. "I'm only asking because maybe you know something else that could shed light on the theft."

"I think I've probably said too much already."

"Look," Andy said, "truth be told, I had never even heard of Logan Kennedy before yesterday. If it weren't for this rotten storm, I'd be down in the Cities right now, getting ready to go to the Blitzers show with a hot date."

"Oooh," Bobby teased, "a hot date, huh? A guy your age? Better not get too frisky, or you might have a heart attack."

"Bobby," Justine snapped, "will you grow up? Not even funny."

"What I'm saying," Andy said, ignoring the taunt, "is I don't have a dog in this fight. If you know anything useful, I'll just pass it along to the authorities and say I don't remember where I heard it."

Justine ruminated a moment. "I can't imagine that I know anything relevant. But there are a couple of items…"

"Go ahead," Andy said encouragingly. "Anything at all."

"Hardly anyone knows this," Justine said, "but after college, Logan actually tried to get a job at the CIA. She hooked up with some guy who was an operative there. He was supposed to be movie-star handsome. And I believe a few of her early plots were inspired by true-life cases he told her about. Rumor has it the agency wasn't pleased."

As interesting as this tidbit would be to a biographer, Andy couldn't see the CIA executing a jeweled frog necklace heist. And that operative Logan had the fling with would probably be a grandpa by now, long since retired from the agency.

All of a sudden, he thought of Ross Ueland and his years working overseas as a "structural engineer." The guy looked awfully fit and buff, like a fifty-something Jason Bourne. Working as an engineer would have been perfect cover for a spy. Could Ross be the CIA agent? Had he decided to track down Logan and reconnect? It was a crazy idea, Andy knew, but no crazier than the guy being a jewel thief.

"And did you know," Justine continued, "that Sara Blake is contractually forbidden from publishing anything of her own during her employment with Logan? If she writes a novel, Logan owns it. And I know for a fact that she's working on a manuscript Logan doesn't know about."

So Sara's dream was to be a novelist. "But why would she sign an awful contract like that?"

"She had to, or she wouldn't have gotten such a plum

job for a newbie in the business. The contacts she's building by working for Logan are invaluable for a novelist starting out."

"Does Sara resent having to give up her first-born to Logan?"

"Wouldn't you? But would she risk jail by stealing the jeweled frog? I don't think so. That'd just be crazy." Justine smiled slyly. "There's one other little tidbit. Actually, the *biggest* tidbit. But a girl's gotta have a secret or two. You'll have to buy my book to read about it." She popped another fry in her mouth, chewed, and swallowed. "Okay, Bobby, that's a wrap. Let's roll. Catch you later, Mayor."

They climbed down off their high stools and headed out of the bar. As they left, the waitress arrived with Andy's clubhouse on rye. Noshing on it, he wondered if Justine and Bobby really had a motive to pinch Logan's necklace, let alone means and opportunity. Justine for sure had a love/hate thing going with the woman. But as much as she might resent the author's treatment of her, Justine's whole professional and personal identity came from Logan and Kat. It would be stupid of her to bite the hand that fed her blog.

Andy was halfway through his clubhouse when two of the T-shirt gals walked in and spotted him. Today they were wearing blouses with long shirttails—still in the same gaudy colors. Waving cheerily, they made a beeline for his table.

"Well, hi there, tall, blond, and handsome," said Hot

Pink. "Okay if we join you?"

Andy wouldn't have minded finishing his lunch alone, but the place was packed. It would be rude not to let them share the table.

"No, not at all. Please, pull up a stool."

"I'll tell you," said Mint Green as she hoisted her short, pudgy figure up on the stool, "we're getting a little tired of the Holiday Faire. I think we've been through it a hundred times, haven't we, Andrea?"

"It sure feels like it. We're so glad the shopping trip down to New Bergen is back on."

Andy was thrilled to hear the news. It must mean the roads were passable. "You're gonna love Skjegstad Street. At last count, thirty-two terrific retail and antique shops and six eateries. We like to call New Bergen the Christmas Capital of Beaver Tail County."

"Eileen here is looking for a bracelet for her daughter," Andrea said. "Something unique. Not the same-old same-old you'd find at the mall. Is there any place you'd recommend?"

"Absolutely. Check out Ludeman's. Bob sells a lot of authentic Art Nouveau and Art Deco pieces to collectors, but he has a nice selection of reproductions that are super affordable. He's just down the street from Ansel's."

"We're eating at Ansel's," said Eileen. "Is it any good?"

"Personally, I think it's the best restaurant north of the Cities." He grinned. "But full disclosure: My sister owns it and I work there."

"Ooh, then it must be good!" Andrea enthused.

"Hope you've got a full bar," Eileen added.

"Fully stocked," Andy said. He remembered that she was the one who had fallen in Grant Hamsden's booth— the one who apparently had a tippling problem. "By the way, that was quite a tumble you took yesterday. Looked like you coulda hurt yourself."

Eileen waved him off. "I'm okay. Just two left feet. Boy, I'm starved…" She flagged down the waitress, who took the women's orders—two bowls of chicken-and-wild-rice soup, house salads, and hot buttered rums.

Andy couldn't resist asking about the attire. "I'm curious. What's the deal with the colored T-shirts and sweatshirts. You guys each wear the same colors all the time?"

Andrea hooted. "Oh, it's just a little thing we came up with on our first trip together a few years ago. I'm in pink most of the time. Eileen picked green. Sherry likes her blue and Kim goes for yellow. It's kind of our trademark."

"Ahh, I guess that makes sense," he said, unable to imagine four guys wanting to coordinate colors. He polished off his clubhouse while the two women yakked away, and then he excused himself. He tried Gilbey again but got his voicemail.

As he emerged from the bar, he almost ran right into Sage. She was standing outside the entrance, as if she had been waiting for him to emerge. She had the strangest look on her face, watching him approach—kind of wide-eyed and twitchy. Harald stood beside her, looking a little skittish himself.

Andy was concerned. "Sage, are you okay?" He wondered if she was feeling ill.

"She told you, didn't she?" Sage whispered. "Verna told you about my old boyfriend."

Andy was taken aback. What was up with her? Was she becoming delusional?

"I swear, Logan didn't say a word to me about him. Nothing. Nada. Zip."

Sage's lips formed a tight, frozen straight line. "Then why is his name on that paper you dropped?"

Chapter Twenty-Eight

Sage glared at Andy. "Why is Ross Ueland's name on that piece of paper?"

"Ross Ueland?" Andy was flabbergasted. "Ross Ueland is your old boyfriend?"

"Until Verna wrapped her claws around him. So why do you have his name?"

Andy fished the paper out of his pocket and looked at it. "Thor gave me his last name," he explained, "and I wrote it down. I thought maybe he has something to do with the jeweled frog theft."

"Thor knows Ross?"

"No," he reassured her. "I mean, well, yes. Slightly. He knows him now. We both do."

Sage seemed baffled by his response.

Andy attempted to clarify. "I bumped into Ross a few times this weekend and we exchanged small talk. First time I ever met the guy. Same for Thor."

"He's here?" Sage's face turned white.

"Yeah, you've maybe even seen him around. Tall,

good-looking fellow with a trim, silver beard. Suppose he looks different from what you remember. Said he was on the way home from a hunting trip."

Sage shut her eyes tight. "Of all the hotels to pick, in all the world, he has to end up at this one."

Andy stifled a smile, remembering a similar line from *Casablanca*. "Well, maybe it's not entirely coincidental. He's evidently a fan of Logan's books."

And knowing now that Ross was the third corner of a love triangle with Sage and Logan, Andy figured his theory that the guy might have been a CIA agent or jewel thief was sounding pretty silly. That's what came of reading too many spy novels.

"Of course he'd be here for Verna and her dog-and-pony show," Sage said bitterly.

"I take it, then, that you're not interested in a reunion."

Sage looked away for a few seconds, then turned back to him, her anger showing. "What would you say to someone who betrayed you? Someone you loved who threw you to the curb? What would you say to a person like that, Andy?"

Andy thought about what he might say. *Let bygones be bygones. It's water over the dam. Forgive and forget.* But he knew that wasn't what Sage wanted to hear. By now, her decades-old resentment was deep down in her bones, a part of her.

"I don't know, Sage. I wish I could help." He reached down and gave Harald a pat on the head. The dog leaned into him as he did. "Would you like me to take Harald?"

She shook her head. "No, that's okay. I'll walk him back to Sonny's booth. Listen, Andy, I'm sorry to put you on the spot. You must think I'm a nutcase. I just didn't expect this weekend to turn into such a nightmare."

That pretty much sums up what I'm feeling, too, Andy thought as Sage and Harald walked away. He looked out the lobby windows and saw some empty spots where cars had been parked. At the far end of the biggest parking lot, he spied his blue Silverado, buried in snow.

On an impulse, he headed outside, coatless and hatless, and, huddled against the cold, made his way to it. Enough snow had been cleared that he could keep his boots reasonably dry. The sky was partly clear now, but the wind was still nasty. Andy could feel the chill beginning to bite. Funny how cold could almost burn.

He opened the driver's side door, causing a mini-avalanche of snow from the roof. He climbed inside, turned the key, and waited for the heat to kick in. It felt good to be back in his own wheelhouse. He grabbed his CD album from the pocket in the door and pulled out one of his special favorites—Earl Klugh on his nylon string guitar. Pretty soon, the warm, tropical sounds of "Midnight in San Juan" were washing over him.

As he looked out on the totally white landscape, Andy wondered yet again if he'd done the right thing, returning home. It had been sensible, his retreat from big-city failures. But it didn't always feel like his heart was in New Bergen. It was safe but unexciting. He ached for the rush of the big city—the energy, the music and art, the hubbub and variety. Sometimes he just felt that life was passing him by.

Not that he wasn't grateful to Kirsten for rescuing him when he was at his nadir. He could always count on his twin sister. And she had never asked for anything in return, other than a good day's work. He suddenly felt the urge to talk with her.

"Hey, little brother," she said, answering his call, "you still snowbound?"

"Yeah, *big sis*, I am."

It was a tired old gag, the big sister/little brother thing. In fact, she'd been born only twenty minutes before him.

"Any chance you could send me a dogsled?" he continued.

"I don't think you'll need one. They say the interstate should be open any time now. Except for some whiteouts north of New Bergen, in the open areas, it shouldn't be too bad. If you go slow and careful, you'll be okay."

"How are things down there?"

"We've had the restaurant open since eleven. It was kind of slow, but it's picking up now. We'll be all ready for the buses Aunt Bev's sending. Every store on Skjegstad Street is staying open till nine. It's gonna be gorgeous, with all the Christmas lights and the beautiful new snow."

At the moment, Andy didn't think that "beautiful" and "snow" belonged in the same phrase. But it thrilled him to know that the roads would be okay. Andy had driven a limo for years, and he knew how to handle a Town Car on ice and in snow. He understood that you had to respect the elements. They could ding you bad if you didn't.

"So," he said, "you think I can make it down to the Blitzers after all?"

"Looks like it. But hey, what's this I hear about that doctor you were with? Aunt Bev really likes her. Said she was *really* cute."

Andy groaned. Even a snowstorm couldn't shut down the Skyberg family grapevine. "Actually, she's a nurse practitioner. And she's *just* a friend. Not that I don't appreciate the help you and Aunt Bev generously give me with my love life."

Kirsten snorted. "Hey there, Romeo, you need all the help you can get."

After he hung up, Andy reached around and grabbed his suitcase. He had been wearing the same clothes since yesterday morning, and he didn't want to have them on for the Blitzers concert that evening. He needed to make a good first-time-in-a-long-time impression on Paula. He could change in Aunt Bev's timeshare and then try to connect with Gilbey one last time before hitting the road.

Andy realized he didn't have much to pass along to

the security guard. His suspicions about Ross had been just plain loopy. For that matter, none of the other people Andy had questioned seemed very strong suspects in the affair of the jeweled frog, either. Sage, the Dillards, and Justine Juveland all had been treated badly by Logan at one time or another, but Andy doubted that any of them would have retaliated by stealing her necklace. Sara Blake maybe had a beef about her contract with Logan, but she wouldn't lash out violently, criminally, would she? And the fact remained that this heist probably involved inside help. The key card to Grant Hamsden's room could have been hacked. But someone knew where the security cameras were located and how to disable them.

Butch Behr—with his old manslaughter conviction—had been the strongest suspect. Would he risk a good job and a happy family life in Beaver Tail County for the sake of a bauble probably worth no more than what he makes in a year? It just didn't make any sense.

Andy trotted back into the resort with his bag, shivering from the cold, and almost ran smack into Aunt Bev, who was making her way through the lobby.

"Hey there," he said, "how you holding up?"

"Got a bit of a crowd control problem," she said. "Logan's signing books in the Holiday Faire, at Copperfield's bookstore. And we weren't prepared for so many people. Logan's assistant was supposed to help out, but she took that dog Nikkie for a walk and hasn't come back yet. I sent Doris to pitch in, and she just texted me an SOS."

Andy peeked at his watch. If he hung around another hour, it wouldn't make much difference. He could still drop off Harald with Uncle Frank and make it down to the Cities in time for dinner and the concert.

"Private Skyberg reporting for duty," he said, giving his aunt a crisp salute.

Her face lit up. "Oh hon, thanks so much! I'd like you to man the ropes and stanchions. To make sure the ladies in line don't get too frisky. And you being a restaurant host, you know the drill. I've seen you charm the pants off malcontents a few times."

Andy had to admit he was pretty good with testy customers. "I'll leave my suitcase with the check-in clerks and head on over there. By the way, you haven't seen Gilbey lately, have you? I want to give him my final report, such as it is. I'm afraid there's not much to say."

"Don't know where he's at." Aunt Bev shook her head. "In my opinion, it's kind of a lost cause anyway. I very much doubt Logan Kennedy will ever see that necklace again."

"I kinda think you're right. Though there are folks here who have speculated she might have concocted this whole scheme herself, just for the publicity. Maybe the darn necklace is tucked away safe and secure in her suite."

"I hope that's not the case, but I wouldn't be surprised." Aunt Bev glanced around, as if making sure no one was eavesdropping. "Don't say you heard it from me, but evidently Logan was considered a bit of a wild one up in Herkimer. A real handful."

That was the second time Andy had heard "handful" in relation to Logan. First from Sage, now from Aunt Bev.

"Doris told me that Sharon Voxland—you graduated with one of the Voxland kids, didn't you? Diana, I think? Anyway, Sharon was friends with Logan's mother's cousin. That would be Babs Olson. And back when Logan was in her early twenties, she started gaining weight and disappeared for a few months. No one could get much out of her mother about it. Claimed the girl was off doing research somewhere for one of those books she was trying to write."

Andy processed that for a few seconds, then the light bulb went on. "Okay, are you saying what I think you're saying?"

His aunt nodded and formed a round belly with her hands.

"Verna had a secret baby." Andy would almost bet that that was the juicy little tidbit Justine had been teasing him with.

"At least, that's what the scuttlebutt was," Aunt Bev said. "But you better scoot off now and help with the signing. And sweetie, thanks so much for chipping in one last time."

When he arrived at the Copperfield's booth, Andy found a line of women—with a smattering of men—

snaking up the aisle and around the corner. Most of them were clutching Kat Taggett books—some of them several titles. Doris Schattenheimer, looking frazzled, positioned Andy at the head of the line. He was to send the fans in to Logan, one at a time.

Like a queen holding court, the author sat regally behind a table piled high with copies of her new book. A big banner in heavy headline type was attached to the table in front of her, proclaiming "**DART SHOT — This Time It's Kat with a Target on Her Back**." Hovering behind Logan were a couple of bookstore employees—one snapping pictures, the other making a video.

Andy could hardly believe he was looking at the same woman who only a few hours ago had been the very picture of despondency. With her hair fixed and her makeup applied, she positively radiated glamor. He could understand why all these people wanted a piece of Logan Kennedy.

As each fan came to the head of the line, Andy asked her to try not to take more than a couple of minutes of Logan's time. Most abided by the request, but one older lady with a widow's hump was talking with Logan a bit too long. He tiptoed over and leaned into the conversation the two of them were having. "Excuse me, ma'am, but we need to move it along here."

The author smiled up at Andy. A million-dollar smile. She could have been a movie star.

"It's okay, Anders. This is Mrs. Burrows, my eighth-grade English teacher. She introduced me to the Brontë sisters and Robert Louis Stevenson. She even tipped me to Ian Fleming. I probably wouldn't be sitting here right now if it weren't for Mrs. Burrows."

The little old lady beamed and proceeded to expound on how Verna—as she called Logan—had been one of her most talented students ever. And it had been clear from the beginning that, if she buckled down, Verna would go far.

A short time later, Grant Hamsden came up the aisle, limping along with a cane. With his sharp black suit he was incongruously wearing bright yellow jogging shoes—the right one untied and open, to accommodate his broken toes.

"Your friend Becky took another look at the toes," he told Andy, "and figured I could wait until this evening to get x-rays. The swelling's not that bad. Anyway, I don't want to miss Logan's big Kat Blast at five. She's going to put up a photo of my poison dart frog. It's better than nothing, I guess."

As Grant hobbled away toward his own booth, Andy happened to glance back in the direction of the double doors that led to the lobby. Through them came Sage Mortenson, marching purposefully in the direction of Logan Kennedy. She looked like a pot about to boil over.

Chapter Twenty-Nine

"Uh-oh," Andy groaned as Sage advanced. He darted over to block her, leaving the line unattended.

"Listen, Sage, you're not planning to do something you might regret, are you?"

"Oh, yes indeedy, I am, Andy," she answered firmly. "Please get out of my way. I need to tell these people the truth about Logan Kennedy."

"No ma'am, you do not! You'll be the one who ends up looking like a jackass. If you really need to vent, then do it in private with her. Cuss her out, throw something at her, call her the all-time rotten beeyotch in human history. Just not here, not now."

Sage blinked up at Andy with a puzzled look. "Beeyotch?"

"That's not important. You just really, *really* don't want to do this. Trust me, I'm right."

"Oh, but I *do* want to do it, Andy. I really, *really* do. I've been waiting for this day for thirty years."

Andy was feeling desperate. He had to stop her

somehow, but he couldn't physically restrain her. What would it take? Well, he could try relying on what they called "Beaver Tail County nice"—people's tendency in those parts to pitch in when you happened to be in a tight spot.

"Please, Sage, I'm begging you. If you throw this hand grenade, I'm gonna get the blame for it. And my Aunt Bev could catch the shrapnel."

She looked baffled. "Why would either of you get in trouble?"

"The manager here's a real jerk, and he's already gunning for Aunt Bev. If there's an ugly incident, he'll make it grounds for sacking her. You don't want to get someone fired, do you?"

Already there were signs of conflict on Sage's face—the little red devil on her shoulder duking it out with the good little angel. She ruminated for a bit, looking as if she was about to surrender. But then her face hardened again.

"Sorry, Andy, I just have to do this."

Andy felt like he was clinging by his fingernails. He needed a *deus ex machina*, an intervention by the gods. And then, out of nowhere, he got one. For there, toward the back of the autograph line, stood Ross Ueland. Andy caught the man's attention and waved him over.

"I hate to do this, Sage, but someone's here who I think you ought to talk to. Turn around."

She swiveled and gasped, looking Ross right in the face.

"Ross," Andy said, "I think you know Sage Mortenson. Now I have to go. Got some fans to wrangle."

Leaving the two of them stupefied and staring at each other, Andy returned to his post. The autograph seekers had managed to police themselves admirably in his absence. Instead of growing shorter, though, the line seemed to be getting longer. Logan looked a little fatigued but still had on her game face.

"Andy, Andy!"

It was Gilbey, pushing past the line of fans. The string-bean security guy lurched to a halt in front of Andy.

"Got some terrible news," he panted. "Logan Kennedy's dog has been snatched."

Andy pulled him across the aisle and down, out of earshot of Logan's fans. "Okay, Gilbey, calm down and tell me what happened."

"Sara Blake was walking the dog over in the timeshare wing. Someone pulled her into a housekeeping closet, tied her up, and took the hound. Sara couldn't get the door open—she had to pound it with her feet until one of the staff heard her."

"Is she all right?"

"She's super upset, of course, but she doesn't seem hurt. Tim is with her. He called the police again, and they said they'd be here real soon. Better late than never, I guess. Tim said there was no reason to upset Logan with the news just yet. With any luck, we can get the pooch back before she even knows it's been dognapped."

"Is there anything you want me to do?"

"Yeah, Tim asked if you'd bring King Harald over. Maybe he could sniff out her trail."

"He's not a bloodhound, you know," Andy said. But Harald's nose was pretty sharp, so it couldn't hurt to have him on the case. Andy looked back at the autograph line, still perfectly behaved. If anything came up, Doris could handle it. "Come on," he said to Gilbey.

The two of them rushed over to the Hofdahl booth, where they retrieved Harald. Thor was busy with customers and just gave Andy a wave.

As they headed out of the Holiday Faire, Andy noticed Ross and Sage at one of the tables in the Coffee Hut booth. They were sitting silently, the very picture of sadness and regret. Andy couldn't tell what had passed between them, but the little scene gave him hope that they might reach some sort of understanding.

The two men hustled over to the timeshare wing. Gilbey pointed out the housekeeping closet where Sara had been found. A bit farther down the hallway he knocked on one of the doors. It was opened by Tim Fisher, whose greeting was an exasperated scowl. A miserable-looking Sara Blake was sitting on the corner of the bed, while one of the housekeeping staff tried to comfort her. Harald went over to Sara and laid his snout on her knee. A tiny smile came across her face as she petted his bristly head.

"Logan is going to kill me," she said, looking up at

Andy. "She didn't even want me to take Nikkie out so close to the book signing. But I figured I had enough time. Now I've gone and totally screwed everything up."

"As if this ghastly weekend couldn't get any worse," Tim fumed, showing not an ounce of sympathy for the distraught PA. "And it doesn't help that Logan tweeted about the theft to the whole world." He shot yet another peevish look at Andy and Gilbey. "I had hoped for better results from you two."

Andy was glad he would never have to work for Tim again, but he felt sorry for Gilbey. It was pretty unreasonable to think that a guy who occasionally broke up a bar fight would be able to make sense of a complicated crime so darn quickly. But the resort manager was just doing what he seemed to do best—being a jerk.

Andy pointedly refused to dignify Tim's comment with a response. He looked down at Sara. "Didn't Nikkie put up a fuss when she was taken?"

"Nikkie's really quite shy, quite timid," Sara explained. "As long as the dognapper didn't hurt her, she probably wouldn't have tried to break away."

"I know you're upset, but could you tell me what happened?"

Sara gave a slight nod. "I'd taken Nikkie out to the lobby and let her outside, for just a minute. Then we headed for the corridor that leads to this timeshare wing. We were walking out there, and I heard someone coming up behind me. I didn't even have a chance to turn around, when I felt something jammed in my back. He said, 'I have a gun, and I want the dog.' I heard him click something. The hammer, the safety, I don't know. I was so scared I couldn't even think straight." She shivered and crossed her arms tightly.

"Let me get you a nice warm washcloth," the housekeeper said. "To hold around your neck. Always works for me when I'm stressed out."

Sara smiled back up at the woman. "Would you? That'd be great."

"If you don't mind my asking," Gilbey said, "how did the perp get you into that closet?"

Sara blinked up at him. "I don't know. He made me give him my phone and took the battery. Then he opened the door, pushed me in, and tied me up. I never even saw his face."

Gilbey looked dubious. "But he would've needed a key. And only housekeeping staff have those, right Tim?"

Tim nodded. "Them and a few managers."

"Well then, he must have been someone on staff."

A subterranean moan issued from Tim.

"It's possible the key card was stolen," Andy suggested. "Maybe it wasn't an insider."

"Thanks for that sliver of hope," Tim muttered.

Andy couldn't tell if he was being sarcastic or not. It was hard to know with this guy.

"And how did the attacker tie you up, Ms. Blake?" Gilbey asked.

She offered up a despairing look. "Sorry, I'm not

sure. It's just all kind of a blur."

"He used cable ties," Tim said. "The housekeeper cut them off."

"Nobody else was around out in the corridor?" Gilbey asked.

Sara glared at him. "I wasn't in any position to notice."

"Did you recognize the man's voice?" Andy asked. "Can you describe it?"

Sara shook her head. "No, nothing familiar about it. He just sounded mean."

The housekeeper returned with a dampened washcloth. "Lift up your hair, honey," she said. "This'll relax you some."

Sara held up her disheveled dark hair and applied the cloth. As she did, something on her neck caught Andy's eye. There were three or four little bird silhouettes ascending, circling around a distinctive birthmark. He had seen it before. That very same tattoo. And not long ago.

"Sara, you *do* know Damian Powers, don't you?" he asked.

She looked up at him with big, dark eyes—now a little red. "I don't know what you're saying. I saw him yesterday at the Tabby Dark reception and I exchanged a few words with him in the café this morning."

"If you met him yesterday," Andy said evenly, "how is it you have those lark tattoos on your neck that are in his slideshow? I know it's your picture because I remember seeing your birthmark."

Sara looked as though he had slapped her.

But before she could say a word, Tim's phone came to life, its ringtone harsh and loud. He tapped the screen and put it up to his ear.

His eyes widened. "What the heck happened?" Pause. "He said what?" Another pause. "Oh, isn't that just great?" he fumed. "I'll be there ASAP. And don't let him move."

He hung up and groaned. "They never told us in the MBA program that there'd be days like this."

"What do you mean?" Andy asked.

"Somebody just found Butch Behr in one of the storage rooms by the loading docks. He was sitting on the floor, confused and woozy. All he could say was that Damian Powers had sucker-punched him."

At that bit of shocking news, Sara Blake burst into tears.

Chapter Thirty

Andy didn't know which way to look. To Tim, for further word about Butch. Or to Sara, whose waterworks were dripping prodigiously.

"Why the hell is she crying?" Tim asked with a scowl, putting his phone away. "Is she friends with Butch, or what?"

Andy shook his head. "No, but she's friends with Damian Powers. Probably a lot more than friends."

Sara sobbed even louder.

"The tattoo guy?" Tim sputtered. "She's hooked up with the tattoo guy? And what in hell does he have against Butch?"

"I don't have all the answers," Andy said. "But I have a hunch that Damian and Sara cooked up this scheme together. It was right in front of me. I just didn't put the pieces together until now. You see, I had asked Damian if he knew what the tattoo of a clock without hands symbolized. He said it could mean different things but didn't give any examples. But my friend Becky told me she had seen it on prisoners and ex-cons, and it meant that you served a long sentence. Now I realize Damian must have suspected I knew about Butch's tattoo, and he wanted to steer us away from that line of inquiry."

Tim looked even more confused than before.

"Because," Andy continued, "if Butch broke down and confessed, he'd probably rat out his accomplices. Am I in the ballpark, Sara?" He shot the young woman a reproving glare.

With a single wobbly nod, she took the damp washcloth from her neck and wiped her face with it. She handed it back to the housekeeper, who looked astonished to have stumbled into what seemed like a scene from a bad soap opera.

"I can't do this anymore," Sara sniffled. "I just can't. Things got out of hand. But no one meant to hurt Grant Hamsden. Damian just wanted to get Logan's attention. He planned to use the necklace for leverage, so she'd talk to him. He would have given it back, but then it got *stolen*."

"Let me get this straight," Andy said. "Damian stole it from Grant. And then someone else took it from Damian?"

Sara gave a hollow laugh. "Talk about rotten luck. And after Logan tweeted out the original theft, she ended up with ten times the publicity she would have gotten if the bloody thing hadn't been stolen to begin with. Damian went ballistic. He decided the only thing that would hurt her was taking Nikkie."

"Hold on," Tim snapped. "Why did this guy want to get at Logan Kennedy in the first place? Why the hell should a tattoo artist care about some woman who writes spy stories?"

Sara looked down at the floor and wiped her eyes with her sleeve.

Andy understood everything now. It was as though he were painting, and some new brushwork or color mixing came out of nowhere, transforming the canvas. All the pieces suddenly fit. Sara's odd, exaggerated "coolness" toward the tattoo artist. Aunt Bev's account of a young Verna's mysterious absence. Logan's "ghosts" from the past.

"Let me take a guess, Tim," he finally said, after an uncomfortable silence. "Damian thinks he's Logan's son."

Gilbey whistled and Tim's jaw dropped. The housekeeper muttered, "Oh my goodness."

"No," Sara said.

Her answer caught Andy off-guard. He was absolutely certain he was right.

"He doesn't *think* he's Logan's son," she explained. "*He knows for sure*."

Andy raised his eyebrows. "And how does he know for sure?"

"I sent him some of her DNA. From a Starbuck's cup. He tried again and again to connect with her, but she refused to meet him. Refused to talk with him. Last night at the reception was the first time she had even seen him face to face. And she brushed him off."

"She knew his name, then."

"Of course."

"So, this whole episode with you in the housekeeping closet was all a setup?" Tim asked.

"Uh-huh." Sara looked as though the tears might start up again. "But I love him. I couldn't say no."

"And you two coerced Butch into helping you."

Sara nodded. "Damian threatened to reveal his prison record if he didn't cooperate. But Butch was getting very cold feet. Damian told me it got a little physical, but I didn't realize he'd hurt Butch."

"What a bunch of morons," Tim said, shaking his head with disgust. "You know I'll have to turn you over to the sheriff when he gets here."

Sara didn't even look up at him, didn't even move.

"I'd like to avoid calling an ambulance." The resort manager's brow furrowed. "The news crews showing up for the Kat Blast might catch on." Then his face brightened. "Maybe we can take care of Butch here. Andy, can I have your girlfriend's number? The nurse practitioner?"

Andy read out Becky number, then muttered, "She's not my girlfriend."

He turned back to Sara. "Where do you think Damian took the dog?"

She kept looking down, her eyes shut, as if she were trying to make all of this go away.

"Sara, you don't want anything to happen to Nikkie, do you? You gotta tell me where you think Damian has her."

She peered up at him, her eyes damp and red. "Probably in his suite. I told him he was crazy to do this, and I tried to talk him out of it. If he hurts her, I'll never forgive myself."

After a quick call to the front desk for Damian's room number, Andy and Gilbey took off at a jog. They got to Damian's suite as quickly as they could.

"Now or never," Andy muttered as they stood in front of the door. He knocked. If anyone was in there, he knew they could see him through the little peephole. The two of them stood there for half a minute but no answer came. Andy tried again, with the same result.

"I have an idea, Gilbey," he said.

"That's good," the security guy said, "Because I don't want to burst in on a crazy man. Sure hope he doesn't have a gun."

Andy knelt down and took Harald's snout in his hand. "I know I've told you not to bark inside buildings, big guy, but now I need you to." To encourage him, Andy let out a few low-volume *woofs* of his own.

Harald looked interested, but didn't reply.

Andy tried again. *Woof. Woof.*

This time Harald got into the spirit of things, his tone low, loud, and impressive. *WOOF! WOOF!*

From behind the door, somewhat muted, came: *Woof! Woof! Woof!*

In answer, Harald started barking again, even louder.

"Damian," Andy shouted, pounding on the door with the heel of his fist, "I know you're in there."

A few more barks came from inside but no human voice.

"C'mon, Damian, it's over. You can't get away."

Now Harald and Nikkie were practically singing a duet. Two baritones riffing. A couple of doors had opened down the hallway. Angry guests were glaring out at the lunatic and his hound. "Will you keep it down!" one of them shouted.

Andy shushed Harald and turned to Gilbey. "Do you have a master keycard for this door?"

"Yeah. But, you know, *gun*? Even a knife'd be trouble. Neither of us is armed. All I got is this flashlight."

Andy thought hard about waiting for the cops. "I know. But we need to open that door and see what's going on. What if he tries to escape?"

Gilbey looked torn. "There's a patio with each of these units, with sliding doors. Thing is, he'd be absolutely bonkers to go out there right now. That wind's whipped up pretty good again, and visibility on the ground is crappy. And we got some serious wind chill going on, too."

"You want 'bonkers,' my friend? I think what he's done the last twenty-four hours is positively fruitcake material."

This wasn't the first time Andy had pursued a bad guy. And even though it was dangerous, he found it oddly exhilarating. He just hoped that Damian could be reasoned with before he went totally off the deep end.

"Open it up, Gilbey," he said. "Let's see what's inside."

"You asked for it." In his left hand Gilbey wielded his Maglite flashlight like a cop's baton. With his right, he inserted the master key card, turned the handle, and pushed the door open.

Andy and Harald went in first. "Damian, you here? Nikkie?"

There was no answer. Andy stepped past the bathroom and bedroom areas into the living room. The joint was empty, but the sliding doors were open about a foot and a half. It was a ground blizzard outside—lots of blowing and drifting. Looking out, Andy saw two sets of footprints trailing into the deep snow—a man's and a dog's. He squinted out but couldn't see anyone. There was nothing but blinding white.

"The idiot's taken that dog out there! He's trying to run! I gotta go after them."

"Now just a danged minute, Andy." Gilbey looked appalled. "Even if you had your winter gear on, it's nasty out there. Let's get on the horn with Tim and the cops and report it in. Nothing more we can do."

Andy almost didn't care what happened to that fool Damian. But Nikkie was another matter. The dog didn't deserve to get hurt or die. If it were Harald out there with that maniac, Andy liked to think someone would try to rescue him. But Gilbey had a point. Andy's coat, cap, and gloves were back in Aunt Bev's cubicle, and it would take too long to get them.

"Maybe there's something here I can throw on," he said, dropping Harald's leash. The dog sat down on his haunches and stared outside.

"Still think it's a dumb idea," Gilbey said. "Nobody's payin' you to be a hero, pal."

"True. But that dog needs help." Andy opened the closet door, hoping for a nice down parka. No such luck, but Damian had brought a heavy, red cotton hoodie that had, by a stroke of luck, a pair of fleece gloves jammed into the pockets. Andy grabbed the hoody off the hanger and tugged it on. A little snug, but it would have to do. He pulled on the gloves and put up the hood.

"I'll phone in when I find them," he told Gilbey. "Let everyone know what's going on."

"Aw, gee, Andy, you really don't have to..."

But Andy and Harald were already out through the sliding doors.

"Who's the fruitcake now?" Gilbey hollered after them.

Andy and Harald trudged ahead, tracking the footprints through snow that reached almost up to the knees. The visibility was only thirty or forty feet, with occasional flashes of blue up above. The hoody and gloves helped, but the wind still cut through them like a knife, and the blowing snow crystals pelted Andy's face. Fruitcake indeed, he thought. If he got out of this without frostbite, he'd be amazed.

They slogged along for a couple of minutes. Andy was able to orient himself during brief breaks in the gusting, biting snow. They were heading northwest from the main lodge, following Damian and Nikkie's tracks. Why Damian was going northwest, toward the farthest fair-way, was a mystery. What was out there that was worth getting to? Wouldn't the guy have gone to his car in-stead? Made a run for it?

All of a sudden, Andy realized that his left boot was feeling loose, and snow was getting inside. He squatted down and began to retie the lace. It being a two-handed job, he had to drop Harald's leash.

"Now sit, Harald. Stay. Really. I mean it."

The big ginger mutt didn't sit, as usual. He gave Andy a look of pure canine joy that could only mean: *You sure do know how to show a fellow a good time!*

From somewhere in the distance, through the veil of blowing snow, a dog's throaty *WOOF* echoed across the resort grounds.

Harald's ears perked up. He barked one lusty bark in reply and surged off in that direction, trailing his leash behind.

"Harald!" Andy shouted, jumping to his feet, trying to grab the leash. "*Dammit! Come back here!*"

Chapter Thirty-One

Harald made for the barking dog, oblivious to the boss's hollering. It didn't sound like the dog wanted to play. She seemed upset or scared or hurt. Maybe Harald could help her.

But the snow was deep, nearly up to his chest, and the harder he plowed through it the more winded he became. He paused a couple of times to catch his breath. He was still dragging his leash, but at least it followed freely over the snow.

Harald heard barking from off to his left, closer now than it had been before. It was higher pitched and more insistent, the sound of a dog in trouble.

It took him a few more minutes to get to her. She was shivering under a big tree. The snow had drifted in around it and the wind came cutting through. No shelter here.

He went up to her and they touched noses. Her tail flicked lightly and she whimpered a little, as if to greet Harald. He sniffed her up and down. Then something else grabbed him by the nose.

There was another dog odor in this place. On the tree trunk. Harald recognized who it belonged to.

Himself.

He had been here just last night, when he was out playing in the snow. And there had been something he had done here. What was it? Then it popped into his head, as his memories often did, out of nowhere.

He had found a treasure buried outside, not far from where he and the boss were staying. It was in a dark-colored bag and it was hard and cold. He had grabbed it, run around in the snow for a little while, found this spot, and tried to bury it here. But the ground was too solid. So he just laid it next to the tree trunk and went back to the boss, who seemed upset for some reason.

Harald began rooting around the trunk, which was wide and rough. And a moment later—digging furiously through the snow, kicking it away with his front paws—he found the bag with the object inside. He picked it up with his teeth and turned around to his new friend.

She didn't seem interested, though. She was still shivering and looked sad. He felt sorry for her, but he was getting tired of the snow and cold. And the notion of being in a warm place with the boss and some food came up to the forefront of his thinking.

He began to walk away from the tree, trudging laboriously through the snow, step by step, lifting each foot as he went. He turned around to look and she was still standing there, rooted to the spot. He tried to bark at her through the bunched-up plastic in his mouth.

Moof. Moof.

She took his hint and began to slowly step through the snow after him.

Chapter Thirty-Two

Andy watched Harald vanish into the gusting snow. "Ungrateful hound!" he bellowed.

Cussing under his breath, he knew he had to make a choice. Chase Harald, who was no doubt heading toward the barking Nikkie. Or follow Damian's tracks. In his heart, he wanted to go after Harald. But Andy knew his big old mutt always found his way back. Harald would be okay. And so would Nikkie, if she followed him. No, best to pursue the tattoo artist. If anyone needed rescuing, it would be Damian Powers.

Andy's face already hurt plenty from the stinging snow crystals and wind. If he stayed out here too long—well, Gilbey was right. This was a dangerous place to be, underdressed as he was.

"Ten more minutes," he muttered, catching a quick glance at his watch. "Then I head back. I'm not frickin' Superman."

Arm held up to protect his face, he trudged ahead, following a track that was more trough than footprints.

From the jumble of impressions in the snow, it looked like Nikkie had broken loose and loped off in the direction that Harald had gone. Damian, for his part, had given up on his canine hostage and forged ahead.

Andy plodded after him across another fairway and through a wooded area, right over one of the resort's cross-country ski trails. Where the man thought he was going, Andy had no idea. It made no sense.

And neither did Damian's mini-crime wave. Sure, the guy was PO'd at his biological mother, who apparently wanted no part of him. But why risk ruining your whole life? Sometimes you just had to accept rejection and move on.

At the far side of the next fairway, the wind suddenly died down and Andy spotted Damian. He was just as underdressed as his pursuer. Andy came up within shouting distance. He didn't want to spook the guy, who seemed agitated as hell, but he had to try to reason with him.

"Where do you think you're going?" he yelled.

Damian turned around, regarding Andy with an angry, frustrated look. "I was heading for that remote lot. My truck's there."

"You're like a mile away, pal."

"I got totally turned around in that whiteout, and then the damned dog got away from me."

"You know, Damian, we can't afford to stay out here much longer. Ever heard of hypothermia?" Andy was shouting, to be heard above the wind.

"You stole my hoodie."

"Yeah, and you took Logan's dog and that stupid necklace."

"Bitch deserved it," Damian snarled. He began to plow forward again.

"Dammit, Damian!" Andy exclaimed. "I got tickets for the Blitzers tonight, and you're gonna mess it up for me."

Damian swiveled and laughed. "Hey, man, I didn't ask you to follow me."

Andy slowly advanced toward the jewel thief, not sure what he was going to do. "That's Caribou Creek in front of you." He could see the stream's undulating course beneath the snow. "You shouldn't try to cross it. The ice might not support you. And even if you get over, where the hell are you going? You're not dressed for this weather. You're gonna die."

"Thanks, but I think I'll take my chances." Damian continued right onto the ice. He made it out about six feet when an ominous cracking sound pierced the snowy air.

He stopped and looked back at Andy. Just as he did, the frozen surface shattered and he plunged through shards of ice, up to his chest. He spat out an ugly profanity. But instead of reversing course, he tried to break through the ice in front of him.

"Damian, you gotta come back," Andy pleaded. "I'll haul you out. We have to get you to the lodge, like pronto!"

Damian kept attacking the ice with his bare hands but was making no progress. Easing down the bank, Andy tried to get close enough to grab the guy if he came within reach.

"Whatever you wanted," Andy panted, "whatever point you're trying to make, it's not worth dying for. Soaked like that, you got twenty minutes max before hypothermia kills you. We can get back in time. Give me your hand."

Andy reached out toward his waterlogged quarry.

Damian finally seemed to have run out of steam. He was frozen in the spot, moving neither forward nor back.

Andy realized that if he didn't do something quickly, Damian would die. But to fish him out of there meant risking his own neck, as well.

From behind him he heard the sound of a truck engine getting louder and louder. How the hell could a truck get anywhere in this mess? He squinted and spied a glimpse of bright orange in the distance. It was a Sno Cat, chugging along on its tracks, making a beeline for them.

Now that he knew the cavalry was getting close, Andy took a deep breath and plunged into the icy creek. The frigid water hit him like a jolt of electricity and almost made his entire body spasm.

"*Oh crap oh crap oh crap!*" he swore.

Pushing aside broken ice, he surged toward Damian, who was quaking like a leaf. Andy grabbed his arm and began hauling him toward the bank. When they got there, both men collapsed onto the snow, out of breath and out of fight.

A moment later, the Sno Cat lurched to a halt about ten feet away. Gilbey leapt from the driver's seat, and Deputy Sheriff Barb Jorgensen shot out of the passenger side like a cannonball, carrying two heavy blankets.

Shivering violently, Andy looked at Damian. "G-g-good news. W-w-we're not gonna d-d-die after all."

Chapter Thirty-Three

Andy was still feeling like a giant Popsicle as he walked down the corridor toward Tim Fisher's office. But at least he was in dry clothes again, from his overnight bag, and he finally had been able to shave. Aunt Bev had found him a pair of cross-country ski boots from the pro shop. They were rentals, kind of beat up, but they'd have to do until his own boots dried out.

Best of all, word had just come down that Doris Schattenheimer had found Harald and Nikkie standing outside the patio doors of Aunt Bev's timeshare unit. Andy felt like a huge load had lifted off his shoulders, knowing his pooch was okay. He phoned Gilbey—out hunting for the dogs in the Sno Cat—with word he could come back in.

As Andy came into Tim's office, all eyes shifted to him. The joint was packed. Tim was hunkered down behind his desk, looking as if he'd just had a root canal. Sheriff Delmar Mandsager perched on the front corner of the dark wood desk, his arms crossed, his bulldog face inscrutable—a sort of Buddha of law enforcement. His cowboy-style cop hat was tilted a bit jauntily to the right.

Sara Blake and Damian Powers occupied the two guest chairs. They both looked disheveled and exhausted. Damian had changed into dry clothes, as well—a resort uniform that looked about one size too big. Behind the two perps stood Barb Jorgenson, an acquaintance of Andy's and a regular at Ansel's.

"Mayor Skyberg, we meet again," the sheriff said with a nod.

"So, how are things in the outside world?" Andy asked. "You guys must've had your hands full."

"We've all been up thirty-six hours," Mandsager replied. "We're running on fumes right now. I've seen worse snowfalls, but this one caught us off-guard pretty bad. Glad things are getting back to normal."

"So the roads are passable?"

"Except for some country roads, we're looking fine," Barb put in.

As much as he wanted to escape Hobartville, Barb's confirmation that he was good to go felt oddly anticlimactic. Andy doubted that anything he would experience down in the Cities—the Blitzers, his reunion with Paula—could top the adrenaline-pumping escapade he and Harald had just played their parts in.

"We're waiting on Ms. Kennedy, who wanted to be here," the sheriff explained. "Normally, I wouldn't host a little conflab like this. But since the young lady there," he said, nodding at Sara, "has been quite forthcoming about what went down, I figure we can make an exception."

"How's Butch Behr?" Andy asked.

"One of our deputies drove him over to St. Luke's. He said he was okay, but we just want to make sure he didn't get a concussion or anything." The sheriff cast a reproving glance in Damian's direction. "They'll check him out. Then he goes down to headquarters to get booked."

Without warning, Logan swept into the office. She had donned her protective armor—her all-black leather Kat outfit. She looked in a grim temper. The charming, effervescent book-signer was nowhere to be seen.

Mandsager gestured to an empty chair next to Tim's desk. After Logan sat, he provided her with the basic facts.

"Ms. Blake," he concluded, "has been fairly cooperative. She's waived her Miranda rights. I believe she knows how wrong-headed she's been, and she regrets it. Mr. Powers, on the other hand, has requested an attorney. But he asked to be here, Ms. Kennedy, so he could see you. I think you have an idea why."

The room went silent. Everyone seemed to be holding their breath, even the sheriff.

"Mr. Powers thinks he's my son," Logan said with no apparent emotion.

"Doesn't 'think,' Logan," retorted Sara. "Knows."

The long burn of the glare that Logan gave Sara could have cut steel. "You little snake. After all I've done for you, all the connections I've provided, everything I've taught you—you betrayed me."

Sara leaned toward her. "For God's sake, Logan, he's your son! What's wrong with acting like a decent human being for once? No one's asking you to bounce him on your knee. Just talk to him."

Damian looked like he was enduring physical torture. Andy couldn't imagine how dreadful his birth mother's rejection must feel. The guy had to be having the worst day of his life.

"When Damian came to New York and tried to see you that first time," Sara said to Logan, "you had security throw him out. *Unbelievable*. I couldn't help myself. I had to know what his story was. And when I found out, I knew I had to help him."

"And just like in the fairy tales," Logan sneered, "you fell in love."

"*You* wouldn't know love if it came up and bit you in the ass," Sara shot back. "Damian was just trying to get through to you. But you're like a damned brick wall. Even when you were face to face with him at the Tabby Dark reception, even when he told you who he was, you didn't have the decency to acknowledge him."

"He was trying to embarrass me in public," Logan responded.

Sara threw up her hands. "He only wanted a conversation, not a confrontation. If only you had taken the time to know him like I did…" She looked over at Damian and smiled. "At first I thought he was a nutcase.

But I started to read the notes he was sending you and I decided to respond. We had a back-and-forth e-mail conversation and then we met. In Chicago, then New Orleans, and back in New York." She fixed her gaze on Logan again. "I don't know what happens now. But I do know that your son is a good man and a talented artist who you could've been proud of. And you've missed out on something wonderful by slamming the door on him."

A chiming sound came from inside Logan's purse. She plucked out her phone, glanced at the screen, and looked up with a suddenly incongruous smile.

"A text from Georgia, my PR woman," she said, almost giddily. "She says we're on the front page of the Sunday *Times*. That's got to be good for ten thousand more hardcover sales. Isn't that wonderful?"

Damian's face went blank. Sara shut her eyes and shook her head. Andy, for his part, saw a narcissist in full bloom. *Lady*, he wanted to say, *you are so clueless*.

"Yes, good for you, Ms. Kennedy," Mandsager said in an even monotone, clearly unimpressed. His eyes focused on Damian. "Now how did you track this lady down in the first place?"

Damian shook his head wearily. "I have nothing to say until I talk to my lawyer."

Sara reached over and squeezed his arm, but he wouldn't look at her. "I can tell you," she said. "He went to the agency that placed him as a newborn. He tried to get the information, but his birthmother, they told him, had asked for no future contact. They had to honor that.

So, somehow, he got someone inside to look in the files. The name that came back was Laverna Klingelhoets. He Googled it and..." She nodded toward the author.

"The theft of the jeweled dart frog was revenge?" Mandsager asked.

Sara shook her head. "More like leverage. He thought he could use it to force her to sit down with him. He was going to give it back, once she talked to him. He recruited Butch to help set the whole thing up."

"Recruited him?" Andy glared at Damian. "Blackmailed him, more like it. You knew that Butch was an ex-con. He must have visited your shop. And you saw the prison tattoo he had on his backside. A clock without hands."

Damian remained silent, staring down at the beige carpeting, in maximum sulk.

"Butch had wanted it removed," Sara explained. "And he came to Damian's shop in Hobartville. After I told Damian about Logan appearing here and the jeweled frog, he remembered Butch. He checked into his background and dug up a conviction back in Nevada. He was driving under the influence and killed a guy on a bicycle. Because he had other DUIs, they threw the book at him. But he got out early for good behavior."

Tim Fisher came to life. "I want to make it clear that Butch was hired by the resort way before I came on board. Back then, they didn't do security checks for part-time employees. I can assure you, though, that his career here is over."

"So, in addition to messing up *your* lives," Andy said with disgust, "you two ruined another guy's. Was Butch the one who put the sleeper hold on Grant Hamsden?"

Sara groaned. "It wasn't supposed to go down that way. You see, Logan asked Grant to reset the safe's combination to 5-1-8-8-1-3."

"Why that number?" the sheriff asked.

"Those figures on the keypad represented something Logan could remember onstage, when she needed to open the safe. All she had to do was tap out K-A-T-T-A-G, for Kat Taggett."

"I'm terrible with numbers," Logan sniffed.

"I gave Butch the combination so he could get the frog from Grant's safe," Sara continued. "Unfortunately, it wasn't in there. Even worse, Grant came back to his room early. Butch hid in the closet. He decided he had to deal with Grant. That's when he found the necklace, which he gave to Damian."

The sheriff gave Damian a cold stare. "So where do you have it stashed?"

"Well, that's the ironic part." Sara glanced at Damian, who let out a quiet groan. "He hid it outside near his patio, and someone else grabbed it."

"Oh, isn't that just perfect?" Logan huffed. "Talk about the gang that couldn't shoot straight."

"If you guys didn't have bad luck," Andy said with a shake of the head, "you wouldn't have any luck at all." All this while he noticed that Logan was purposely avoiding looking at Damian, instead saving her little eye daggers for Sara.

What would it be like, Andy wondered, to be confronted by a kid he had given up? No way could he do what Logan was doing. It was so harsh. But people at the top of the pyramid, the one-percenters, lived on a different planet. He had driven some of them back in his chauffeuring days—CEOs, billionaires, big celebrities—and he knew from being with them for just a few hours how very not-nice some of them could be. Acting like jerks was in their DNA.

Andy scratched the top of his head. "So why did Butch and Damian get in a dustup?"

"Ask Damian," Sara answered, making a nod toward her lover. "All I know is that Butch was getting very cold feet. Damian went to have a talk with him."

The sheriff stood up from his perch on the desk and crossed his arms. "And why abduct Ms. Kennedy's dog?"

"The frog theft turned out to be a PR bonanza for Logan," Sara answered. "It was even better for her than having the frog in hand. She's getting a million dollars in free publicity. By this point Damian just wanted to hurt her. He said, 'Let's go after something that matters to her. She cares about that damn mutt more than her own son.'"

Logan's hard-boiled façade showed a tiny fracture. A glimmer of regret? Just briefly. Then it disappeared. She wasn't going to give Damian and Sara any satisfaction.

"I shouldn't have agreed to bring Nikkie to him, but I

did." Sara gave Logan a regretful look. "It was stupid, and for that I'm sorry."

Ignoring the apology, Logan stood. "If you'll excuse me, I have a book launch to attend to." She took a few steps and then turned to Damian. For the first time, she looked him in the eye.

"If you are who you claim to be..." Her voice was icy. "And let me tell you, your so-called DNA test doesn't convince me. But if you are who you say you are, I would tell you this. I gave you nine months of my life, and I'm afraid that's all you get. I never wanted to be your mother, or anyone else's. Okay? I understand that you crave a connection, but I have nothing to give you. Your adoptive parents should have provided all the love you needed."

There was a long, grim silence before she spoke up again.

"For what it's worth," she said evenly, "I would prefer that these two and Mr. Behr are not charged with anything. I'll certainly encourage Grant to not press charges."

"That's as may be, Ms. Logan," the sheriff said. "But Mr. Fisher and his employers will have something to say about it, as well."

The author shrugged. "Well, I do hope you can contain the personal details of this matter. I'd rather the press weren't rooting around in my private history."

Sara gave a bitter laugh. "Logan, you're too smart to think this will stay a secret. It's all going to go public. It wouldn't surprise me if Justine's caught wind of it already."

Logan blinked and crossed her arms defensively.

"And what happens, Logan, when all those mothers who read your books... Hundreds of thousands of them. What happens when they find out?"

Andy glanced at Damian as Sara spoke and was certain he saw the glint of tears in his eyes. But the man stared straight ahead, looking at no one. Despite what the three conspirators had done, Andy hoped their lives wouldn't be entirely trashed. If he were the county attorney, he would go light on them. He felt especially bad about Butch. Having been a hardworking family man for so many years, the poor guy deserved some kind of break.

"What will they think of a woman," Sara continued quietly, "who treats her own child like dirt?"

Andy saw a flash of doubt on Logan's face, a flash of fear. Sara had found a chink in her armor. But that lasted just a few seconds, before Logan rallied, a slight smile popping up.

"Georgia will know how to spin it."

Sara looked as though she wanted to strangle her former boss. "I think even Georgia is going to have a hard time figuring out what to—"

She was cut off by a distinctive, deep *WOOF* that echoed into the office. Andy twirled around just as Harald came clomping in, towing Aunt Bev. Doris followed along with Nikkie. An air of *eau de wet dog* suddenly wafted into the room.

"Oh, Nikkie, darling!" Logan gushed. "Come here, baby girl." She squatted down to hug the dog. "I was *so* worried about you."

Damian looked like he had been kicked in the gut. Sara put her hands over her face.

Harald trotted over to Andy and leaned against him, dampening his nice dry pants. That's when Andy noticed the plastic bag in Harald's mouth. "Whatcha got there, boy?"

"I tried to take it," Aunt Bev said, "but he wouldn't let me. He even growled a little."

"C'mon, bud," Andy said. "Hand it over."

Harald hesitated for a few seconds, then gently set the bag down on the carpeting. Andy picked it up—dog drool and all—and peered inside.

"Well I'll be a…"

Reaching into it, he slowly pulled out an exquisite silvery chain with the jeweled dart frog. Its sapphires and black diamonds scintillated like tiny, fiery stars. He held it up, displaying it for everyone to see.

Logan laughed, and Aunt Bev giggled. Damian looked nauseated and Sara flabbergasted.

"I think that I know," Andy said, looking down at Harald, "who filched the frog."

Chapter Thirty-Four

Gilbey caught up with Andy and Harald as they were leaving Tim's office. "Well, Andy, guess the case is closed and the necklace recovered. You and I and Harald there," he said, winking down at the pooch, "make a pretty good team. Maybe we oughta think about hanging out a shingle and opening a detective shop."

Andy didn't want to rain on his new friend's parade with things like the apprenticeships and licenses that a detective agency would require. "Well, maybe *you* oughta. Me, I prefer a saner line of work, like hosting at a restaurant or painting pictures. But I'll tell you what. Next time you're in New Bergen, call me and we'll catch a coffee or brewski somewhere. I'd enjoy keeping in touch."

The security guard grinned at him. "I will definitely do that. And by the way, my boss Warren just sent over some video on those jewelry thefts down in the Cities. Wanna take a look?"

Andy didn't, really. He already knew who had stolen the frog—not just once, but twice. It would be a waste of time, and right now all he wanted to do was blow this pop stand. But he liked Gilbey, and he didn't want to hurt the guy's feelings. "Sure, why not?" he said. "But it's gotta be quick, okay?"

They made a U-turn back to the security office. Gilbey brought the video up on a monitor. It showed some glitzy jewelry store at the big mall. And as soon as the short, stout woman fell to the floor, distracting the clerks, Andy knew exactly who he was watching. He started to laugh.

"I know those gals," he hooted. "The one who took the pratfall, that's Eileen. She's Mint Green. Andrea is Hot Pink. I only remember those two by name."

Gilbey looked baffled. "Huh? What?"

"They're here for Girls' Weekend Out."

"They're *here*?"

"Yeah. And they told me they're going to New Bergen on the bus tonight. You should be able to track them down pretty easily."

"Eileen and Andrea?" Gilbey said.

"Yup."

"I gotta go tell the sheriff." Gilbey scurried off, grinning like an idiot.

With Harald in tow, Andy popped into Aunt Bev's cubicle to retrieve his bag, gifts, and coat. She had offered to take care of his damp clothes and boots. Leaving the resort offices, Andy and Harald nearly collided with Tim Fisher.

"Oh, Mayor Skyberg," the manager said, flashing an insincere smile, "Beverly slipped out of my office before I had a chance to talk with her. I just wanted to commend her for a job well done. I have to admit I was skeptical that she could handle things this weekend, but she definitely stepped up. She's done okay."

Andy thought the praise a bit underwhelming. "I'm sure Aunt Bev will value your comments for all they're worth."

Looking momentarily confused by Andy's syntax, Tim quickly recovered his managerial air. "And we're very grateful for all that you and the dog have done. Please keep in mind, if you should need to host a world-class event or meeting, we'd be happy to offer you a ten percent discount on our facilities and services."

Watching the haughty hotelier walk away, Andy was thinking where he'd like to stick that generous ten percent discount. But there were more important things to focus on—Andy Skyberg was finally blowing town.

Out in the lobby, the Moose Junction Bolts were tramping out the door to the team bus. One tall, dark-haired player lingered, staring mournfully down into the eyes of Becky's pink-haired pal Shannon. She looked equally as bummed.

Oh, to be young and in love, Andy thought. He wondered if the pair's snowbound infatuation would endure beyond the twenty hours they had been together. Stranger things, he supposed, had happened in the game of love.

Andy was pulling on his coat when his phone ding-donged. He was half-inclined to ignore it, but he saw Thor's name pop up.

"Yo, super-geezer," he joshed. "What up?"

"You still here, Andy?"

"Yessir, but about to split."

"Not gonna stay for Logan's book launch?"

"Nope. That's a big negatory." After just witnessing Logan's cold, calculated cruelty, he had no desire to spend any time at her Kat Blast.

"Can't you come for just a little while? I've got the darnedest story to tell you."

"Well…" Andy glanced at his watch and figured he could spare a few minutes. "Okay, but it's gotta be PDQ."

Andy and Harald almost made it out of the lobby when Aunt Bev appeared, approaching at flank speed.

"Glad I caught you, Anders. I was afraid you'd gone." She gave him a quick hug and Harald a brisk rub. "You've been such a trooper, sweetie, and I love you to pieces, and I wanted to thank you so much. Now go enjoy your Twisters concert."

"It's Blitzers, Aunt Bev. I figured you'd be over helping with Logan's big show."

"I left Doris there to hold down the fort, but Logan's got some gal named Justine giving her a hand."

So, with Sara Blake sitting in the hoosegow, Logan had to turn to Justine. Logan gets an assist and maybe a

RICHARD AUDRY

more sympathetic appraisal from Justine. And the blogger gets an inside line to all matters Logan and Kat. A
good deal for both of them.

"You know something, Aunt Bev? The Beaver Tail
Resort is darn lucky to have you."

She put on a Cheshire cat grin. "Well, not for much
longer. As soon as Rosemary comes back, I'm quitting.
Doris and I are going to start our own event-planning
outfit. Gotta decide if we're gonna be an LLC or an S
corp. We're ready to think outside the box, take it to the
next level, and interactively maintain operational
synergy."

Andy smiled at her corporate word salad. If nothing
else, this job had given her a whole new vocabulary.
"Well, Aunt Bev, congrats!" He wished he could see
the expression on Tim Fisher's face when she told him.
"Listen, I'm gonna catch some of Logan's show, and
then I'm outta here. Talk to you next week."

Thor was waiting for Andy and Harald at the doors
to the ballroom. They slipped in, standing in the back,
and Andy put his bags down. The place was packed. An
excited woman—probably one of Logan's superfans—
was giving the author a gushing introduction. A camera
on a tripod was set up onstage, probably for the live
stream online, and Justine was operating it.

"So, rumor has it that the young tattoo artist was the
culprit," Thor whispered. "Did you and the pooch here
have anything to do with tracking him down?"

"We helped a little," Andy whispered back. "But

what's this big story you got for me?"

The ballroom erupted in applause as Logan Kennedy, leading Nikkie, swept onto the stage, radiating charm and glamor. No one would have guessed what she had just been through in Tim Fisher's office. No one would have guessed she had just seen her own son and thoroughly rejected him.

"Sage invited Sonny and me to have drinks with her tonight," Thor said, as Logan began her remarks. "Said she wants us to meet an old boyfriend of hers. You'll never guess who it is."

"Ross Ueland."

Thor's eyebrows shot up. "Now how in heck did you know that?"

"Long story, Thor. If I told you the whole thing, I'd end up missing my concert tonight."

"Sonny thinks he's the guy Logan stole from Sage."

Andy thought a moment about the possible connection between Ross Ueland and Damian Powers. If someone tracked down Damian's birth date, it wouldn't take much to figure out whether or not Ross could have been his father. If so, maybe Ross would be willing to provide the younger man with a connection that Logan had refused to. Who knows? Maybe Ross would be over the moon about suddenly having a son.

"I need a favor, Thor. If you get a chance, pull Ross aside and tell him he should ask Logan about that baby she gave up for adoption thirty years ago."

A look of astonishment lit up Thor's face as the

words sank in. "Whoa, do you mean…?" He paused for a couple of seconds. "Sorry, my friend, but no can do. I make it a practice never to stick my nose in other people's intimate affairs." He crossed his arms and pondered it for a few seconds. "I'll ask Sonny to do it."

"…and due to the help of some very capable people," Logan was announcing from the stage, "Grant Hamsden's exquisite dart frog necklace has been recovered."

The audience went nuts with applause as Justine's boyfriend Bobby—with some help from a still-limping Grant—wheeled the safe out onto the stage behind Logan.

The author raised her hands to quiet her fans.

"Before we announce the details of the contest, I just want to express my gratitude to the people who saved this seemingly lost weekend. First, I want to thank the resort staff, most particularly Tim Fisher, Beverly Engebretson, and Virgil Gilbey." She paused for more applause. "Also, I want to express my gratitude to a special pair of investigators. One of them apprehended the primary culprit. And the other not only recovered the necklace, but rescued my sweet puppy Nikkie. I'm speaking of Anders Skyberg and his canine companion, King Harald. Are Anders and Harald here with us?"

Andy tried to shrink down a few inches, his cheeks growing warm.

"Here they are," bellowed Thor, jabbing the top of

Andy's head with his index finger.

"Ah, Thor," Andy whined. "Dammit."

"Can we bring up the lights in back?" Logan requested.

The illumination promptly brightened, and Thor repeated his pointy finger jab. Everybody in the joint had twisted around to look at Andy and Harald, and another round of applause broke out.

"Now I don't usually reveal details of future stories," Logan said after her audience quieted down, "but this time I will. The next Kat adventure is going to feature a tall, handsome Norwegian named Anders. Kat's new valet. And on the Caribbean island where she lives in anonymity, Anders wears as little as possible."

Hundreds of fans hooted and shouted their approval. Andy could feel his cheeks turning crimson now. But he knew he had to be a good sport. He waved to the cheering ladies and shot Logan a distant thumbs-up. As the lights lowered again, he said goodbye to Thor, grabbed his bags, and slipped out of the ballroom, hugely relieved.

He and Harald were halfway across the lobby when he spied Becky Reingold sitting in one of the leather chairs in front of the big fireplace. Her coat was across her lap. She was staring pensively into the flames and didn't notice Andy until he came right up next to her.

"Oh, hi, you two," she said, popping up. "You look ready to rock and roll."

Andy set down his case and bag of gifts. "Yup, all

done here."

"Blitzers, here you come."

"Can't feel my eyes, can't feel my nose," Andy crooned. *"Can't feel my legs, can't feel my toes."*

"Wanna feel your cheeks, wanna feel your lips," Becky joined in. *"Wanna feel your waist, right down to your hips."*

She tilted her head and regarded Andy intently. "Aw, you shaved. I liked that stubbly look. Kinda sexy."

Andy laughed but figured he might try it again sometime. "And what are you doing out here all alone? You're missing the Kat Blast in the ballroom."

"Yeah, I know. I'm just feeling a little burned out. I needed some alone time, so I figured I'd wait here until the New Bergen buses arrive."

"You're gonna have a fantastic time, Becky. All the Christmas decorations and lights are up on Skjegstad Street. The shops are full of great stuff. And my tip for Ansel's is the salmon with polenta. One of my faves. Wonderful."

"Wow, I can see why you're the mayor," Becky teased him. "You know how to sell your town."

"And I absolutely believe every word. When you come down for that lunch and glass of wine, I'll give you a personal tour of the historical spots. Like where Andy Skyberg learned to ride a bicycle. Where Andy Skyberg was *the worst* lineman in the history of New Bergen football. And where Andy Skyberg played doctor with Sylvia Borgstrom."

Becky laughed and as she did, Justine's boyfriend Bobby slouched by. He made a slight detour and came over to them.

"So, *this* is that hot date you were talking about. *Fox-y la-dy.*" He gave them a leer and a wink. "Now you guys behave yourselves. Don't steam up the windows too much." He chuckled and headed for the bar.

Dammit, Andy thought. He could sense Becky tensing up and backing off.

"Ah, you've got a hot date for tonight," she said. "That should be fun."

"Practically a blind date," Andy muttered. "Someone I used to know back in the day."

"An old friend. You'll probably have lots to catch up on. And who knows..."

Andy hated to leave things like that, with the cold water Bobby had inadvertently dumped on them. But he had to hit the road. He picked up his bags.

"Well, have fun in New Bergen, Becky, and I'll expect you at Ansel's real soon."

Man and dog headed out the door into the dark. The cold bit something fierce. But at least the blowing snow had stopped and the air was crystal clear. A couple hundred feet out, Andy turned around. Becky was standing behind one of the windows, waving to him. He waved back, beaming a big smile, then kept walking.

The Silverado started up right away, and Harald occupied his usual perch in the passenger seat. Andy spent a few minutes clearing off snow and climbed back into the cab. He called Phil.

"Well, if it isn't the prodigal son," his friend answered. "I hope I won't have to scalp that ticket."

"Don't you dare. Just gotta leave the hound in New Bergen, and I'll be on my way. I don't think I can make it in time for dinner, though. I'll grab a burger en route."

"Hey, I've been thinking. Why don't you stop at my place and drop off your bag and pooch. Our daughter's home, and she'll take good care of him. We'll rendezvous in front of the box office."

Andy thought that was a terrific idea and quickly agreed. It would save time, and Harald would love the ride.

"Man, Andy," Phil said, "Beaver Tail Resort's all over the news, with that, uh, what's-her-name, the author. And a jewel theft and stuff. I bet you're glad to be escaping that loony bin."

Andy looked back at the lobby windows, aglow in the darkness and ringed with Christmas lights. Becky was gone now.

"Well, you know, Phil, there were parts of being snowbound that I kinda liked."

He said bye and turned to his faithful mutt. "Got an offer for you, buddy. Want to go see what life is like in the big city?"

Harald gave a loud, affirmative *woof* and off they went.

Acknowledgements

My team of editors and beta readers continues to make a big difference in the world of Andy Skyberg and King Harald. Kate Collins, Kelly Germain, and Jeri Smith do a terrific job as my beta readers—offering many insights, new ideas, and corrections. My editor, Marlo Garnsworthy, confirms that I'm on the right track. Marie Joseph gives the manuscript one final proofread to hunt down those stubborn little errors that I've missed. And Sue Wichmann keeps the story focused and on task throughout the writing process. Without her, there would be no Andy, no Harald.

About the Author

Richard Audry is the pen name of D. R. Martin. As Richard Audry, he is the author of the King Harald Canine Cozy mystery series and the Mary MacDougall historical mystery series. Under his own name, he has written the Johnny Graphic middle-grade ghost adventure series, the Marta Hjelm mystery *Smoking Ruin*, and two books of literary commentary: *Travis McGee & Me* and *Four Science Fiction Masters*. You can follow his musings and stay up to date on news about his books at drmartinbooks.com. And be sure to visit and like Richard Audry at facebook.com/richardaudryauthor.

If you enjoyed *King Harald's Snow Job*, please consider reviewing it. And be sure to check out these mysteries...

The Karma of King Harald
by Richard Audry

When springtime arrives in picturesque New Bergen, so too do the tourists and antiquers. This year, though, there are some unwelcome visitors. Extortion. Arson. And murder.

Join Andy Skyberg and his crime-sniffing mutt King Harald as they embark on their first mystery adventure.

Available as a trade paperback and e-book.

King Harald's Heist
by Richard Audry

As the leaves begin to change color in New Bergen, Andy Skyberg wants to turn his full attention to his sister's new café and art gallery—and to the beautiful Finnish architect who's managing the project.

But King Harald has a kennel full of trouble in store for Andy, beginning with a pilfered thousand-dollar bill and a naughty garden gnome. Havoc and hilarity ensue, as Andy and his happy hound get to the bottom of *King Harald's Heist*.

Available as a trade paperback and e-book.

A Mary MacDougall Mystery Duet

by Richard Audry

The year is 1901 and young Mary MacDougall has a rather improbable ambition—to become a consulting detective. *A Mary MacDougall Mystery Duet* features the two cases that establish her as a force to be reckoned with.

In the first novella, *A Pretty Little Plot*, Mary's painting instructor is charged with kidnapping two of his students. The second novella, *The Stolen Star*, follows Mary as she unpeels layers of deceit and duplicity in the hunt for a purloined precious stone during the Christmas season.

Available as a trade paperback and e-book. The two novellas are also available separately as e-books.

A Daughter's Doubt

by Richard Audry

Mary MacDougall is hired to visit a little town in Michigan's Upper Peninsula to make inquiries. Did Agnes Olcott really die there of cholera? Or were there darker doings in Dillmont? Mary's mentor, Detective Sauer, thinks it's merely a case of bad luck for the dead woman. But Mrs. Olcott's daughter suspects foul play.

As Mary digs ever deeper, the enemy she provokes could spell disaster for her and the people she loves. But in the end, it's the only way to banish a daughter's doubt.

Available as a trade paperback and e-book.

Smoking Ruin

by D. R. Martin

Minneapolis P.I. Marta Hjelm failed to prevent a murder that was waiting to happen. Her guilt has brought her right to the edge of burnout and dropout. But a prize specimen from her ancient past—her cheating ex-husband—appears out of nowhere with a gig too good to turn down. One last job, Marta figures, can't hurt. But hurt it does, as Marta tries to make sense of a terrorist plot at a major ad agency.

Available as a trade paperback and in various e-book editions.